Spouse on Haunted Hill

E. J. COPPERMAN

BERKLEY PRIME CRIME
New York

BERKLEY PRIME CRIME
Published by Berkley
An imprint of Penguin Random House LLC
375 Hudson Street, New York, New York 10014

ISBN: 9780425283387

First Edition: December 2016

Printed in the United States of America
1   3   5   7   9   10   8   6   4   2

Cover illustration by Dominick Finelle/The July Group; photographs: flock of birds © AlexussK/
Shutterstock # 68613040; painted background © iStockphoto/Thinkstock # 92043813n/a
Cover design by Judith Lagerman
Book design by Kristin del Rosario

For Shannon Jamieson Vazquez.

ACKNOWLEDGMENTS

This is the eighth Haunted Guesthouse novel, which blows my mind. Before this my standing record was three books in a series, achieved twice. Now I can honestly say I've written one more book in a series than J. K. Rowling, the only such statistic in publishing that will come out in my favor via straight-up comparison.

Loyal readers of the series will know that I believe the writing process is one that does not consist strictly of an author in a room typing solitarily (is that a word?), if you don't count the inevitable Muse sitting on the writer's shoulder, which seems to me would make typing that much more difficult. Many people worked hard on this little tome before you got your hands, ears or any other body part on it, and they deserve much credit for the product you're now, with any luck at all, about to enjoy.

Indeed, there was a somewhat larger cast of characters involved in bringing my cast of characters to you this time. Thanks to Michelle Vega and Amanda Ng, both of whom served as editors on this book. They read over the rough—a grand understatement—draft and helped turn it into this more polished story. Such efforts are invaluable to an author. Any writer who simply wants an editor to read the work, gush over it and submit it without a comma displaced is doing him- or herself and the reader a grand disservice. Editors exist as an institution because history has proven authors can't be trusted with their own work. If not for editors, Charles Dickens might have written *A Tale of Only One City* and we would have been deprived of half his brilliance.

In this case, Ashley Polikoff worked as production editor and Dan Larsen as copy editor on this book in capacities I can't adequately list here. Suffice it to say you'd be reading a much rougher book if they hadn't gotten their hands on it.

Dominic Finelle again wiped me out with his cover artwork and Judith Lagerman with her cover design. They found the essence of the book and communicated it. They say a picture is worth a thousand words. In this case, it's worth about 86,000.

As ever, my sincere thanks to the wizards (I'm not stealing that, J.K.; don't take the extra-book thing to heart!) at HSG Agency, Josh Getzler and Danielle Burby especially, who keep me from going too far off the deep end and who actually keep me employed straight through the year. They are lovely people and very talented at their jobs, which is a combination you don't get to see all that often. Thanks again to Christina Hogrebe at Jane Rotrosen Agency for getting this series to exist all those years ago.

Readers are the people who keep a series alive and make a writer willing to shuffle over to that desk and try again. Thank you sincerely for taking Alison, Paul, Maxie, Melissa, Loretta and all the others into your minds and your hearts and letting them be themselves. It has been a privilege to send them to you every year. No writer could be more grateful.

E. J. COPPERMAN
DEEPEST NEW JERSEY, 2016

One

"This is the end," I said.

I was mostly talking to myself. It was one of those things you say to yourself when things aren't exactly going your way, and they weren't going mine right now. I was standing just short of the security line at Newark Liberty International Airport (the longest name for an airport in the continental United States, but that's just a guess) where at any moment—I had been told—my daughter, Melissa, now thirteen but no less sensible than she ever had been, would be returned to me after having been held captive against my will for almost a whole week.

Okay, she'd been visiting her father in Los Angeles during a school break that took into account all presidential holidays and the remainder of a week, but to me that was the equivalent of kidnapping. Sure, Liss had been willing to go visit Steven, but that didn't make it the right thing to

do. He had not been given (in my mind) the nickname The
Swine without some cause.

"What's the end?" Maxie Malone, to my right, was
watching up the corridor as I was, despite my urging that
she head on down past security and see what was holding
Melissa up. Maxie could do that because very few people
could see her.

She was dead. More on that in a minute.

"The end of my patience," I said into the little Bluetooth
device I wore on my ear so I could talk to Maxie without
people thinking I needed psychiatric observation. "She
was supposed to be back here three hours ago."

"It was snowing," Maxie reminded me as if I didn't
know that. "You're lucky she's coming home today at all.
They almost closed the airport."

Since when was Maxie the Weather Channel? "That's
not the point," I explained through semiclenched teeth.
"The point is that I was supposed to have my daughter
back at two and it is now five fifteen. That is worse than
two."

"You're overreacting," said Maxie.

I looked around for a kettle and a pot to see what color
they each might think the other was. Oddly I found none.

"So she's a little late. You know how the airlines are."
Maxie had once told me she'd never been in an airplane
in her life. Maxie had been murdered at the age of twenty-
eight and now existed—*lived* would be inaccurate—in my
huge Victorian guesthouse back in Harbor Haven, New
Jersey, roughly an hour's drive from here when it *wasn't*
snowing.

"It's not the airlines. It's Liss's father. He probably made
it snow so I wouldn't get her back."

Maxie rolled her eyes and clicked her tongue. I gave
her a sharp look, which drew a quick glance from the TSA
guard at one of the fluoroscope machines. Great. Now

they'd think I was a hijacker because I was trying to glare significantly at one of my resident ghosts.

Perhaps I should explain.

After divorcing The Swine I had taken some money from the settlement—okay, *all* the money from the settlement—and some from a lawsuit I'd settled with an ex-employer with wandering hands and bought the big house in Harbor Haven, the town where I'd grown up. While restoring the house with an eye toward opening it to tourists, I'd taken a bucket of wallboard compound to the head (Maxie to this day swears she wasn't responsible), and once I'd come to had seen two people in my house I had not known were there.

Maxie was one of them. Paul Harrison, the aspiring private detective who had been Maxie's bodyguard for the last twelve hours of her life, was the other. The reason I hadn't seen them before was that almost nobody could see them—they were ghosts.

It seemed seeing ghosts ran in my family. My mother and Melissa apparently had the ability since birth, which they told me about only after I'd been clonked on the head and thought I was having dangerous hallucinations. This was the dynamic in my clan.

Paul and Maxie had been murdered in my new house and oddly were not happy about that, so they'd insisted I find out who had done the murdering. We eventually did sort that out, the perpetrator was now in prison and would be for quite some time and I figured the two ghosts would move out and let me have my guesthouse on the Jersey Shore.

No such luck.

At first neither of the ghosts was able to move beyond my property line, which was the beach in the back of the house, the street in front of the house and some nebulous line between houses on either side. Eventually Maxie spontaneously developed the ability to travel, but Paul was still housebound and grumpy about it. He was a lovely guy, but he tended to take things like being cooped up in one house for all eternity personally.

"Why don't you go up and see if she's in yet?" I suggested to Maxie. "They're not going to arrest you for breaking security."

"Will you calm down?" she said. "I miss Melissa, too, but you don't see me getting all antsy."

It was true. Maxie considered herself something of a big sister to my daughter, and Liss adored the brassy ghost, particularly since Maxie loves nothing better than to annoy me to the point of distraction, which Melissa considers hilarious. Even so, I was anxious to see my daughter after a week away. Five years to college. There was a thought I didn't want to have.

"I just—" I began.

Maxie rose toward the ceiling to get a better viewpoint. "They're coming out," she reported.

Immediately I started to jockey for position, but so did every other person waiting for a loved one (or maybe someone they didn't even like) to walk down the corridor. This area could see as many as three flights arrive at once, so even in this weather it was fairly crowded with New Jerseyans, and there's nothing we like better than nudging each other out of the way.

Unfortunately many of the New Jerseyans (don't *ever* call us "Jersey-ites") in front of me were tall, or at least tall enough that I couldn't see Melissa—or anything except the somewhat hairy neck of the guy in front of me—as the ex-passengers approached. "Do you see her?" I asked Maxie.

Maxie started to giggle, and that was *always* a bad sign.

"Yeah," she managed to squeak out.

"Why is that funny?"

The hairy neck in front of me wasn't laughing. Neither was anyone else in line. That let out the possibility that Jon Stewart had disembarked here or that a group of chimpanzees in flight attendant uniforms were juggling on their way out of the tunnel. Because chimps are funny.

"You'll see," Maxie chuckled, and then she rose higher either so that I'd have to yell to talk to her or so she could see better. There were no hairy-necked ghosts hovering near the ceiling, although one rather distinguished elderly gentleman dressed for a flight in 1974 was hip-deep in the floor of the terminal. He checked his watch as if time was actually a consideration of his.

I didn't have time, I'm saying, to assess Maxie's proclamation before my very own Melissa, who seemed taller after being gone only a week, squeezed her way through the crowd (practically hip-checking Hairy Neck) and gave me a measured but affectionate hug.

"Where's Josh?" she asked. That was the kind of greeting I got from my daughter. A lot of girls would have said, "Mom! I missed you so much! Thank goodness I don't live with that demon full-time!" But no. I got a thirteen-year-old asking where my boyfriend of two years might be.

"He couldn't make it tonight; he has to shovel out in front of his store." Josh Kaplan owned Madison Paints, an independent store in Asbury Park. "The town issues summonses if you don't shovel. But hey, don't worry, he managed to send your next favorite adult." I gave Liss a consolation hug with my right arm.

"I thought that was me," said a voice I knew too well. A voice that I couldn't be hearing. A voice I absolutely didn't want to be hearing.

"Don't make me play favorites, Dad," said my daughter.

Sure enough, standing just to the left (mine, not his) of Hairy Neck was my ex-husband, Steven Rendell.

The Swine.

"What are you doing here?" I sort of growled as Maxie, guffawing her way down from the ceiling, pointed at me.

"You should see your face!" she gloated. Melissa shot Maxie a look to indicate she was taking the gag too far. Maxie didn't notice, or that was what she wanted us to think.

"Nice welcome," Steven said. "Can't I come out and visit once in a while?"

"No."

Melissa dragged her carry-on-size bag with the one sort of shaky wheel, and started toward the exit. "Come on," she said, I think to Maxie. The ghost nodded and floated on behind her.

"I just wanted to come out and see you for a couple of days," my ex continued as if I hadn't made it clear that was a bad idea. "Do you have a room empty?"

It was February and the tourist trade down the shore (as real Jerseyans call the coastline) was not exactly booming. I had a grand total of three guests at the moment and none scheduled for the following week.

"We're all full up," I told Steven.

"Good for you!" The Swine liked to pretend that any business success I might have would be a complete surprise, because he thought I didn't actually know what I was doing. Yeah, I only had three guests. February. Shore. Remember? "You have somewhere you can stash me, right?"

I noticed he was walking slowly, more so than I remembered, but then, maybe age was starting to catch up with him. Steven had to be in his early forties by now, because I was in my late thirties. "Not really," I said. "Why not catch a flight back out to California while you can and save the cost of a hotel?"

"Ally." Steven knew for a fact that I absolutely hated

being called "Ally." I gave him a look. "Sorry. Alison. Can you just wait up a second?"

Melissa (and by extension Maxie) already had a ten-yard lead on us. "Steven, I haven't seen our daughter—*my* daughter—in a week. Why would I hang back with you, when I didn't want to see you at all?" It seemed a logical question. The Swine had left us when Melissa was only eight, and he had done so to go live the Southern California lifestyle (which as far as I could tell was like New Jersey but with less gluten) with a woman named . . . Bambi? Barbie? That was four women ago, so I couldn't really remember.

"I have a problem." It was hardly worth noting that The Swine *always* had a problem. That was why the child support checks were late, when he managed to send them at all. That was why it hadn't been, until now, a "good time" for Melissa to come visit him in sunnier climes. Steven saying he had a problem was like LeBron James mentioning that he was taller than some.

"Fine, you can have a room at the guesthouse," I relented. "But only for a couple of nights. I have a new group of guests coming in a few days." That was an outright lie, but fight fire with fire, I always say.

"That's not it." Steven held my left biceps to slow me down, which considering that I was barely walking at this point, meant I had to stop. "I mean, yes, I want the room, but I figured I could get that. I have a *real* problem."

"And a charming way to convince me I should help." I shook his hand off my arm and started after my daughter, who was conversing openly with the invisible woman over her head. "What's the problem?"

"Some people want to kill me."

I kept walking. "Again?" I asked.

Two

The drive home was slow and, from Steven's end, quiet. Melissa and Steven did not have a lot of details to share about their week together—they'd gone to Disneyland (of course) and the Chinese Theater (even more of course) and gotten their picture taken under the Hollywood sign. I would have to consult with Maxie, who had "mad computer skills," she said, about Photoshopping The Swine out of that one.

Maxie was sitting with her head out of the car, which made it look as if she were feeling the breeze despite the fact that she couldn't. So she did not contribute much except when she decided to drop down and see if anyone was saying anything she would consider interesting. We were, apparently, not doing that very much.

I had not mentioned Steven's comment at the airport to Maxie, since I'd had no time alone with her and didn't want to alarm Melissa over what I was sure would not be a

serious issue. Steven was always getting involved in somewhat sketchy business deals, confident in his ability to talk
his way out of trouble, and about seventy percent of the
time he was able to do just that.

It was the other thirty percent that offered him some
challenges, and probably would have ended up contributing
to our divorce if Bobbi (or Bitsy, or something) hadn't
gotten in the way first. I was really young when we got
married. That's not an excuse, but it is an explanation.

"So, what's Dad's house like, Liss?" I asked when the
slick roadway on the Garden State Parkway eased to the
point that I could stop leaning forward, coaxing the Volvo's
ancient defroster to make the highway visible.

"Um . . ." Liss wasn't often at a loss for words. "We
didn't exactly stay at Dad's house."

"I'm having some renovations done," The Swine
jumped in. "We had a suite at a hotel for the time Melissa
was there, because nothing is too good for my girl."

I couldn't actually turn my head at the moment, but I
could picture Liss rolling her eyes at that one. Her father
could snow her (if you'll pardon the expression), but he
had to work harder than that.

"A hotel?" None of the texts or phone calls had mentioned that.

"It was really nice," Liss told me. "One night we got
room service and all they brought was a soft pretzel."

"Uh-huh." I didn't care much for the way this particular
vacation was sounding. We didn't talk again for a while.

The truth was, what had fallen on New Jersey that day
was hardly a significant snowfall. But it was the third one
in a week and we were running out of places to put the
stuff. I know some people see snow and think of lovely
evenings spent watching it pile up. You never hear rhap-
sodic tales of shoveling and driving in snow on a dark
night.

Still, this was not a huge threat and the drive, while requiring attention, was anything but dangerous. People tend to stay off the roads when there's weather in February, so I didn't run into any real traffic and we were back at the guesthouse in Harbor Haven about an hour after we'd gotten into the car at the airport, pretty much the time it would take on a clear night in May, which was something I was dreaming about tonight.

Melissa had just the one bag and Steven had no luggage at all, so there was not a huge procession getting into the house. It was just after seven and two of my guests, Mel and Anne Kaminsky, were still out at dinner. I don't serve food at the guesthouse unless there's a serious emergency because I am among the worst cooks on the planet, and besides, I have an agreement with a few of the local restaurateurs—I send them customers and get a percentage of the check back—so I recommend local eateries and the guests are usually happy to go there.

The one remaining guest, Yoko Takamine, was in the library when we arrived. Reading the latest Lee Child thriller, she was engrossed in the book and barely looked up when Melissa's suitcase rolled by followed by her mother and father, who were making a point of not discussing *anything* at the moment. The ghost floating over our heads was not Yoko's concern. I didn't see my other resident spirit, Paul Harrison, which was odd. Paul was bound to the property and usually showed up the second the door opened.

Liss took the stairs up to the second floor and then rolled her bag into the dumbwaiter/elevator that went up to her attic room. Maxie ascended the easy way through the ceiling as my daughter, saying she'd be down for dinner, pulled her way up to what she surely considered sanctuary. The level of tension always rises when The Swine and I are in the same room. We don't have to say or do anything; you can just feel it. I regret that Melissa has to deal with that, but we don't see Steven often, so it has never seemed like a huge issue. Now he was following me around the guesthouse, where he'd only been once before. He kept looking around at each room as if he were trying to decide whether he wanted to buy the place, but I knew he was storing away information he could use for . . . something. The man was insidious.

The best thing to do was ignore him, but to do so in ways that would get him annoyed. I was a pro at that. I began by calling Josh and letting him know we'd made it home safely. I made a point of telling him that Steven was in town and would be staying in the guesthouse for a day or two at the most. That last part I mentioned while my ex looked on so he'd know the accommodations were not a permanent solution to his problem.

"You want me to come over and beat him up or anything?" Josh asked.

I laughed. "I'd be much more adept at it. I have all the anger. You'd just be doing it out of loyalty."

"It's more than that. I hate the way that guy has treated you and Melissa."

Josh and I had known each other for a long time. A really long time. Since we were kids, playing in his grandfather's paint store. Now Josh owned the store and we'd been seeing each other for about two years. At one point six months before, we had discussed his moving into the guesthouse, but it wasn't practical to his store in Asbury Park, where he had to be extremely early in the morning, when the painters arrived for their daily supplies. And I, clearly, couldn't move in with him, since my business was sort of predicated on the idea that I'd be in the house when people were staying here.

"Don't worry about me," I assured him. "I can definitely handle myself."

"Yeah, but it's more fun if I do it."

"You'll be here for dinner tomorrow?" I asked. I looked at Steven then, too, just to make sure he knew this was a regular thing.

"Unless there's more snow. Maybe even if there is. I haven't talked to you enough lately, and I miss it." Josh belonged in the Boyfriend Hall of Fame. I said I'd see him the next night, gave my ex a dismissive nod and went upstairs.

I walked into my bedroom to take out my earrings and change clothes. I only got to do the former because my ex-husband didn't take a closed door for an answer and barged his way in.

"Hey!" I snapped at him. "We haven't been married for years. You don't get to come in here." All he'd gotten to see were my naked earlobes, but it was the principle of the thing.

"I need to tell you about my situation," The Swine said in what he considered to be an urgent yet subdued voice. It actually sounded like he was whispering to the back of the room at Madison Square Garden.

"Let me save you the time," I told him as I saw Paul push his face through the wall to look in. Paul was polite, but when he heard me shout he might have thought something was wrong. I gave him a quick look to indicate he should come in, and he did, looking baffled. He'd met— okay, seen—The Swine before and held the opinion that he was, you know, a swine. "I've seen this before. You got into a shady business deal with somebody, you lost their money, they are mad as all hell and threatening you and so you need to get out of your house and hide in a hotel. And by the way, that's a swell time to invite our thirteen-year-old daughter out to spend a week with you. Are you even aware you're a father, Steven?"

Paul immediately started stroking his goatee. He was in private investigator mode.

When we had finished finding out who poisoned Paul and Maxie, Paul had approached me with a proposition: He wanted to keep doing some investigations because he seriously had nothing but time on his hands and considered the mental puzzle necessary to his sanity. But he had a problem—he was dead. He couldn't leave my property and he couldn't interview people about cases, because if they were alive they wouldn't see or hear him (unless they were as wonderfully gifted as me, and that, if you're not from New Jersey, is what we call Sarcasm). So he wanted me to be his "legs in the field" for investigations, something I did not want to do. I had a business to run, and investigations tend to deal with angry people, the very type I like to avoid.

But then *I* had a problem: I was just opening my guesthouse and needed a steady stream of clients to keep the place running. A business called Senior Plus Tours, which features vacations with "value added" qualities—in my case, staying in a "haunted house"—had offered me a contract for a number of guests per month that could definitely help me along.

I needed Paul and Maxie to do ghost things so the guests would feel satisfied with their vacations. Paul made it clear: He'd talk Maxie into doing two "spook shows" a day if I'd agree to get a private investigator's license and help him with the occasional case, which he promised would not be dangerous.

Since then I'd had a number of deadly weapons aimed or in general pointed at me, but Senior Plus had held up its end of the bargain. That is, they had done so until very recently. The number of guests had tailed off, mostly because it was indeed winter in New Jersey, but this was worse than previous winters had been. I got the feeling the company was running out of seniors who wanted to stay in a spook house and might be reconsidering renewing its contract when it came due this coming autumn. So I had about ten months to pick things up.

"Of course I'm aware I'm her father," The Swine answered. "That's why I wouldn't let her stay in my house where it might be dangerous. Nobody knew I was in a hotel."

"Except you had to put the stay on a credit card because you don't have any money, so they probably traced you, right?" I countered. "I've seen this bit before, Steven. You should have canceled Liss's trip and you know it."

The Swine shook his head. "It happened too fast. All this hit the fan the day before she was flying out; I didn't have time." He sat down on the bed, saw the look I gave him and stood up again. He could be oily, but he wasn't stupid.

"Okay, let's have it. Who's ticked off at you this time and why are you so scared you had to fly all the way to New Jersey to get away from them?" That was mostly for Paul's benefit and he nodded to me in thanks.

"I got into a deal with this guy Lou Maroni."

"Huh. I didn't know they had guys named Lou Maroni in L.A.," I said. "I thought they didn't get any farther west than Trenton."

"You gonna be a pain in the butt or are you going to help me?" my ex asked.

"I'll aim for both, but given the choice I'll settle for just being a pain in the butt." Divorces are rarely as amicable as the participants would like you to believe. "So, how'd you get Lou mad at you?"

Steven, even in the rather tight confines of the room—I made most of the larger bedrooms guest accommodations— found a way to turn away from me so I couldn't see his expression. Paul, having no such difficulties, simply flew through me (it feels like a warm breeze when he makes contact, where Maxie is more of a cool one) and took up a position where he could view The Swine unobstructed.

"The original deal was simple," Steven said. "We were providing seed money for a start-up that was going to be huge. Bigger than huge. Planetary."

"Spare me the sales pitch. I'm not investing. My ex is late with the child support." I looked at Paul's face; he smiled. Good. That meant Steven had not.

"You never believed in me, Ally."

"Maybe it was the lying that cut into my confidence."

Paul sighed—it wasn't breathing exactly but it had the same effect—and shook his head slightly. "This is not a time to rehash your divorce, Alison," he reminded me. "We are taking information from a client."

I must have turned my head suddenly at that remark, because Steven narrowed his eyes. "What?" he asked.

"Go on. Lou. The planetary-sized deal. And how it went completely wrong. Start from there."

Paul nodded approvingly.

"The idea was this company was going to put out software called SafT that would make your personal data absolutely unhackable." The Swine was back in salesman mode. "No chance anyone would ever be able to see anything you'd done online."

"Perfect for cheating husbands everywhere," I pointed out. He ignored that.

"A real boon to anyone concerned with identity theft," Steven went on. "Could be bought by Google or Apple, and the guy's a billionaire."

"I'm still not an investor, Steven. What happened? How come Lou's got his goons on your tail?"

Maxie chose that moment to drop down out of the attic. "Melissa wants to know if you're ordering in or if she has to cook," she reported. Because, as I've pointed out, I am a terrible cook, Melissa, my mother or a combination of both often makes dinner at my house. Then Maxie caught sight of The Swine again. "What's he doing in this room?"

Because Steven believes the ghosts are a genius market-ing tool I made up to get more guests, I do not interact with them when he's around. I am constantly thinking of an imaginary custody hearing in which his high-powered attorney (as if he could afford even a public defender) tries to question my sanity by noting the front of my home and business bears a sign reading "Haunted Guesthouse." So I did not directly answer Maxie.

Paul, unencumbered by the need to appear sane and freed of having The Swine aware of his presence (there are some advantages to being dead after all), looked at Maxie and said, "I'm betting takeout."

I nodded a touch and Maxie rose into the ceiling again.

"What happened was that the project was doing really well," The Swine said. It was his defensive tone. I could have written what was coming weeks ahead of his arrival, but I let him say it because, well, it warmed my heart a little to hear him embarrassed. "But some of the investors got a little . . . antsy . . . and decided they wanted to get their capital back."

"Imagine. People getting cold feet after giving you their money."

The Swine blinked but did not take the bait. Paul, how-ever, should have been wearing a Deerstalker cap and cape, he was concentrating so intently.

"Investors, especially inexperienced ones, will often get nervous when a deal is taking slightly longer than they might have anticipated to get off the ground." He had decided to face me directly, a mistake on his part, since I knew what every expression meant and which ones were lying. Most of them were lying.

"Your pal Lou was not an experienced investor?" I asked.

"Not in this kind of opportunity, no. His area is more in importing/exporting."

I could tell Steven wanted me to ask what Lou imported and exported. I could imagine, so I did not.

"It's an easy fix, then," I suggested, knowing no such thing ever existed in The Swine's universe. "Give the man back his money and he'll stop sending people after you."

My ex turned away again. This was going to be the tricky part. For him. "It doesn't really work like that, Alison. You see . . ."

"You don't have the money, do you, Steven?" I would like to point out that I could have let him twist in the wind indefinitely, as he never would have gotten to the point. But I was getting hungry and was sure Melissa was on the phone ordering our dinner even now.

"Not exactly, no."

He turned, and I got the naughty-little-boy-wanting-forgiveness look. It had worked on me once. Then it hadn't, ever again.

"So you'd taken the Kickstarter money and probably begun yet another can't-miss project and you didn't have the cash on hand, is that it? You know, a lot of people would call that a Ponzi scheme. Like the ones who work for the FBI."

The Swine had the nerve to look insulted. "It's not like that, Ally."

I had the nerve to look annoyed.

"Okay, sorry. It's not like that, *Alison*."

I raised an eyebrow. "Okay, then. What's it like?"

He raised a hand, index finger pointed toward the ceiling as if he were about to make a major point. He even opened his mouth to speak. Then he stopped and his face seemed to sag a little. "Okay. That's what it's like. I wasn't trying to steal their money, Alison, you have to believe me. I just had some expenses and—"

"And you were going to put all the money back as soon as you got it from your other business venture, right?" To be fair, The Swine had been a legitimate stockbroker when we were married, but after he'd left the Wall Street area for Blonde Central, he had not found the same success in the financial services business. Hence the robbing-Peter-to-pay-Paul (not the Paul in the room) business tactics. Hence the late alimony and child support payments, when there were payments at all. Hence the need to put his whole life on credit cards issued by banks foolish enough to think they would be repaid.

"That's exactly right," Steven said. "I was maybe five days away from having all the cash back in the bank when Lou Maroni decided he has to have his seed money back, and he means *now*."

"How much?" I asked. It was not—believe me—out of character for Steven to charge a plane ticket from Los Angeles to Newark in order to ask me for the money he needed to pay off his scarier investors. Mentally I calculated how much I could spare from my savings, with the understanding that despite his assurances, I would never see the money again.

"How much what?" That kind of bargaining tactic wasn't going to get him what he wanted from me.

"How much do you need to pay off Lou Maroni?" It's possible my tone was not the most patient one you would ever have heard, had you been there.

"Six hundred thousand dollars."

"Whoa." That was Paul. I think it was the most surprised I'd ever heard him sound.

My mental checkbook closed shut with a resounding snap. "Well, I can offer you some pizza," I said.

Three

"This is not a case, Paul." My British/Canadian ghost friend was "pacing" a foot or so off the floor of my basement, where I'd found him when I came downstairs the next morning. Paul spends his "alone time" in the basement, while Maxie frequents Melissa's room in the attic. She considers herself Liss's roommate, which isn't getting uncomfortable . . . yet. Maxie will also occasionally situate herself on the roof when she really wants to be left alone. "We don't have a client, so we don't have a case to solve."

I got out my trusty tape measure and took, for the fifth time, the dimensions of the part of the basement closest to the stairs and away from the boiler that runs the heating system. We also have a freezer down there where I mostly keep bags of ice because I never have more food in my kitchen fridge than I might need.

"I understand divorces are often contentious, Alison," Paul said, eyes down toward the floor. That's his "thinking" pose. "But your ex-husband appears to be in some danger and we have the ability to do something about that."

The area of the basement I was measuring was exactly twelve feet and three inches across and ten feet, two inches deep. The ceiling was a quarter inch over seven feet. Write that down in case I ask you for the dimensions later.

"No, we don't," I told the goateed ghost. "There's nothing to investigate. Steven got himself into trouble. He does that on a regular basis. Now he thinks there are people after him who want six hundred thousand dollars. So he skipped town and is hiding out in my house for what I assure you will not be more than a couple of days until he figures his next move. We don't have a role in this, and I'm especially not interested in getting involved with Lou Maroni and his orchestra, so let's drop it, okay? Here, hold this."

I handed him the end of the tape measure so I could figure out the distance from the post holding up the ceiling (and the rest of the house) to the wall. The plan was to convert part of the basement to living space so I could have an extra guest room when I needed one. I got the measurement— don't worry, I wrote that one down myself—and relieved Paul of the tape measure. "Thanks."

"I'd really prefer you leave the basement as it is." Paul sniffed. "It's the only place I can go when I need to think. Having guests down here would not be conducive to my process."

"That's the way we do things in the Lower Forty-eight, stranger," I said. I had no idea why. "Look. Nobody's going to bother you, and I'll only rent out the room when I need it. It'll be the cheapest one in the house because there's really only that little casement window at the top."

"I don't see the point," Paul said. "You can't fill the rooms you already have for guests."

That was hitting below the belt. "It's February, Paul. It always slows down in the real winter months. Things will pick up again in the spring."

"They didn't last year."

The previous year had been my least profitable since opening the guesthouse three years before. With the diminishing roster of Senior Plus guests and some let's say unsavory happenings that had taken place here the year before, publicizing the guesthouse was becoming something of a challenge. So that last remark stung a bit.

"They will this year," I said drily. "Besides, it just increases the value of the house to have living space down here. That's off-topic anyway—we're not going to do anything about Steven and his current screwup. He's done it before and he'll do it again. He won't learn if we help him every time."

I stood in the center of the space I'd blocked off and tried to envision a bedroom here. Unfortunately at the moment it looked a lot like a basement, and that wasn't helping. A concrete floor, exposed beams in the ceiling and walls. It was over a hundred years old and it wasn't as if there was a portrait stashed in my attic of a basement that looked much older; this place was showing every year clearly.

"He could be in danger," Paul countered. "If something happens to him, wouldn't that be a terrible blow to Melissa?"

"You're really playing dirty today, Paul," I said. "What's bothering you?"

He looked surprised. "Bothering me?"

"When you repeat me, you're just stalling for time. You're acting uncharacteristically cranky and I want to know why. So let's hear it."

Paul's face registered irritation initially. He was going to try to protest. But he realized the pointlessness of that and shrugged. "It's starting to wear on me, Alison," he said.

"What's starting to wear on you?"

"This existence. I've been in this house or on this property for over four years now. I don't want to upset you, but being in the same place for this period of time would become tedious no matter where I was confined. Do you understand that?"

This was not a new sentiment. Paul envied Maxie's ability to move around outside the boundaries of my property, which had appeared out of the blue. Paul says the afterlife does not seem to have rules that apply evenly to each person. Some people die and never become ghosts; those like Paul and Maxie who do sometimes move on to some other level of existence, but that doesn't seem to have any rhyme or reason to it, either.

In short, whoever is running the afterlife has a mean streak, or ADHD.

"Of course I understand, Paul. I wish there was something I could do to help you. I realize you get more antsy when we don't have a case to investigate. But that's not a reason to get involved with one of Steven's ridiculous schemes and subject me and my daughter to any risk that might come with it. Okay?"

Paul, in midpace, looked into my eyes and saw my conviction. "Of course not," he said. "I was not trying to suggest we should investigate simply to make me feel better. You're absolutely right about the danger. I will find something else to occupy my mind." With that he vanished, which was something he rarely did. Maybe he was more upset than I had realized.

I decided that was unfortunate but unavoidable. Steven was going to be out of the house by the next day (another decision I'd just reached) and he'd have to deal with the consequences of his actions just like everybody else. It wasn't my problem and it wasn't something I wanted our daughter to see happen before her eyes. I'd tell my ex to find alternative accommodations as soon as I saw him.

Once upstairs again, I barely had time to clean up the den before Anne Kaminsky came in from the downstairs guest room. Anne, a lovely woman in her early seventies, looked concerned. After four days with a person—especially when she, her husband and another woman were the only guests in the house—you could read her expression.

"Something wrong, Anne?" I asked.

She looked up, having been watching her steps as if she were afraid she would fall. "What? Oh no. No, Alison. I'm fine." Some guests are so horrified at the idea of being a bother that they wouldn't tell me if they saw a headless man parade through the library. Which had happened once; it's a long story.

"It's okay," I said. "If there's something troubling you and I can help, that's what I'm here for." That, and to make a living for myself and my daughter, but that part wasn't really relevant to the conversation.

"Well . . ." An innkeeper is part hotelier, part concierge, part tour guide, part local liaison and part psychotherapist. But we only get paid once.

"What can we do to help?" I asked. I say "we" because Melissa was something of an assistant manager, and the ghosts were . . . there in the house, too. In fact, Maxie, who rarely showed up before the first spook show at ten in the morning, was uncharacteristically descending through the ceiling as I asked.

"I was wondering if I might have another room," Anne said.

That was strange; the downstairs guest room was the largest and most lavishly furnished one I rented, originally intended as the master suite for the house. It had a separate bath and a walk-in closet. I couldn't imagine what would make Anne request a better room. Maybe Mel was offended by the chenille bedspread or thought they were being cheated by being housed on a lower floor than everyone else. That must be it—some people are afraid of being isolated and might think being on the ground floor in a strange house constitutes a security risk. "Why do you and Mel want to move out of the room?" I asked.

"Not Mel," Anne said. "Just me."

Um . . . "I don't understand." Actually I was afraid I *did* understand, but I wanted to buy myself a moment to think about that.

"I have had enough of sleeping with that man and I want to stay in another room," she said. "Can you accommodate me on that?" That last sentence sounded like the request of a small girl and not the demand it might have been from someone less polite. You get a lot of people less polite than Anne Kaminsky in the innkeeper trade.

"I can, certainly," I said. "If you like I can move you into a room upstairs right now."

"Good," she said. "That's a relief. I'll get my things." She turned toward the door and then stopped and faced back toward me. "How much will the extra room cost?" she asked.

This raised an ethical question. On the one hand, I was underbooked and had plenty of rooms available in the house. There would be no huge expense involved in moving Anne to a new room. Aside from cleaning her new space every day, something I would do once a week for an unoccupied room, it was basically the same as having her stay where she was.

On the other hand, I was underbooked and wanted more money.

Actually it wasn't all that huge an ethical question after all. "Well, it's only a partial week," I said. I quoted her a price that was less than the nightly rate I usually charged for the room I had in mind, and Anne agreed.

She brought out a rolling suitcase about five minutes later and I showed her a second-floor room that wasn't as large or luxurious as the one she'd been staying in with her husband. "It's very cozy," she said when she saw it. I'm not partial to that word, but Anne seemed pleased.

As I turned to leave her in the room, a thought occurred to me. "Have you discussed this with Mel?" I asked. It would be awkward if I saw him first and he asked where Anne and her luggage might be.

"Not yet, but I will when he's awake."

I thanked her and left her to unpack. Again. Walking back downstairs, I made a mental note to avoid the area of Mel Kaminsky's room until I could be sure he was up to date on the status of his marriage.

It's one thing to leave your husband. I'd done that. It's another to leave your husband and stay in the same house as him. Actually I'd sort of done that, too. But at least The Swine knew he had to leave, and had booked a flight to California the day after we decided to split. By "decided to split," I mean when I told him he had to haul his sorry carcass to the West Coast or face severe bodily injury, which I described in a great amount of detail.

In Anne's case, the process seemed a little more cold-blooded. She was leaving him while they were on vacation and staying in the same accommodations—and she hadn't mentioned any of this to Mel yet. That seemed uncharacteristically mean for Anne, but I supposed she had good reasons. It's not the hostess's responsibility to know what those reasons might be.

Luckily Mel was not at the landing of the stairs when I descended. I made sure to scoot past that section of the front room quickly and started toward the kitchen, where

I get tea and coffee ready in urns every morning and cart them out to the den for the guests. With only three extra people in the house, I was using a smaller coffee urn and a standard teapot, but the same cart.

Before I could get to the kitchen, however, the doorbell rang.

From upstairs I heard a tiny amount of barking. Melissa had adopted a small dog in the golden retriever family, probably a puppy, who also happened to be a ghost. He barks whenever the doorbell rings, but nobody living hears him except Liss or me, or my mom when she's around. So I didn't have to worry about Lester barking upstairs.

Maxie and Paul followed as I headed toward the door. It's not incredibly unusual for the bell to ring, as I get deliveries and such for myself and the guests, but it was not at all typical at this time of the morning. Guests get their own keys to the front door, which is more often than not unlocked until everyone is in for the night anyway.

"What's going on?" Maxie wanted to know. She sounded annoyed that she'd been disturbed from whatever it is she does at night. The ghosts don't actually sleep but they do seem to need some kind of downtime. Paul says they are probably made of energy, so perhaps that needs to be replenished the same way a living person needs sleep.

"You see me approaching the door. How would I know?" I said.

Paul, still in a contemplative mood apparently, said nothing but floated in behind me. Maxie stuck her head through the door, a talent of hers that makes a peephole somewhat unnecessary.

"It's some guy," she reported when her head was back inside. "He's wearing a coat."

"It's February," I reminded her. The ghosts don't feel heat or cold, so they tend to lose track of the weather. "Thanks for the useful information."

Before she could reply I unlocked and opened my front door and was face-to-face with "some guy," whom indeed I did not recognize. "May I help you?" I said. It seemed the thing to say.

The man, in his mid-forties, was wearing a woolen overcoat, which wasn't inappropriate given the rush of cold air that met me when I swung the door open. It wasn't the usual parka you see in the area; it was more formal. It went with a cherry red scarf that circled his neck and was tucked into the front of the coat. His gloves were real leather. In short, this man had not bought his ensemble at Kmart.

"I'm looking for Steven Rendell," he said in a voice that wasn't at all unpleasant. "I have a message for him."

"There's a bulge in his right front pocket," Paul said. "It could be a gun."

The day was starting off swimmingly.

"There's no one here by that name," I told the man. "Are you sure you have the right address?"

"Oh, I think so," Overcoat said. "This is 123 Seafront Avenue in Harbor Haven, New Jersey."

"Yes, but—"

"And you are Alison Kerby, Mr. Rendell's ex-wife. You and your daughter, Melissa, live here and run a public accommodation, and according to the sign to my left, the house is haunted. That's very quaint."

"Uh-oh," Maxie said. "You want me to hit him with anything?"

I shook my head slightly.

"Perhaps you should find something, just to be safe," Paul suggested. I thought he might have been trying to get the excitable Maxie out of the picture for the moment. "But don't let him see it." Maxie was gone in a second.

"Mr. . . ." I began.

"I'm a friend of a friend," he said.

I wanted to get some of my own back. "You are a friend of Lou Maroni," I told the man. "You're here because my ex-husband owes Mr. Maroni some money in relation with a software development project your *friend* was helping to finance. And you've come apparently to threaten Steven in an attempt to get the money, which I can assure you he doesn't have. So let's not pretend anyone is fooling anyone here."

"Nice," Paul said.

Maxie swooshed in behind me; I could feel her more than see her without turning around. I saw a tiny flash of a trench coat she wears to conceal especially big items from the eyes of the living, something the ghosts can do with the clothes they wear. I didn't want to think about what she might be carrying now.

"Very good, Ms. Kerby," Overcoat said. "May I come in? It really is very cold out here."

"I don't think so. Steven isn't here. But I'm sure the car you drove here has a very efficient heater, so why not use that and try to find him elsewhere?" I started to close the door.

I stopped when the man spoke again. "Mr. Rendell flew here on United flight 1947 from Los Angeles International Airport last night," he said. "He and your daughter got off the plane and were driven home in the red Volvo station wagon that is currently parked behind your house. So I agree, let's not pretend anyone is being fooled at the moment. May I come inside?"

"I've got a shovel," Maxie said. "Should I use it?"

"Why not let him in?" Paul suggested. "He doesn't know Maxie has a shovel." It was a decent point.

Without answering I stepped aside and watched as the man walked in. He was polite enough to scrape the snow off his boots (expensive, leather) before crossing the threshold. If he was a hit man, he was an unusually fastidious one. Of course, I had no idea if assassins were generally sloppy and didn't want to make unfair assumptions about a person based on his choice of profession.

"Thank you," he said.

I made a mental apology to hit men everywhere.

"Now if we can get past our distrust and talk plainly. You know why I'm here and I know your ex-husband is here. So would you please tell him that I have arrived so we can meet?"

I wanted to make sure I worded this next part very carefully. "Let's say hypothetically that Steven was here, which he's not. Why would I want you to meet with him? What's the benefit?"

The man did not take off his gloves, which I found ominous, but did loosen his scarf. "That's better," he said. Then he turned his gaze on me. His eyes were a gentle blue, which was incongruous. This whole man was incongruous. "I'm going to stay here until I get to talk to your ex-husband. I realize you have four guest rooms available, assuming he is staying in one, but I sincerely doubt you want to put me up for an extended visit. So the benefit to you is that the sooner you produce Steven Rendell, the sooner I will leave your home and never return. I would think that's a fair incentive."

Actually I now had three guest rooms available because Anne had just occupied one of the unused ones in the process of leaving Mel, and I took a tiny bit of comfort in the fact that this guy didn't know that before Anne's husband found out.

"I still have the shovel," Maxie said. "Is it time yet?"

Melissa would be coming down the stairs in a minute or two. She'd head for the coffee urn in the den and make herself a cup of what she calls café au lait, which is about half milk/half coffee. She'd pass right by where we were standing. That, I decided, was not acceptable.

"I'm sorry I can't help you," I told the natty man. "Steven isn't here."

And I swear to you, that was the moment my ex-husband's voice came calling from behind me, "What's for breakfast?"

The man in the overcoat gave me a withering look. I shrugged. "You can't blame a girl for trying," I said.

He did not answer. By then, Steven had walked up behind me and then stopped short when he saw Overcoat in the front room. I heard his sharp intake of breath.

"That was quick," he exhaled.

"Steven," answered Overcoat. "Your lovely ex-wife has been trying to protect you from me."

The Swine chuckled so unconvincingly I didn't think Lester the golden retriever would have bought it. He walked to my side and I could see he was wearing the same clothes he'd had on when he got off the plane—a pair of old jeans and a T-shirt that was plain and navy blue but had seen better days. "She's a keeper," he said.

I started to regret having tried to stop this man from killing him.

"We need to talk," Overcoat said.

"Um . . . sure . . ."

I'd heard The Swine sound nervous and I'd heard him sound concerned, but I'd never heard him sound scared before. And he never forgot a name.

"Maurice," Overcoat said. "You remember, don't you?" His eyes got a little colder.

Before anything happened that I'd have to try to erase from my visual memories for the rest of my life, I interrupted. "Look, guys. I understand you two have some very important business to discuss. But my daughter is going to walk down those stairs at any second and I'd prefer she not see . . . anything you're going to do or hear anything you're going to say. Can we move this conversation somewhere else?"

Overcoat looked at the stairs, probably without realizing he was doing so. Steven continued to look at Overcoat.

"Of course," the more well-dressed of them said. "Where would you prefer? Someplace more private?"

I thought hard. The kitchen was the one room guests almost never enter because I don't serve food at the guesthouse. But it would have any number of sharp objects that could be used in ways I preferred not to think about. The movie room did not have doors that closed so much as archways that served as entrances. I sure as hell wasn't letting this guy go into any of the bedrooms, and somehow the thought of his beautifully maintained woolen overcoat in my dusty basement was incongruous.

"How about the library?" I said. If the guy wanted to beat Steven to death with a copy of *The Big Sleep*, it wouldn't only be more difficult, it would be appropriate.

Overcoat nodded and Steven, his face paler than usual, followed me as I led the two of them into the house and then down the hall to the library door. As they entered I looked at Maxie, who caught my eye. I tilted my head in the direction of the library, and she nodded and went through the wall, still in her trench coat. She'd have the shovel with her if it became necessary.

Paul did not follow her but stayed with me as the door closed behind Steven. I looked at him. "Should I stay here?" I asked.

"I don't think there will be anything going on in there but talk," he answered. "Maxie will protect your exhusband, but I doubt even that will be necessary."

"Why? That guy seemed quietly ominous."

Paul made a "yeah, well?" face. "He's here to collect a large sum of money. He won't be able to do that if your ex is not . . . available to deliver it. This meeting is a warning. It's about that man making clear to your ex-husband that he knows he was capable of finding him here, to indicate that running is not an option."

But I was still reeling from one aspect of the morning I had not been able to properly absorb. "I . . . I . . ." was the best I could muster.

Paul's face showed concern. "What is it, Alison?" he asked.

Finally I could manage to get the word out. *"Maurice?"*

Four

We stood by the door (well, I stood and Paul hovered) for about a minute. No loud shouts or thuds of a shovel blow were audible, and it wasn't that great a door. When I saw Liss walk into the front room, I walked toward her and stopped about halfway.

My daughter is not what you'd call a *morning person.* So the look on her face indicated she should not be approached or engaged in any way for fear of a cutting remark or, worse, an eye roll. I stepped backward to let her pass. As she did, she muttered, "Coffee." She shuffled into the den and headed directly for the urn.

Yoko Takamine, a very small but vivacious woman in her sixties, practically tap-danced into the room from the stairs. Yoko was a dear, but I found it hard to accept all this cheerfulness so early in the morning. And I'd already been up for two and a half hours.

"Good morning!" Yoko chirped. "Isn't it a lovely morning?"

It was twenty-seven degrees and I needed to put more ice melt out on my walk before someone slipped and slid directly into the nearest litigator's office. "It sure is, Yoko," I said unconvincingly. "What are your plans for the day?"

"I'm going to walk on the beach," she said. Of course she was. The windchill by the water would put it into the single digits.

"You're a stronger woman than I am, Yoko," I said. Over her left shoulder I saw Maxie sticking her head through the wall and talking to Paul. "I don't want to hold you up. There's coffee and tea in the den. Anything I can do for you?"

"No, I'm fine." Yoko pranced on into the den, where I was hoping she wouldn't cross paths with Melissa. Liss knows how we treat guests (and is actually better than I am at it) but might let her new teenage hormones rule her better judgment. It doesn't happen much, but it does happen.

I walked over to the library door as I saw Maxie duck back inside. "What's the latest?" I asked Paul.

"I was about to go inside myself," he said. "But Maxie says they're actually discussing the matter pretty reasonably. There have been no threats."

That seemed weird. "This is one crazy shakedown," I told him.

"If that's what it is," Paul answered.

"You want to go in? Go in."

Paul looked at the door as if considering. Then he shook his head. "I don't want Maxie to think I don't trust her report."

I saw Mel Kaminsky's door open and hid behind the staircase. Paul, watching me with an expression of complete bafflement, actually moved back to give me room, as if I wouldn't have just passed through him if we'd

intersected. "What is it?" he said in hushed tones. Sometimes I think Paul forgets he's dead.

"It's Mel," I hissed.

Paul's eyelids lowered a bit to bring his eyes back to
their normal shape. "He's been here for four days," he
reminded me.

"I know." I snuck a peek around the corner. Mel, looking puzzled, was headed toward the den. So he would pass
directly by us, and see only me. I took off as quietly as
possible toward the movie room.

"So, why are you suddenly afraid of him?" Paul wanted
to know. He followed a little behind me.

"I can't talk now," I said as quietly as possible.

"Alison!" I heard Mel's voice behind me. *Busted!*
"Excuse me, Alison!"

I gathered my face into a professional smile and turned
back to look at him. "Good morning, Mel," I trilled. "How
are you this morning?"

"Confused," he said. "Have you seen Annie?"

I considered saying I had seen the movie and not the
stage musical, but Mel probably wouldn't have laughed. I
couldn't lie to him; he was a guest. You get a bad reputation
that way. "I have," I told him. That was true.

"Do you know where she is? She seems to have taken
all of her things out of our room."

Again, I certainly could have told Mel that I did know
where his wife was and left it at that, but it would just be
delaying the inevitable. "I believe she's in one of the guest
rooms upstairs," I said. "The second one on the left."

Mel Kaminsky seemed to think I was speaking in some
foreign tongue. I only wished I was at this point. "One of
the upstairs guest rooms?" he parroted back.

Liss, no doubt on her second cup of coffee because she
was less grumpy, walked by us as she headed for the stairs.

"Morning, Mel," she said. "Did you know Anne was upstairs?" My daughter, ladies and gentlemen.

"Yeah," he answered, but he didn't sound all that sure of himself. Liss kept walking and was halfway up the stairs before Mel looked up at me again. "Why?"

This time I was legitimately confused. "Why what?" I asked.

"Why did Annie take all her stuff out of our room and move it upstairs?" he said.

As an innkeeper, your job is not to get involved in the lives of your guests. Your job is to make their stay comfortable and enjoyable. Since it seemed "enjoyable" was going to be a stretch for Mel from now on, and comfortable was not on the table at the moment, I did the only thing I could do.

I punted.

"That's something you'll have to ask Anne," I told Mel.

He nodded. "Which room, again?"

I directed him to Anne's new room and he walked off looking determined. Paul, who had been watching the whole sordid scene, stifled a laugh. "Jerk," I said to him in a low voice.

We turned just as the library door opened and out walked Overcoat, who had not removed one article of clothing despite being out of the frigid temperatures on my doorstep. I'll admit I held my breath for a moment, but The Swine walked out right behind him, and the strangest thing was going on as they approached us.

They were laughing.

"You should have seen him!" Steven said, his arm thinking about wrapping itself around Overcoat's shoulder and then thinking better of it. "I thought he'd—oh, hi, Ally."

It was "Ally" again. I was already starting to regret being worried Overcoat might have killed him.

Maxie floated out and started talking to Paul, who looked interested and a little baffled. But they were too far away and talking too quietly for me to make anything out. "I guess you two have worked out your differences," I said to the two completely three-dimensional men in the room.

"Differences!" Steven was overdoing the jocularity to a point that even Overcoat was looking embarrassed. "Simply a misunderstanding. Everything is fine. Right, Maurice?"

Overcoat looked less ebullient, but still calm. I got the impression he'd be calm if the house were being bombed. He might even be the one doing the bombing. "It should be," he allowed.

Whatever Maxie was saying to Paul at that point must have been a doozy, because I could hear his "What?" from across the room. I looked up involuntarily.

The Swine turned and looked where I was looking. "What?" he echoed. He didn't *know* he was echoing, but that didn't really matter. "What's going on?"

"Nothing. I thought I heard something." What I wanted right now was to usher Overcoat toward the front door, where all his clothing would go to good use against the cold and I could have my house back. Win-win. I looked at him. "Well, I'm sure you have a lot to do." I moved in the direction of the front room.

"Yes," he said. "Thank you."

But The Swine, for reasons I could not begin to understand, put up a hand. "Nonsense!" he said. "Stay for breakfast."

"I don't serve breakfast," I reminded him.

"We can bring something in. I'm sure you have something in the kitchen that you and Melissa were going to have." The fact was, Liss would have her two "coffees" and I'd probably grab a glass of orange juice and that was breakfast at the guesthouse. We were a lean and spare people. Steven looked at his new pal. "I want you to meet my daughter."

"Steven!" It was out of my mouth before I had a chance to think. Paul looked over at me and he and Maxie moved closer to us.

The Swine stared. No doubt my outburst had been a terrible breach of whatever new bond he had established with Overcoat. "Alison, the man is a guest," he said through clenched teeth.

"Not at all," Overcoat told him. "I need to be somewhere else, and I completely understand Ms. Kerby's reluctance to introduce her daughter to your business dealings." He nodded at me and we walked into the front room.

Steven, apparently not having gotten the memo on quitting while you're ahead, was still arguing that Overcoat should stick around awhile, but the other man would have nothing of it. "I appreciate the hospitality," he told my ex. "Now we must be sure that our business arrangement is solidified. So I assume I will hear from you soon?"

The Swine lost a little color from his face, but only someone who'd been married to him would have noticed. "Of course," he said.

"Tomorrow," Overcoat said a bit more ominously.

"Yes."

Overcoat smiled at me and nodded again. "Nice to meet you," he said, and left before Steven could try to talk him into taking a ride to the IHOP and sharing some blueberry pancakes.

As soon as I closed the front door behind him, I turned a hundred and eighty degrees and glared at my ex-husband. "You want the hit man to meet our *daughter*?" I said.

Steven laughed. "Hit man," he said. "He's not a hit man."

"He ain't from the Chamber of Commerce."

Maxie moved over closer to me, hovering about a foot off the floor. She was no longer wearing the trench coat. "Get rid of him," she told me. "We need to talk."

That was unusual; most of the time Maxie would rather avoid talking to me. I was too much like an . . . older sister to her. Maxie was poisoned when she was only twenty-eight, and I was no longer that age. Let's leave it at that. Maxie's emotional age was probably somewhere around eighteen, which was why she mostly preferred to hang around with Melissa.

"He's just doing his job," Steven said.

I decided the best thing to do was act like we were still married. It wasn't hard; I just needed to tap in to my vast reserves of annoyance with him. "Fine!" I shouted, reaching for the ceiling. "I can't ever talk to you!" I turned my back on The Swine, which felt both familiar and satisfying, and went into the kitchen. Having lived with me for ten years, he would know not to follow me there, especially if he wanted something to eat.

Paul and Maxie actually beat me into the room, not having to deal with things like gravity or solid objects. They waited until I was inside and heading for the fridge— that orange juice was sounding good about now—before they both started to talk at once.

"That guy was here to—" Maxie started.

"Your ex-husband is going to—" Paul began over her words.

I poured some orange juice into a cup with the logo of the local pizzeria on it and took a sip, holding up my hand for a quiet moment. Then I took a deep breath and looked at the two ghosts. I pointed at Maxie. "You first. You were there."

Maxie gave Paul her best triumphant smile, to which Paul simply nodded. "They started off sounding like it was gonna be bad. I had the shovel right in my hand if I needed it. Then they got friendly even when the other guy said the ex owed him a bunch of money and he knew the kind of people he was dealing with, so he'd better pay up. To which the ex says he hasn't got it."

"I imagine that went over big," I said.

"Yeah, that was my most shovel-ready moment," Maxie agreed. "I thought I saw your buddy in the coat go into his pocket, but all he took out was a handkerchief. Wiped his head, but he wasn't nervous; he was hot. He wouldn't take off that wool coat."

"Yeah, what was that all about?" I asked.

"What Maxie is leaving out—" Paul began.

"I'm *getting* to it!" Maxie cut him off. "So anyway, that's when they start getting chummy. Coat Guy keeps insisting your ex call him Maurice, like they're pals, making a joke about how he forgot the guy's name. Then *Maurice* tells the ex he's got until tomorrow morning to pay off or something bad is gonna happen."

I bit my lip. "Did he mention Melissa?" I asked. My voice sounded raspy.

Maxie shook her head. "He wasn't specific, but your ex definitely got the message, because he started begging for more time. He hasn't got four hundred grand on him, he just flew out from L.A., yada yada."

That caught me. "Hold on," I told Maxie. "Back up. He owes Lou Maroni *four* hundred thousand dollars?"

"He didn't mention any names," Maxie said. She started twirling around listlessly in the air, the Maxie version of casual. She was enjoying her moment in the spotlight. "But it's clear he's in pretty deep to somebody."

"Paul," I said. "You were there when I talked to Steven."

Maxie scowled a bit that I was asking Paul something

when she wanted to continue, but she didn't have time to protest, because our resident ghostshoe (I just made that up) knew where I was going and floated forward.

"Yes, and he said he owed *six* hundred thousand," Paul said. "But that's not the part—"

"*If* you don't mind." Maxie, who had risen along with her blood pressure if she'd had blood pressure, huffed a bit and looked at me. "I was telling you the story."

"Of course." If I didn't let her speak, there would be no living with her for at least half a day. And you know the thing about ghosts: You can't live with 'em, because they're not living. "Please go on." But I tucked away the discrepancy in The Swine's accounting to be discussed later.

"*So*, Maurice is laying it on thick about he's gotta have the money tomorrow, and the ex is pleading, but not very convincing. I mean, he didn't cry or anything. He just keeps saying he doesn't have the money and there's got to be a way they can work this out."

"I don't see how this ends with the two of them walking out of the library guffawing," I said. "Where did it turn around?"

Maxie folded her arms and descended to my eye level. "It got a lot friendlier when your ex said he had a way to pay the money, but it would take some more time." She gave me a look that got me angry at Steven, and I didn't know why. Paul sort of looked away like the way you do when you're watching a horror movie. You know something awful is about to happen, but you can't entirely stop watching. He was looking at me through the corner of his eye.

"Did he say how he was going to do that?" I asked. I had no idea what the answer would be, but I could tell from the whole dynamic in this room that I wasn't going to like it.

And I was right. What I hadn't anticipated was that

Paul, unable to contain himself, blurted out the response as if it were one word, fast and blurred. He managed not to slam his hands over his mouth when he was finished, but the effect was the same.

"He wants you to sell the house and give him the money," he said.

Five

Maxie finally got to use the shovel.

Unfortunately she was using it as an obstacle, blocking the kitchen door to keep me from leaving the room and going to kill my ex-husband. Technically I could have just ducked under the shovel, held horizontally across the doorway, and run through Maxie. But that was always kind of gross and she was also very quick and kept adjusting the height of the shovel as I attempted the maneuver.

"It'll just take a minute!" I protested. "In fact, give me that shovel. It'll take less than a minute, and we can use it after to hide the body!"

"Alison, you know you're not going to do that," Paul said. He was behind me, probably looking for some other item he could place in my way, but I couldn't tell from here. His voice sounded as though he was trying to be soothing while looking for the syringe with the sedative in it.

"You're right. I'll burn the body in the boiler downstairs. Then we can renovate the basement and replace the unit with a gas furnace. The cops will never know." My mind was racing. Sell the house? After all I'd done to buy it and fix it up to make my home and my business here? Was he nuts?

Maxie blocked yet another attempt at going under the shovel. I couldn't go *over* it without a trampoline, so I sat down, deflated, on my kitchen floor and looked around. "He thinks I can get six hundred grand for this place?"

"Don't you have a mortgage?" Paul asked.

I stared up at him. "You're going to try and convince me with facts and logic? Where have you been living all this time?"

Paul allowed himself a small smile. "My mistake," he said.

Luckily I wasn't leaning on the kitchen door, because it opened and Melissa walked in, saw me on the floor and knelt down. "Mom! Are you all right?"

"Yes, sweetie. I'm just dealing with your father."

"It's no big deal," Maxie told Melissa. "I had her under control."

I gave her the latest in a long series of dirty looks.

Liss held out a hand and helped me to my feet. "I'm getting a ride to a movie today with Wendy's mom. It's supposed to stay in the twenties today. Do you want to pick us up, or should I walk home?" When you're thirteen, all that matters is you. No. All that *exists* is you.

"I'll pick you up," I said to my daughter. "You and Wendy?"

"And Jared. But we can walk if you're busy." Jared was a boy in her class whom Melissa definitely did not have a crush on. If you asked her.

"If something comes up I'll text you."

Liss nodded. "Is Dad doing something especially crazy?" she asked.

Now, I tried very hard not to be the divorced mom who

tries to poison her daughter's relationship with her father. My daughter's father. My ex-husband. The Swine. I saw no reason to tell her about her father's insane plan to get me to sell our home so he could pay off his Ponzi scheme. The best thing to do here was to smile and put a brave face on it.

"He's being a swine," I said.

Melissa nodded. "I figured when he had to fly to Newark all of a sudden and didn't stop to pack a bag. Should I be worried?"

Paul looked away to avoid eye contact with Melissa. He's not a good liar to begin with and is not great at dealing with children, even Liss. In fact, he probably would have a harder time selling her a fake story than anyone else. Liss is really smart, and Paul has a softer heart than he'd like you to know.

"No. About what?" Had Steven said something to her?

"About Dad. Usually when this kind of thing happens he ends up moving somewhere else and we don't hear from him for a while."

"Well, I can't vouch for him, but we're not moving anywhere."

Liss gave me an odd look. "I know."

I was saved by the honk as her best pal Wendy's mom was clearly outside waiting to get the kids to the movie. Liss hit the swinging kitchen door and said she'd see me later. I could hear her scurrying for the front room, picking up her backpack and her parka along the way. Life is so much smoother when you're young; one movement just blends into the next without a thought.

When I turned toward the kitchen door, Maxie raised the shovel horizontally again. "Forget it," I told her. "I'm past that part. But I do have to confront Steven about this selling-the-house deal so he can come up with a Plan G."

"You mean Plan B," Paul suggested.

I shook my head. "You don't know him like I do. He's

already been through a few and rejected at least one more. I just have to make sure I keep ahead of him, especially if he really thinks I have enough money to bail him out. If I'm the mark he'll try anything, and I just don't have the patience I used to have."

"No kidding," Maxie agreed. But she put down the shovel.

It wouldn't go over well if I let The Swine know I had heard about his plan. For one thing, the only way I could have gotten the information was to have had someone in the room, which I had, but she was dead and Steven wasn't going to hear about that. (See previous comment, re: custody hearing.)

"I'm probably better off not letting him know I'm onto him," I mused. I was talking mostly to myself, but the ghosts didn't know that.

"What?" Maxie sounded appalled. "No fight?"

"Maxie," Paul admonished. "How will that help, Alison?" Paul likes to understand the way people think. "You weren't saying this a minute ago."

I sat, this time on a stool we keep by the center island in lieu of an actual table to eat dinner at like real people. Wait. I was channeling my aunt Alice there for a second. "If Steven knows that I heard he was planning for me to sell the house, he'll want to know how I found out. And since I heard about it from Maxie, that's a problem. But that's not the reason."

"I'm a problem?" Maxie was not always focused on the issue at hand. Unless it was her.

"Yes, but that's not what I'm talking about," I answered. "The thing is, if I go right after Steven, he'll pivot. Go to the next plan, and that one we won't know about. It's better to play him for a while, let him go on with his plot and maybe even let him believe he's making progress so he can't maneuver his way into something worse."

"Your marriage must have been hilarious," Maxie said. "I wish I'd seen it."

"But—and I'm just playing devil's advocate here—if you let your ex-husband waste his time on a solution to his problem that you know will fail, you give him much less time to find a solution that really will solve the dilemma." Paul wasn't pacing or stroking his goatee, because there was no case to consider, but he did look serious. "You could be helping the people trying to do him harm."

I considered saying, "And?" But despite whatever differences The Swine and I'd had—and an encyclopedia couldn't contain all of them—he was still Melissa's dad and they actually loved each other. I couldn't let him come to any real harm.

"So we have to figure out how to raise four hundred thousand dollars or scare Mr. Overcoat away," I said.

"Scare him away?" Paul squinted at me.

"Sure. This is a haunted house, isn't it? But I'm going to need some reinforcements."

This time Maxie squinted. She's oddly shy of people she doesn't know and will sometimes leave the house completely if strangers (other than guests, whom she considers somehow necessary irritants) are due to show up.

"Yeah. It's a good thing we're cooking dinner tonight." I got my cell phone out of my pocket.

"We?" Maxie laughed. "You don't cook."

"We. Melissa and my mother. That we. That means my dad will be here and Josh is definitely coming. But maybe we need just a little more brain power." I swiped the phone into active mode and called my best friend, Jeannie Rogers.

We almost couldn't fit everyone into the kitchen for dinner, and that didn't even count the people who were dead and therefore not eating.

My mother and father arrived first. Mom, her backpack stuffed with dinner preparation materials, bounded in through the kitchen door and started unloading immediately. "Your father's bringing the rest," she said.

"The rest?" I looked at the small pantry she was unloading on my center island. "Did you invite the Philharmonic Symphony Orchestra?"

Mom waved a hand. "Don't be silly. We'll be lucky if there are leftovers."

"Oh, there will be leftovers." My father, carrying two heavily stuffed shopping bags, floated in through the open door, which was lucky, since he would not have been able to hide anything this big under an article of clothing unless he was dressed in the big tent from the Ringling Brothers collection. "You'll be eating brisket for a couple of days easy."

"We're having chicken," Mom corrected him.

"Brisket fit the joke better." Dad hovered above the island and placed the bags down. "How are you, Baby Girl?" Dad didn't get to hug that much anymore, but his words could have almost the same effect on me.

"Don't play with me," I said to my parents. "I told you who flew in last night."

Both their faces registered certain levels of disgust. My mother lives in the delusional belief that I never make mistakes. Except for The Swine. Neither of them was at all pleased with my husband, for reasons that became obvious (to me) about halfway through our marriage. They were right, of course, but classy enough never to have uttered the words "I told you so." When we split, they took Melissa and me in for the time I couldn't afford the rent until I was able to put together the money to serve as a down payment on the soon-to-be guesthouse.

"We know," they intoned almost in unison.

Melissa pushed the door open and smiled when she saw

our guests. "Look who's here!" she said. She got a real hug
from her grandmother and a virtual one from her grandfather. She's more "sensitive" to spirits than I am, so she
can feel their touch better than I can. It's an advantage,
except when Maxie wants to touch us.

"World's best girl," my father said, smiling the most
grandfatherly smile you wouldn't have been able to see if
you were in the room.

"World's best grampa," Liss responded.

"You ready to cook?" Mom wanted to know. She and
Melissa do most—okay, all—of the cooking in our family.
It began as a way for Mom to teach Liss a skill she saw
had clearly skipped a generation but lately had been a case
of the pupil exceeding the master. Liss is a really good
cook, and likes to show Mom variations she's either found
online or thought up herself.

"Sure. Did you bring the orange?" Liss started rum-
maging through the shopping bags.

"Yes, but I don't see why orange juice from a carton
isn't good enough."

Liss smiled and shook her head. "Grandma."

They set about cooking, which nearly always drove me
out of the kitchen. I served as much purpose in the room at
such moments as would a harp. Pleasant to have nearby,
perhaps, but mostly you just keep having to walk around it.

Dad followed me out and then down to the basement,
where I could get his assessment of my renovation plans.
My father was a handyman in life and knows more about
the workings of older buildings than Bob Vila ever did.
He and Josh are my consultants in such matters. And Jeannie's husband, Tony, who's a contractor.

I'm rarely at a loss for advice, is what I'm saying.

Dad dropped himself down through the first floor,
which meant that he got to the basement before I could
using the conventional means of getting down there. He

was stroking his chin, giving the impression of a clean-shaven Paul who was forty years older.

"You can turn it into a room, Baby Girl, but I don't see this ever being a real comfortable living space." This, and I hadn't even made it down the stairs yet.

"Oh, thanks a lot. Between you and Paul, you're about as encouraging as a bowl of gruel." I sat down on the steps. "But the thing I hate most is that you're right, and so is Paul. I don't need this to be a room. Why do I want to turn it into one so badly?"

Dad dropped his arm down and turned to face me fully. "Maybe you're done with this house," he said softly.

Had he been talking to The Swine?

"What do you mean?"

He shrugged. "I've seen it happen. A contractor takes on a job that seems like it's going to last forever, and eventually all the work is done. It's just maintenance now, keeping things the way they are instead of making big exciting changes. Maybe you're trying to create a project where none exists because you don't want to believe you're done doing the big stuff."

"You think I should get rid of the house?" I was almost misting up. Almost.

Dad chuckled. "No. You've made a home and a business here. You don't have to move away because there's nothing left to fix. Believe me, a place like this will give you plenty of projects going forward. You just don't have to turn anything into anything else now. It's time to stop renovating and enjoy the work you've done."

I let out a breath. "You always make me feel better, you know?" I said.

My father smiled. "No charge, Baby Girl."

Upstairs I heard feet tramping around on the floor above, and before I could even get to my feet, Jeannie's voice was reverberating around what I could only assume was the whole house. "Alison!" she yelled. Jeannie did nothing halfway.

"I'm coming! Don't yell anymore; there are noise ordinances in this town." I stood and headed up the stairs. On the way I caught a glimpse of my father, who had his hand over his mouth. He always had thought I was hilarious.

Jeannie was helping her son, Oliver, now two years old, off with his winter jacket while her husband, Tony, was bringing their baby daughter, Molly, inside. Molly was eight months old and just figuring out that she was alive, so her default expression was one of complete awe and confusion. Her adorable brown eyes were constantly opened as wide as they could go. Molly always looked as if you just told her the best secret ever.

"Stop wiggling," Jeannie told her son. Ollie had done everything he was supposed to do (walk, talk, run, do logarithms) pretty much on the day Dr. Spock had assigned to him more than sixty years before he was born, and now he was determined to prove to his mother that the expression Terrible Twos was not arrived at randomly. He was twisting his body back and forth, making it difficult for his mother to pull his arms through the sleeves of the jacket.

But Jeannie, resilient creature that she was, had adapted. She had spent the first year of Oliver's life obsessing over every detail of his existence to the point of madness, but once she settled into the idea of having her second baby, she had relaxed her parenting methods almost supernaturally. She let go of Ollie's sleeve and let him spin himself into the den, something I wouldn't have minded if every breakable item I owned did not reside in that room. "Fine," Jeannie told her son. "Wear the jacket inside. If you get hot, come ask me and I'll help you get it off, okay?" Oliver toddled off, still spinning, happy. Jeannie beamed at him and then came over to me.

"Okay, where is he?" Why bother with pleasantries like "hello" when there's an ex-husband to snarl at?

"Steven is out 'running errands,' he said," I told her. "I imagine that means trying to get a real estate agent to give him an appraisal on my house."

Tony, having gotten Molly out of her snuggly outerwear, shook his head as he carried her over. "He can't do that. He's not on the mortgage, so he has no right to an appraisal."

"Will the average agent ask that?" I said.

Tony flattened out his lips and tilted his head: *Maybe, maybe not*. "Probably they would, but you can't count on it happening immediately. The key is to make sure *he* understands this is not his house."

"I can handle The Swine," I said.

They had the nerve to look skeptical.

"He's not going to sell my house," I protested. "He's not legally entitled to, and I'm not going to agree to it, so the deal is over. What I need you two for is a council of war. The question on the table is: Do I tell him I know about his plan, or do I let him go on thinking he can get away with it and watch him waste the little time he has to pay off this Lou guy?"

Jeannie grinned evilly. "It would be entertaining," she said.

"How serious did this guy seem when you saw him this morning?" Tony asked. If their children turn out to have practical sides to them, it will be from their father's side of the family.

Maxie dropped down into the room carrying Lester the puppy for no obvious reason. Lester, who might have been born as many as a hundred and fifty years ago for all we know, had never outgrown the puppy behavior most dogs give up around two. This made him a match temperamentally for Maxie, who had bonded with him from the day we'd "rescued" him, as Melissa would say. The fact was, he came in through a wall one day and never left.

I sniffled a little. I'm allergic to dogs. A year of visits

to the allergist had provided a cocktail of antihistamines that had taken away the bulk of my symptoms, but I still felt it when Lester strayed outside Melissa's attic room, which Maxie knew full well he wasn't supposed to do. I gave her a look. I think Tony noticed it, but then, he understands the whole ghost situation.

Jeannie, the captain of the Olympic denial team, refuses to believe Paul and Maxie (and any other spirits we happen to encounter) are anything but a clever marketing ploy and a game I like to play with my mother and my daughter. Jeannie has an interesting mind.

Maxie caught the glare I was pointing in her direction and rolled her eyes. "He needs to get out of that room once in a while," she said, secure in her knowledge that I wouldn't answer her with Jeannie around.

I decided to concentrate not on my suddenly watery eyes but on Tony's question. "He didn't scare me much, if that's what you mean," I said. "But he definitely had an agenda, and it didn't include singing the greatest hits of Peter, Paul and Mary."

"Do you think he'll do Steven any real harm?" Tony asked.

"I didn't give the guy a deep psychological profile test," I said, more annoyed at Maxie, who was letting Lester run around my den, to which we had adjourned to better get the full spectacle of Oliver, who was continuing to spin. No doubt he was making an attempt to get dizzy enough to throw up. Little boys are fascinated with bodily fluids. "I didn't even give him a BuzzFeed test on which Disney princess he really is. I can't answer that question."

"What question?" I turned my head and the day got better.

Josh Kaplan stood in the archway to the den, smiling in his affectionate, slightly amused style. Josh knows about the ghosts but can't see or hear them, so he didn't notice

Maxie or Lester. He came over and gave me a kiss on the cheek and then settled in with his arm around my waist.

"You know my ex is in town," I reminded him, then filled him in on the psychodrama Steven had brought with him this time. The last time The Swine had arrived in Harbor Haven, I had not remet Josh yet, so he was still a vague childhood memory. Now, seeing the concerned look on his face, he was completely real and engaged. Josh was what his grandfather Sy, now in his mid-nineties and still coming to work at Madison Paints four days a week, called a "mensch."

"So you're trying to figure out if you should tell him you know about his scheme to have you sell your house and then give him all the proceeds?" Josh seemed not to understand how that was even a question. "Of course you tell him, while showing him precisely where the front door is and insisting that he use it, but only in the direction of out."

Mom pushed her way out of the kitchen. "Your daughter is a genius," she told me, wiping her hands on a dish towel.

"And you're not the least bit biased." Jeannie gave Mom a kiss on the cheek and Mom responded as she should, by paying attention to Jeannie's children. First she stopped Ollie's spinning and directed him to a soft easy chair, which he appeared to need, eyes wide and head wobbling. He flopped down and sat there staring into space.

Then Mom walked over to Tony, who was still holding Molly. She shucked the baby under the chin, as proscribed in the Grandmother's Handbook, made some cooing noises and then turned her attention on Josh, whom my mother probably likes better than she likes me, and that's saying something. Both my parents have been completely in love with my boyfriend since he arrived back in my life. Dad, in fact, had known Josh from the days at Madison Paints when he was alive. He has repeatedly informed me that my boyfriend is "a keeper." Who am I to argue?

Dad, who had followed Mom out of the kitchen after a few moments, no doubt after having had a quick affectionate word with our chef for the evening, floated up toward the ceiling when he saw the gathered crowd. "Is it Thanksgiving?" he asked facetiously.

Mom hugged Josh, who smiled but still seemed a little stunned by our ongoing conversation. My mother noticed his face and asked, "What's wrong?"

Josh does not lie much. For one thing, he's bad at it and for another, he doesn't want to, which might be why he's bad at it. This once again highlights his complete difference from my ex-husband, who would lie if asked whether he was alive. It's a reflex.

"Your daughter is pondering whether to play it straight with your ex-son-in-law," Josh told Mom. "I'm trying to persuade her that there's no point to playing along with his little game, and then to shove him out into the cold to take his schemes and their consequences elsewhere."

Mom raised an eyebrow and looked at me. "There's something you weren't telling me?" she asked.

"Deal with it," I said. She was my mom. By definition you don't tell them everything. Except Melissa. She has to tell her mom everything. It's a special case.

Mom scowled but did not respond. My father, whose normal reaction to such a show of defiance would be "Don't sass your mother," appeared fixated on Josh, waiting for more information. I immediately apologized to my mother, who waved a hand and told me to forget it. Compared to my teenage years, this was a Hallmark Mother's Day card.

"The point," Josh went on, his eyes with more fury than I'd seen before, "is that this man has been scamming you since the day you met him, and you need to show him exactly where the road to the airport is, today."

That was worth thinking about, since Josh never

interfered with any business between me and The Swine, and only got involved with Melissa issues when she asked him a direct question, usually to back me up. The fact that Jeannie and Tony were both nodding in agreement bore some weight as well.

But I didn't have time to decide on a course of action. There was the sound of the back door opening, which was unusual, since Mom, Josh and I were the only ones who ever used it. Within seconds, The Swine swung open the kitchen door and, snow still clinging to the shoes he had worn from Los Angeles that were probably wondering what this cold, wet white stuff was, barreled into the room looking absolutely frantic, eyes darting back and forth. He did not say hello to any of the people who had come since he left and did not react to Josh's arm around my waist, which was only odd, since he'd never actually laid eyes on Josh before. Instead he hustled through the den, the largest room in my house, and headed toward the stairs without breaking stride.

As he went past me he did not stop or even slow down, but got close enough that only I could hear when he muttered, "Remember, you never saw me."

Then he went directly to the door and the sound of his shoes reverberated on the stairs as he climbed up to his room.

Six

Steven did not immediately join us for dinner.

"You didn't see him?" Jeannie repeated after I'd told the crowd (some of whom could not be seen by three of the assembled) about The Swine's weird statement as he rushed by me. "What does that mean, you didn't see him?"

Melissa, who had never been excluded from the conversation even when we were discussing stabbings and shootings, looked more bothered than usual, which made sense. The subject today was her father, and his behavior was not inspiring a great deal of confidence.

You can only shield them for so long. Besides, there was no way to keep Liss out of the room while we ate. She was the chef.

Josh, Jeannie, Tony, Mom, Liss and I were on barstools situated around the large center island I'd installed in the kitchen back in the days when I thought I might learn to cook. And that was *before* I'd been hit on the head by a bucket of wallboard compound and started to see ghosts. Luckily my mother and daughter had made the kitchen relevant.

But also present was Oliver, seated at a small table I'd used for Melissa back in the day and looking very pleased with his solitude, mostly because it meant that he could avoid his younger sister, who was in her father's lap and clearly co-opting a good deal of attention that was clearly supposed to be his. Ollie was pretending that didn't matter. He was biding his time.

Hovering at various points around the kitchen were Paul, Maxie and Dad. My father seemed to be examining the bolts holding the light fixtures and the hanging hooks for pots and pans, making sure they weren't going to fall any time soon. I knew that meant Dad was listening to the conversation and considering his response, which he would undoubtedly give me later on when he could get me alone. Dad doesn't like to intrude.

Paul was lower down, almost at eye level. He had clearly decided The Swine's situation was as close to an investigation as he was liable to get in the near future and so was going to treat it as such; he was paying intense attention to all that was said.

Maxie, sharing some of Oliver's maturity level, was not pleased with the idea that the focus of the group was on someone who dared not to be her. She hovered, lying on her side, looking as if she were posing for Botticelli as one of Venus's handmaidens. She was fully dressed, I hasten to add, and looking as bored as a person could be when a mystery of sorts was being discussed in close proximity.

"Clearly he thinks someone is going to ask if we saw him, and the answer is supposed to be no," Josh said. He had waited through a delicious bite of orange chicken before responding, because he has excellent manners. I tend to talk through food, which my mother says is due to my high spirits and my daughter informs me is gross.

"Yeah, but what do you think it means that he's telling Alison to cover for him?" Tony asked. I watched him closely. Everybody has better table manners than I do. Even Oliver, who was eating the cut-up pieces of food Jeannie had given him, and was using a spoon. At that age Melissa would have used her fingers. I haven't asked my mother, but I'd bet I would have flung the chicken across the room to see how far it would go.

Josh considered his answer, and I did notice him glance at Melissa. "I think we're better off not thinking about what it means," he said. He looked at me.

"I have to guess that he ran into someone he doesn't want to talk to, and if they come looking for him, he wants me to deny he's here," I said. "It's not unusual when you come back after a long time away."

Melissa, who sometimes watches me as if deciding who to be when she's an adult, looked . . . I'll say skeptical. Exasperated would be going too far.

My father seemed even less convinced. "He's up to something and that's never good," he said.

Josh, who naturally hadn't heard Dad, was still looking worried/annoyed. "What are you going to do, Alison?"

"Pushy, isn't he?" Maxie was doing her "bored monarch" voice, which indicated she had gone more than a minute without being the center of attention. "What do you see in him?"

"I told Steven he could stay here for a couple of days," I told Josh. Ignoring Maxie had become something of a reflex for me. "Today was the first day. If he doesn't find himself somewhere else to stay by tomorrow, I'll make it clear he has to go. I don't see how I can do more than that."

"Mom," Melissa said, "I saw how he was living in California. I don't think Dad can afford to stay in a real hotel."

It was nice how she saw our business as a cute little indulgence that clothed and fed her. But I was being unfair.

Anything that made her sound sympathetic to The Swine rubbed me the wrong way, and I had to fight that urge. "He has friends in the area, Liss. He grew up here. He has family here. He'll find a place to stay. But if that Overcoat guy is going to come back soon looking for him, I want to be telling the truth when I say that your dad's not here."

Tony and Jeannie exchanged a glance. "Maybe he could stay with us," Jeannie said. She sounded about as enthusiastic about the idea as I would be about going back to the job I had at the lumberyard before I'd bought the guesthouse. With money I'd gotten from suing the lumberyard.

"No," I said. "You have two kids in a two-bedroom house now. Besides, I don't want Overcoat finding Steven at your place, either. Let him go crash on a couch by one of his old stockbroker buddies. They probably have pretty nice couches."

Mom was about to say something when the kitchen door swung open and The Swine, looking pale (which was weird for a guy who'd come from the land of the sun only a day earlier) and nervous, skittered in. He stopped short, surprised at the crowd he saw staring at him.

"Steven," my mother said. My father said something else, and for once I was not pleased that my daughter could hear her grandfather.

"Hello, Loretta," The Swine said. He bravely—I'm sure he considered it bravely—smiled and walked over to embrace my mother, who looked like she'd rather hug a boa constrictor. Behind Steven's back I saw my father pick up a rolling pin Melissa had left on a counter from her preparation of dinner. "It's good to see you."

"Yes," Mom said. I guess it was all she could think to say.

"You want some dinner?" Melissa asked her father. She reached for a plate on the center island.

"No, pumpkin, that's okay." Melissa once told me she

didn't like her father calling her *pumpkin*. She was younger
then and didn't understand what was endearing about a
large orange gourd. "I'm going out in a minute. But thank
you."

"So, what's new, Steven?" Jeannie could ask an innocuous question and make it sound positively sinister if she
wanted to. And she wanted to.

"All the usual, Jeannie." The Swine looked at the baby
in Tony's lap and put on that sickening baby talk voice
adults use to show how in touch they are with their inner
children. "And who is this? Huh? Who is this?"

Tony gave him a look that had icicles attached to it.
"That's Molly."

"Hi, Molly." Steven put out his finger, which Molly
placidly ignored, staring at her father. Already Molly was
showing better taste in men than I had at a considerably
more mature stage in my life.

"Ask him what he meant," Paul suggested softly. "Ask
him why you have to lie about his whereabouts."

My father tightened his grip on the rolling pin. Hitting
Steven would probably fulfill a dream he'd been having
for at least fifteen years.

"Steven," I began, "about what you said before."

The Swine turned quickly and dropped his adorable
talking-to-an-infant cadence. "I didn't say anything
before," he said. His tone was slightly threatening.

But I'd heard it before and besides, Dad had a rolling
pin and wasn't afraid to use it. "Yes, you did. You passed
by me and said that I never saw you. What did you mean
by that?"

My ex-husband looked like he'd been slapped in the
face, which would have fulfilled a dream *I'd* been having
for at least fifteen years. "I didn't say that," he attempted.

"You did. Now, what did you mean by it?"

Steven glanced quickly at Melissa, then back at me, as

if reminding me our daughter was in the room. He had clearly misunderstood: I was doing this specifically because she was present. She needed to understand her father.

"I think you must have misheard me." A second try and a lame one.

"Why'd you marry him, again?" Maxie wanted to know. It was a fair question. There were two reasons I couldn't answer it at the moment.

"Steven," I said in my best grown-up voice. "This morning a man came to my house and made it clear he was looking for you and then mentioned that he knew Melissa and I lived here. You left to 'run errands' this afternoon and when you came back you told me that I never saw you. Now you're going to tell me *exactly* what is going on or you can leave this house tonight and not come back. Is that clear?"

Josh looked as proud of me as I'd ever seen. For some reason that didn't make me happy. The last thing I needed was to be the object of competition between these two. Not that Josh had a chance of losing; it was the principle of the thing.

Part of it was surely the look on Melissa's face. She's always had conflicted feelings about her father. When we divorced, Liss was little and simply sad, but now she had been talking to me about how living with just one parent almost all the time might have biased her feelings. That was a large part of the thinking behind her trip to visit Steven in L.A. He'd always tried to be the "fun parent," which was natural, since I was the one making the rules about ninety-nine times out of a hundred. I hadn't gotten a real read on whether that dynamic had changed in the days they'd just finished spending together.

Right now she was studying Steven and not liking what she saw. When she looked back at me, I wasn't sure whether that was admiration or disapproval I saw in her eyes.

Teenagers, it should be noted, are scary people. Much scarier than ghosts.

Steven's mouth opened and closed a time or two. Okay, two. His eyes darted between Melissa and me as if we were playing an especially spirited match of Ping-Pong and he didn't want to miss anything. Part of his success with people had always been the ability to make everyone believe he was on their side. That was undoubtedly what had gotten him into this current predicament. He was being judged by his daughter and found wanting. He knew it.

"You want the truth?" he managed.

"No, please lie to us all," I answered, the anger in my voice palpable. "That's always served you so well before."

That's when the scary teenager turned on me. She didn't say anything or even do much more than change her facial expression, but I saw it happen. I was being mean to her dad and she didn't like it.

"I deserved that," The Swine said. "I have lied to you and I've lied to you a lot. But this time I'm trying to protect you, and you have to believe that. You don't really want to know all that's going on right now, Alison."

"That doesn't help me," I told him. "I can't let you put us in any kind of trouble. And from what I've seen, that's all there is surrounding this deal of yours."

"Just one shot to the head," my father muttered. He backed off when he saw the look on his granddaughter's face. "Sorry, peanut." Silently he put the rolling pin back on the counter.

"Let me tell you this," my ex said. "I'm doing everything I can to keep any danger away from you and Melissa. If that includes moving out of this house until it all blows over, that's what I'll do."

"You don't have to do that." I knew *I* hadn't said that, but it was still something of a shock to determine that the words had come from my daughter's mouth. "We can help. There's a lot all of us can do. Max—"

"No," Maxie said quickly. "Don't say it." Melissa stopped.

"Maximally we prefer that you stay somewhere else while you're dealing with this," I said. "If there's anything one of us can do to help, you can let me know."

"Mom," Melissa protested.

"She's right," my mother said. I wasn't sure which one of us she meant.

"No, Liss. Your dad has gotten into some real trouble, and you're not a little kid anymore, so I can't just pretend it isn't there. But I can make sure that it doesn't get to you, and that's what I'm going to do." I turned toward my ex-husband. "You're going to have to move out tomorrow."

Steven looked like I'd hit him with the rolling pin. His eyes widened and his face, already pale, drained itself even more. His lips pursed. Then he nodded. "You're right. I'll pack up and leave in the morning." Honestly, Joan Crawford on her best day had nothing on Steven in the melodrama department. It even took me a second to realize he didn't have anything to pack up.

"You can stay with me if you want." It wasn't the last voice in the room I expected to hear, but that would have been Oliver's, so it was close.

Josh Kaplan stood and gestured toward Steven. "I don't have a second bedroom, but you can have the couch," he continued. I tried to wrap my mind around what he was saying.

"Really?" The Swine asked. And that was going to be it. The two significant men in my life were going to be roommates. A sitcom waiting to happen.

"If you want," Josh repeated.

Steven looked at Josh with wonder, then at me. For permission, I guess, or something. I couldn't do anything but shrug.

"I'd like that," The Swine said.

"Okay. I'll take you there tonight after dinner."

That was something of a disappointment, as I'd sort of thought Josh might want to spend the night at the guest-house. But there was my hard-line stand to consider. We all had to make sacrifices.

Steven nodded, looked like his eyes were misting up, and left the kitchen without another word.

It was Jeannie who broke the long silence that followed. She looked down at Oliver, who had gotten up and was playing with a toy car on the floor. She didn't see Lester the puppy, who was trying desperately to sniff the chicken Ollie had left behind. Then Jeannie looked at her daughter, who had fallen blissfully asleep in Tony's lap. Liss pretended not to be looking at me by checking her phone.

"Well, that was weird," Jeannie said.

Melissa got up, glared at me and ran out of the kitchen, presumably to go find her father. Her expression indicated I shouldn't talk to her again, perhaps until after she received a master's degree. In something.

Maybe it had been a Ping-Pong match after all.

Seven

"Melissa, you have to talk to me sooner or later," I said, pacing back and forth. "I'm your mother and we've always been able to talk to each other. What's different now?"

"That was good," Paul said, looking down from the ceiling. "Until you asked that question at the end. You're opening the door for her to tell you exactly what you did wrong, and then she'll get angry again."

"I dunno." Maxie was watching intently, a green visor over her eyebrows, the Maxie version of serious. "She's just mad at you. Maybe you should let that go for a while and see if it wears off."

Maxie, who considers herself Melissa's closest confidante (when it is in fact her friend Wendy), likes to be the good cop when I have to play bad. Since Maxie never has to be the bad cop, that gives her a lot of opportunities. I wasn't buying this one.

"Rehearsing is stupid," I said, flopping down on my

bed. "I'm talking to my daughter, not to a grand jury. I shouldn't have to worry this much about a simple conversation."

I closed my eyes to avoid seeing the ghosts, but I could still hear Maxie. "Well, you kicked her dad out of the house. She's not going to be too happy with you. Maybe that's the new normal."

Mom and Dad had left an hour earlier, citing Mom's night vision but really because things had gotten uncomfortable in my house. Tony and Jeannie had packed up their children not long after, Jeannie offering to call later and "help you through this," no doubt with her vast experience raising a teenager through a divorce.

Steven and Josh had left together. That seems weird even to say, but it was true. Josh had tried to explain his rationale when the two of us were (as far as he knew) alone in the kitchen: "I figured I could keep an eye on him and make sure anything he said to you was true. Besides, you wanted him out of the house and I agreed with you. Seemed the easiest thing to do."

I held him close to me for a moment. "I lived with Steven a long time," I told him. "It's not as simple as you might think it is."

Josh laughed lightly. "The circumstances are going to be a little different this time."

"I would hope so." I liked the feel of his arms around me and he was just enough taller than me that I could duck down and fit my head under his chin if I bent a little. It sounds painful, but it actually feels nice.

"I think we should leave," Paul told Maxie.

"Yeah. I'm getting a little nauseated myself." They vanished, Maxie through the ceiling and Paul, the floor. Two vastly different spirits stuck existing in the same space.

"You sure you don't mind having him there?" I asked Josh for only the fifth time.

"Of course I mind, but it's a better plan than having him stay here, and I'll know if someone comes looking for him. That would mean they have someone watching your house." A cheerful thought.

We agreed that I'd call him if Overcoat showed up again and that Josh would call if anyone came to his apartment for business with Steven. And then I let go of him, although that was not my strongest impulse.

But Melissa was not convinced and she was not impressed with the possible danger to her if her father and his massive debt to Lou Maroni remained living under our roof. On one of the few moments she spoke to me before dumbwaitering up to her room, she said, "The ghosts can look out for us. They've done it before."

"Yes, but it's safer to keep the danger away rather than try to control it here."

"You're just doing this because you're mad at Dad," my daughter spat out. "It's not fair and you're going to get him killed!" Teenagers are the best in the world at ramping up the drama. She turned on a dime and ran up the stairs. We hadn't spoken since.

So I was practicing for an imaginary conversation I was hoping to have with my own daughter. Lying on my bed with my eyes closed, I thought it seemed so much easier to simply stay where I was and sleep until she had to leave for college.

"Come on, get up," Maxie said. "Melissa has to go to bed soon. If you want to have this fight with her, you need to do it now."

"It's not a fight," Paul corrected her. "It's going to be a healthy conversation." Paul is British but grew up in Canada. Strong emotion doesn't run with his people.

Maxie, I had to admit, was right. If I wanted to clear the air with Liss, I should do it tonight and not let this fester. I stood up. "Don't follow me," I told the ghosts.

I heard Maxie make a disappointed noise, but they did not seem to move when I left the room and headed for the pull-down stairs I could climb to Liss's attic room.

But I didn't make it that far. The phone in my pocket vibrated, and thinking it might be a conciliatory text from my daughter, I grabbed at it. But the message was coming from someone considerably more disturbing. It was from Detective Lieutenant Anita McElone of the Harbor Haven Police Department, and it read "I'm on your front porch." McElone, although she has come to accept there are ghosts in my house and having been told repeatedly that they are not scary, does not care to come inside unless she has to.

I wasn't crazy about hearing from the police . . . ever, really, but this time of night it was more disturbing. It wasn't something that could wait until morning. Did something happen to Steven? To Josh, because he was with Steven? (That would unquestionably have been worse. In case you're seeing this, Josh.)

I rushed down the stairs, passing Yoko on the way. Luckily she didn't seem to have anything to ask me about, but at the speed I was traveling it was hard to tell. I loved having guests, but Josh was my boyfriend and Steven was . . . Melissa's father. That's right. So they had to take priority at the moment.

Of course, I could have just texted McElone (if you have problems with your hearing, you would pronounce it "macaroni") and told her to come inside, but she would have argued and I didn't have time. I opened the front door and looked out for her.

McElone is nothing if not reliable. She was standing (despite the very inviting glider I installed almost immediately after closing on the house), fingers intertwined behind her, just to the left of the door. She looked like she was waiting for someone to give her the at-ease command.

"What's wrong?" I asked. Some people would have

started with "hello." I was cutting the niceties to get to the point. That might have had something to do with the fact that it was ten degrees outside.

"We had a call from Hanrahan's," she said. McElone doesn't believe in niceties either. Hanrahan's is one of the slightly rowdier pubs in Harbor Haven. Of course in Harbor Haven a rowdy pub is one where a game of darts can get a little heated. "They found the body of a man in the alley next to the bar."

My voice didn't sound smooth when I spoke. In fact, it sounded like I'd just swallowed a handful of sand. "Whose body?" I asked. *Let it be Steven, not Josh. Sorry, Liss, but your father is a Swine and Josh so isn't.*

The hands came from behind McElone's back, and they were holding a small notebook. She opened it and looked at a page. "A guy named Maurice DuBois," she said. "Address in Santa Monica, California."

Maurice. Overcoat.

McElone looked up from the notebook and seemed to be looking for a reaction. The one she got from me was probably relief. "You ever hear of this guy?" she asked.

"Me?" That wasn't an answer, mostly because it wasn't meant to be. "Why?"

McElone's gaze did not waver. "Mostly because we consulted with the Santa Monica PD, and they say this DuBois guy might have had dealings with a Steven Rendell." She did not pause for a reaction that time. "Is your husband in town?"

I blinked. "*Ex*-husband," I said.

"Why don't I come inside and look?" the lieutenant suggested. "It's pretty cold out here, in case you hadn't noticed."

"You're the one who's afraid to come inside," I said. I opened the door and held it for her. "After you. But you won't find Steven here."

Even as we were walking inside, Paul's head stuck out through the door, which was abrupt enough to make me start just a little. McElone looked at me. "Ghosty thing?" she asked. The lieutenant looked a trifle worried. It was going to take a long time for her to be comfortable with the dead people in my house. I shook my head.

"Just the shock of what you said," I lied.

Paul, meanwhile, followed us into the house, where it was thankfully warmer. "Why is the lieutenant here?" he asked. He sounded excited. There's nothing Paul likes as much as a fresh mystery to investigate. "Is it something about the man from this morning?"

I didn't react—I try not to when McElone is around—but it seemed strange that Paul would leap to that conclusion.

"So you say this Maurice DuBois was found dead outside Hanrahan's," I told the lieutenant, as if she didn't know that. "How did he die?"

"Not from old age," she said. "He had two bullet wounds, one in the leg, from behind, probably to stop him from running. Then one in the head. Execution-style, as they say."

And here I thought Overcoat was the guy I should have been afraid of. "Like a mob hit? On a guy from Santa Monica? That seems so impolite."

McElone shrugged. She walked through the front room, looking from side to side, no doubt trying to determine if my ex was somehow concealed within the plaster walls or behind the painting of the old (before Superstorm Sandy) Point Pleasant Boardwalk I'd bought from an artist named Dominick Finnelle at a fund-raising sale for the middle school's theater club. "Don't want to jump to conclusions," McElone said.

I followed her into the den as Paul marveled at the idea of a murder related to Steven's business difficulties. "It's especially perplexing that he traveled all the way here from California," he mused. "The victim couldn't have known very many people in the area."

I know Paul; his mind was racing faster than . . . some NASCAR guy. (What do I know about NASCAR?)

McElone spent some time looking around the den, which was empty but for Mel Kaminsky, sitting in one of the easy chairs, just staring out the glass doors at the beach. People like to do that, especially when it's this cold out, but Mel still looked stunned. I gathered whatever conversation he'd had with Anne had not gone well, for him at least.

"Did you ever meet Maurice DuBois?" McElone asked. She turned after having perused the room and headed for the kitchen.

"I don't know," I answered. *I mean, I met a guy named Maurice. But really, doesn't that happen at least a couple of times a week?* "Why should I know him?"

"Like I said, he had some business dealings with your hus—ex-husband."

We glanced into the kitchen, which was empty of people. McElone still gave it a long view, like it was possible Steven was there but had become transparent. Which wasn't the case, assuming he was still alive.

"Wow," Paul said. As usual, he was one step ahead of me.

Wait. If Maurice had been shot, and Steven was with Josh . . .

"Steven is at Josh's apartment," I told the lieutenant. "You need to give them protection."

McElone turned to look at me. "What did you say?"

"I know you heard me. I'll give you the address. Steven went to stay there because I told him he couldn't be here. Now please, make sure nobody is going after them, okay?"

The lieutenant pulled a cell phone out of her pocket and

pushed a button. "This is McElone," she said after a moment. "I need a cruiser at an address in Asbury Park in connection with the homicide at Hanrahan's. I'm putting someone on to give you the address." She extended the phone to me. "Go ahead."

I took the phone and said Josh's address into it, spelling the street name. A male voice came through and said the cruiser would be on its way as soon as he could contact the APPD, which I assumed meant Asbury Park Police Department. The voice, which never identified itself, instructed me to give the phone back to McElone and I did without question.

"Get back to me when they report in," she said, and without a good-bye she disconnected the call and put the phone back in her pocket. Then she looked at me again. "Why didn't you tell me your ex was here before?" she asked.

"You asked if he was here. He wasn't here. It's not my business to get him in trouble if I don't have to." I wasn't making eye contact. It's harder with McElone since she and I had . . . an adventure together. I sort of saved her life, and even though she's done the same for me more than once, that's her job and not mine, so it's been a little weird since then. For one thing, lying to her is more difficult. The fact that she can arrest me whenever she feels like it contributes as well, but she could always do that.

"Okay, I'm asking you now. What do you know about this whole business with Maurice DuBois?"

I leaned on the arm of one of the overstuffed chairs and glanced again at Mel, who was still staring out at the surf and probably wondering what the hell had happened to his marriage. Paul flittered down from the ceiling and hovered right where he could look into my eyes.

"You have to give her the whole story," he said. "You know the lieutenant and you know she'll help if she can."

All that was true. I didn't look up, but I said out loud, "Steven owed this Maurice guy's boss a lot of money. He came looking for it this morning and Steven told him he'd have it in a couple of days. When Maurice left he and Steven were laughing like a couple of old friends. That's what I know."

McElone had her notebook and a pen out and was jotting down what I'd said, even though I knew she would be able to recite it chapter and verse if you woke her at three in the morning six months from now. She is unbelievably efficient.

"Who's the boss?" she asked without looking up.

"Um . . . Tony Danza?" I admit I knew what she was asking, but I needed a moment to process the situation and decide what I would say in response.

"Tell her everything," Paul reiterated. "Lying to the lieutenant isn't going to help you."

"Maurice DuBois's boss," McElone said with a little edge in her voice. She doesn't always appreciate my hilarious sense of humor.

"His name is Lou Maroni, and I take it he's in L.A., but that is really everything I know about him," I told the lieutenant. "I don't know what business he's in or what side of the law he might be on. I never even heard his name before last night." Had I really just picked up Liss and Steven from the airport *yesterday*? It felt like two weeks ago.

It was possible my thinking of my daughter had awakened some karma in the house or something, because she appeared at the door to the den and looked at McElone, registering some panic. "Lieutenant," she said. "Is something wrong?"

That was the moment McElone's cell phone rang and she pulled it from her pocket and pushed a button. "McElone." She listened for a moment. "Okay. Keep me informed." The phone went back in the pocket.

"Mom?" Liss moved close to me and I put an arm

around her. McElone's face was serious, but that was true all the time.

"It's okay, baby," I said. Then I looked at the lieutenant. "Right?"

"Mostly," McElone said. "That was the Asbury Park PD. They checked in on your boyfriend in his apartment."

My stomach was not feeling the way I wanted it to. "And?"

Melissa held me a little closer.

"He's fine," the lieutenant said. "He answered the door, they went inside and looked around. There was nobody there. I'm surprised you haven't heard from him yet."

"I turned my phone off when you texted me," I told her. "It was low on battery and I didn't know how long we'd be."

"Turn it back on. I'm sure you'll see messages."

Melissa let go of my arm and composed herself. "What about my father, Lieutenant?" she asked.

McElone pursed her lips a little. "That's a little more complicated. He wasn't there when the Asbury Park uniforms got to the apartment."

"Where is he?" Melissa asked before I could.

"We're not sure. Josh told the cops your dad had slipped out not long after they got there and he didn't know where he'd gone."

One of the things I like about McElone is that she talks to Melissa like an intelligent person and not a little child who needs coddling.

"Why is this a problem, Lieutenant?" I asked. "Do you think Steven is in danger?" If Melissa was going to hear that, she'd hear it from McElone and not me.

"Not necessarily. If this DuBois guy was the one threatening him, the danger has been removed." McElone folded her arms in front of her in what appeared to be something of a challenging gesture.

"So, what aren't you saying?" I asked.

Her eyes darted to Melissa, then back to me.

"I appreciate it, Lieutenant, but Melissa is a smart and mature thirteen-year-old. Anything you can say in front of me you can say in front of her." I looked at my daughter, who appeared confused as to how she should feel. On the one hand, I was still someone who had kicked her dad out of the house. On the other, I had just given her a compliment in an area she considered important. She appeared to choose bracing herself against whatever news McElone might be preparing to deliver.

"All right, then," the lieutenant said. "I still need to find your ex-husband, because if this guy *was* the threat, your ex was the person who stood the most to gain from his death."

Liss's eyes widened. "You think—"

McElone held up a hand, palm out. "I don't think anything yet. I'm just saying that your dad is a person of interest in the murder of Maurice DuBois."

Eight

"I have no idea where he went," Josh said. "That guy is slippery."

"No kidding." Having been married to Steven, I had learned to wear gloves with Velcro fingers to keep him in one place.

McElone had ignored my suggestion that we drive to Josh's Asbury Park apartment to make sure he was all right. She assured me the cops were keeping an eye on him and that once Steven had left his sight, Josh was probably removed from any danger. But she seemed skeptical of Josh's explanation and was now listening on speakerphone to see, as she said, if she could "figure out what's true and what's not."

Maxie had shown up at some point and was talking quietly to Melissa in a corner of the den. Paul was watching the lieutenant intently as he always did when she was around. I think he wants to be just like McElone when he grows up.

Liss didn't look upset in that she wasn't actually crying. She loves her father but is not blind to his faults, which gives me an extra case of the willies when she looks at me sometimes. She knows Steven is not a perfect man by any stretch. But the idea that Lieutenant McElone, whom Melissa greatly respects, might think Steven was responsible for the death of the man who had been in our house this morning was a lot for her to handle. Frankly I was annoyed that McElone was keeping me from my daughter for this phone call, but when Josh's number had shown up on my cell phone, she insisted I answer it.

Josh was fine, of course. I was relieved but hadn't really thought he was in danger once I'd heard Steven had left. Trouble follows my ex-husband around; my boyfriend does his best to avoid it. It's one of the reasons I'm with Josh and not Steven these days.

"How did he manage to get out without you knowing it?" I asked Josh.

"We came up and I showed him the couch, where he'd be sleeping. I went into the closet to get some sheets and a pillow, and he was gone when I got back. I'll give the guy one thing: He's quick." You could practically hear Josh shake his head in wonder. I assumed he was wondering what made me marry that man to begin with. It was an excellent question.

McElone, who was not trying to make her presence a secret, said, "Did he say anything about Maurice DuBois?"

Josh took a second, although he'd heard the lieutenant's voice just a few minutes ago. It's disconcerting to hear two people, particularly of the same gender, on a speakerphone. I was hopeful he'd be able to discriminate between my voice and the lieutenant's, and luckily he came up just right.

"Nothing really, Lieutenant," Josh answered. "I tried asking him about what was going on with the software and all that, but he said it was something he didn't want to discuss."

"Did he say where he'd been all day?" I asked. If McElone thought he had something to do with Overcoat's death, it would have been during the time of day Steven was "running errands," the time he'd told me to lie about if asked. I'd been asked, and I'd told the truth right down the line. Never ask a divorced person to do something even slightly inconvenient for his/her ex. That's a rule to take with you.

"I didn't ask," Josh said. "Of course at the time I didn't know this guy was dead. Lieutenant McElone, are you sure Steven is a suspect in the killing? It seems a stretch."

"I didn't say suspect," McElone answered. "We'd like to ask him some questions, is all." That's what cops say when they mean "suspect."

Paul looked over at me. "Tracing those missing hours is the key to the murder," he said. He sounded positively thrilled. Paul loves nothing better than investigation. I tried to give him a sharp look, but there was no point in upsetting McElone.

Melissa stood up and walked past Mel, whose midsection I examined closely to be sure he was still breathing, to sit next to me (apparently we were okay again) and watch the proceedings.

"Well, it never occurred to me to ask him," Josh told McElone.

"That's okay," the detective answered. "It's not your responsibility. Did he give you *any* indication where he might have gone? Mention anybody he wanted to go see? Anything like that?"

Josh seemed to think for a moment. "No," he said finally, sounding disappointed. "Maybe he went out to get some food. He said he was hungry." We'd had a lovely dinner Melissa had cooked, but Steven had not eaten any of it.

I must have looked skeptical, because McElone asked, "You don't believe him?"

Her question startled me for a moment and I hesitated. Over the phone I heard Josh say, "I have no reason to lie about that."

"Oh no," I said. "It's not you I have trouble believing here. Just because Steven said he's hungry doesn't mean anything. If you asked his name, he'd lie to you out of habit."

McElone raised an eyebrow. Then she looked at Melissa, again wondering if she should bring this up in front of my daughter when the last time a sensitive question about Steven had clearly rattled Liss. But McElone is a professional and lets nothing stand in the way of her investigation.

"Did you try to get in touch with him after he left here?" she asked. Maybe this was a new way of attacking the problem.

"You've been here the whole time I knew about this Maurice guy getting shot in an alley," I reminded her. "I haven't had the chance to alert my ex that he should stay on the lam, if that's what you're suggesting."

"Remember to whom you're talking," Paul said. He can admonish me about subject matter and grammar at the same time.

"I'm asking if you wouldn't mind texting your ex now to see how he answers," the lieutenant answered. Not a hint of annoyance in her voice. Okay, maybe a hint.

"Happy to," I said. "Josh, I'm going to have to hang up on you."

"I was wondering when it would come to this," he joked.

"I'll call you tomorrow. You call me if The . . . if Steven comes back, okay?"

Melissa caught the slip and curled her mouth a little, but said nothing.

Josh agreed he'd call the lieutenant, then me if The Swine was foolish enough to show his face back at the apartment tonight. We ended the call and I looked at McElone.

"What do you want me to say?" I asked.

We decided I would pretend that everything was as we'd left it when Josh and Steven had gone. So I sent Steven a text that read "You get there okay?" I know that in the true texting spirit I should have sent "u get there ok," but I just didn't have it in me.

No answer was quick to come. Melissa's eyes grew more worried. Paul started pacing. Maxie, watching Liss, twitched her mouth back and forth trying to decide what she could do to cheer up my daughter as if that was her job.

Mel just sat and stared out the back doors. He touched the side of his nose at one point, but that was about it for his participation or interest in the ongoing proceedings.

McElone, who has never sat in my house, leaned against the doorjamb. It was the most blatant display of impatience and tension I'd seen her exhibit despite her clear discomfort with the ghosts in the house. Luckily they were being unobtrusive at the moment. From her point of view.

"Maybe he is injured and needs some assistance," Paul said, midpace. Melissa looked up in alarm, which McElone noted by looking around the ceiling, which is where people think ghosts are in any room. They're usually not, but go tell people that. "I'm sorry, Melissa." Paul doesn't always think through what he's saying when he dissects a case.

"Do you think he's in trouble?" Liss is very good at talking to the ghosts when appearing to address a living person. She's been doing it since birth and I've been at it a few years. So I carry a Bluetooth headset with me when I go outside. In the house you're on your own.

"It's pretty clear there's some kind of trouble," McElone said, "but I don't know if there's any danger. There's a difference."

Paul, to whom the question was actually aimed, was now in "let's not upset Melissa" mode. "I doubt it," he said. "I was thinking of a car crash or something like that."

Liss's eyes indicated Paul's mode was not having its desired effect.

"I've been through this kind of radio silence before," I said to Melissa. "If your dad's not answering, it's because he doesn't want to or hasn't come up with the proper story to tell yet. Don't worry."

That is the kind of remark that Liss would have simply nodded at and accepted two weeks earlier. Now she was in the throes of spending time with her father when he was trying to be charming and I can tell you from experience that is a powerful thing to overcome. So she clucked her teeth and turned away from me. "You just say stuff like that because of the divorce," she said.

McElone kept looking at the ceiling, but now I think it might have been because she was trying to find a safe spot to aim her gaze.

Of all people, the one to break the tension for me was The Swine. My phone vibrated and I looked at his text message.

It read, "Fine. Why?"

I showed the message to McElone, who walked over from the door, and to Melissa, to prove to her that her father was alive and still being a jerk. She wasn't entirely wrong about my behavior, but divorce is something you don't really just put in the rearview mirror and leave at the side of the road. It sticks with you like Greek yogurt.

Paul hovered over McElone's shoulder as she read the text, which admittedly didn't take long. "He's suspicious," he said. Paul has a talent for the obvious.

"Tell him Maurice came by again and asked to see him," McElone suggested.

"Won't that alert him something's wrong if he knows Mr. DuBois is dead?" Melissa asked. She was trying to protect her father now.

"Yes, but it will also alert us about whether he knows about the murder," said the lieutenant. She pointed to my cell phone. "Go ahead."

So I did. I texted: "Your pal Maurice was here. Wants to know where you are." And I sent it.

I noticed everyone—except Mel—was closing ranks around me, looking over my shoulder at a phone that at the moment wasn't doing anything.

Even Maxie swooped down and glanced. "What's with this guy?" she demanded. Patience is not one of Maxie's virtues. Don't ask me what they are unless I really have time to think. She's very good to Melissa. That's one.

At the moment, my daughter looked like she needed a hug, so I put my arm around her. She didn't acknowledge it, but she didn't move away, either. This wasn't easy for her.

Then my phone buzzed again and Steven's text message came through. I actually closed my eyes for a moment before I looked at it.

"When?"

That wasn't much. I looked at McElone, who nodded.

"Right after you left," I sent back. "Why?"

This time the answer was swift and disturbing. Instead of a text message, the phone rang with Steven's number in the caller ID. I didn't look for approval from McElone and just accepted the call without putting it on speaker, which I'm guessing the lieutenant would have preferred but which would have made my ex-husband suspicious.

He started talking even before I could say hello. "Who's there with you?" he asked.

Maxie, who was closest to my ear, said, "Uh-oh."

Melissa flinched a little and I tightened my free arm around her shoulder.

"What?" Paul asked. Maxie didn't answer him, probably because she likes knowing things others don't.

"Just Liss," I said casually. I felt it was best not to mention the detective in the room who might suspect he was a killer, and the two ghosts were simply off-limits to any conversation I had with my ex. Mel was practically forgotten in his corner of the den. I checked again. He was breathing. "Why?"

Steven's voice was strained; it wasn't like he was under pressure so much as he seemed to be trying to force the words out when they weren't coming naturally. "You're lying about Maurice and I need to know why."

"What do you mean, I'm lying about Maurice?" I could let McElone (and by extension Paul) know what was being said without giving away anyone's presence in the room.

"I mean I know for a fact that Maurice didn't come to your house after I left there tonight, and you know it, too, so I'd like to know exactly why you're lying to me about that. Alison, what's going on there?"

It was time to end the games. I had reached this point countless times with The Swine, and it always ended with me blinking first. "You can't turn this one on me, Steven," I said. I saw McElone shaking her head, but I didn't care and I didn't stop. "You're mixed up in something way over your head and you need to come clean about it. Right now."

The Swine fell back on his usual line. "I don't know what you're talking about."

I was fairly sure McElone's eyes popped out of her head when I said, "I'm talking about the dead man in the alley next to Hanrahan's and what exactly he has to do with you," I said.

Paul, usually so undemonstrative, moaned. Loud. If you could hear him.

"Mom," Melissa said. This time she did pull away from my arm.

"Give me the phone," McElone said.

But Steven had already hung up.

Mel stood up, smoothed his pants and walked out of the room past us without so much as a nod. He headed for the downstairs room he had until recently shared with his wife, and I heard the door close behind him.

"I think he just went from person of interest to suspect," McElone said.

Nine

"We don't have a case to investigate," I protested. "It's McElone's job. We don't have a client. Let her do the work."

I was sweeping—not shoveling—the latest dusting we'd gotten off my front porch the next morning. Melissa had said all the right things the night before, told me she didn't blame me for her father being the prime suspect in a murder and then gone up to bed saying she had school in the morning.

It was about twenty degrees this morning, so I was dressed in jeans, snow pants, a work shirt, a fleece, a parka, a scarf, a pair of knitted gloves and a woolen hat as well as earmuffs. Paul, hovering just off the porch, was in his usual jeans and T-shirt and even though he was dead I resented him for that.

"I understand your reluctance," he said. "And I'm not just saying this to engage us in a case so I can relieve the boredom. I'm working on my energy experiments and don't need anything else to engage my mind."

Paul had been working for over a year on the idea that he and Maxie and people like them were actually composed of energy and that this information held the key to their moving on to some higher plane of existence, something Paul has been pursuing pretty much since I met him. I'm sort of ambivalent about the subject, since Paul moving on would remove from my life one of the closer friends I'd made since moving back to Harbor Haven.

If just Maxie was moving on, I'd have been happy to buy her the bus ticket and pack her a lunch for the trip.

"Then what's your point?" It hadn't taken long to get the snow off the porch and I'd already done the steps and the walk. Now I needed to spread ice melt and then I could bolt for my kitchen, where my *real* closest friend, coffee, was waiting.

I went to the bucket of pet-friendly ice melt I kept next to the door this time of year. (Lester wouldn't have minded the stuff on the ground, but other people bring actual living dogs and cats around now and again. I sneeze more but I don't take it out on the animals.)

"The point is that your ex-husband is being hunted by the police now. You can't simply ignore that. Clearly you have information that can lead to his being found, but you haven't given it to the lieutenant, which indicates to me that you don't want her to locate him right now. So in order to clear him of the suspicions surrounding him, the best thing for us to do is figure out where your ex-husband is at this moment, for you to go there and try to convince him to go to the police and cooperate with the investigation. It's better for him, it's better for you and most of all it's better for Melissa, who can barely hide her tension every second. I don't think Maxie has left her side since last night."

Since those were probably the most words I'd ever heard Paul say in a row, it took me a moment to process everything he'd said. There was some truth in what he'd brought up, but he was skimming over some serious issues, too. It wouldn't do me any good to ignore that.

I'd tried repeatedly to get Steven to call me back, but he was going straight to voice mail. Even when Melissa had texted him at McElone's behest, he had simply texted back to tell her mother (me) he'd be in touch and that he was sorry.

At least the "sorry" thing was showing progress. He'd never said that to me.

McElone was all business, reminding me to let her know if I heard from The Swine at any time and assiduously avoiding telling me not to worry. She did make a point of saying to Melissa, "We're going to get this worked out," which probably didn't make Liss feel any better but was at least an attempt.

"Look," I told Paul as I flung some ice melt onto my front walk. I love that stuff; it makes ice go away, and ice is my sworn enemy. Innkeepers live in fear of having a guest slip on the walk and then suing for all said innkeeper is worth, which in my case would be a distinct disappointment to the suer. "The fact is that I don't know where Steven is and I didn't give McElone any names of friends because it's been years and I don't know who his current friends are. But if you're asking whether I want the police to lock up Melissa's dad for killing a shady business associate, no, I'd like to avoid that if we can."

Paul, trying to show off his energy theory, stuck his finger up into one of the bulbs in my outside lamp and turned it on. I looked up. "Just trying to give you some more light," he said.

"It's morning. The sun's out. You're showing off."

He looked sheepish as he floated down. "Just trying to help."

I threw the last handful of ice melt onto the sidewalk and headed quickly back to the porch. Warmth was starting to sound really good. "No, you're not," I told Paul, the Bluetooth device—not connected to anything—starting to chafe against my ear behind the earmuff. "You're stalling for time because you don't have an answer."

"Not true. You've made my point for me. In order to keep your ex-husband out of jail, we need to do some investigating."

We made it inside the house. I used the door; Paul just phased through the wall, which was showy but second nature to him. "Are you overlooking one possibility?" I asked him.

"I don't believe so." Mel and Anne were nowhere to be seen, but Yoko was doing yoga, which seemed redundant, in the library, probably the quietest room of the house. I headed for the kitchen, where she wouldn't be disturbed and I could get that coffee. Everybody wins. "I have weighed the facts and determined that the police hold the best solution to the case unless we do our own digging, in which instance I believe we might discover the truth faster."

In the warmth of the kitchen I decided a cold day actually screamed for something other than coffee. I started a burner on the stove and got a small saucepan out of the cabinet. Mom and Melissa could cook, but I could make the best hot chocolate on the planet. Well, on the Jersey Shore.

"That's the problem," I said. "Maybe the truth is exactly what we don't want to discover."

Paul actually stopped in space, which was disconcerting because he was halfway through my refrigerator and I was reaching for the milk. "You're saying you think your ex-husband actually killed that man?" he gasped.

I closed the refrigerator door perhaps a little too hard, which had no effect on Paul but made the little Peanuts statuette on top of the fridge shake a bit. Snoopy did not appear to be especially concerned, so I walked to the stove and poured some milk into the saucepan.

"I'm not saying that, exactly." I was still trying to figure out what I really did think, but my stomach was knotted with the idea. Steven had never been violent that I knew about, but he'd also never been completely honest. About anything. There was always something a little disturbing about his business dealings. It had not been a surprise when Overcoat showed up on my doorstep with vaguely threatening words. I'd always sort of expected something like that to happen. "I'm saying I don't know, and that bothers me enough. I worry that if we find out something we don't want to know, it'll hurt Liss and I absolutely don't want that to happen. Can you understand?"

Paul moved out of the fridge—his head had always been outside anyway—and he nodded. "I do understand. But consider this—the police already suspect your ex-husband. And while Lieutenant McElone is a very good detective, police officers tend to stick with a theory until it is disproven without question. She isn't necessarily looking for other suspects, and from what I can tell, your ex is not especially good at covering his tracks. Maybe he didn't kill this man. If that is the case, the lieutenant might not find the evidence that exonerates him. If we investigate, we might."

Maxie dropped down from above slowly and deliberately. She did not try to determine what the conversation in the room might have been about or whether we were indeed paying any attention to her. "Melissa just got up," said. "She's not in a great mood."

A teenager in a cranky state of mind. Stop the presses.

I sighed. The milk on the stove was warm enough, so I turned off the heat and poured it into a mug I'd already readied with cocoa powder and some sugar. You don't need anything else. Anyone who tells you otherwise is mistaken or lying. And marshmallows are a ridiculous distraction. "Tell me something I don't know," I said.

Maxie, in her current subdued mode, was doing her best to be uncharacteristically understanding. She floated to an eye-to-eye position with me and made sure her "sincere" face was on. "I know this is tough. Usually she likes you as much as she likes me." Maxie was in her own world, which was probably a good thing for the rest of us.

I knew one thing I could do. But I had to set some ground rules first. I looked at Paul. "I'm going to make a phone call," I said. "This *doesn't* mean we're investigating the murder, okay?"

"I don't understand." Paul understood just fine. He didn't want to commit to anything without thinking it over.

"Yes, you do. I just don't want you jumping to conclusions. This is one phone call and it's simply a fact-finding mission." I didn't ask if it was okay again, because I had already decided on this course of action and didn't want to discuss it. I pulled the phone from my pocket and hit the speed dial for Phyllis Coates.

Phyllis, who owns, runs and sweeps out the offices of the *Harbor Haven Chronicle*, continued to print a paper edition of the weekly paper in the face of . . . all the rest of society. She's not stupid, though; she also has an online version of the paper that charges for access.

She likes me because she considers me a work in progress. I think Phyllis believes that at some point I will realize my mistake and come write for the *Chronicle*. This is based on the erroneous belief that I have any talent whatsoever for journalism, and the fact that I did indeed deliver

the *Chronicle* for her when I was the very same age Melissa
was right now. Liss used to talk about following in my
bicycle tracks, but the number of paper copies Phyllis has
to distribute these days can't even sustain a part-time job.
Which is fine with me. Newspaper journalism isn't necessarily the growth industry to which you want your teenager
to aspire.

"You're calling about the murder at Hanrahan's," Phyllis said as soon as she picked up the call. That's the Phyllis
version of "Hello! How have you been! It's been much too
long since we've spoken!"

Maxie rose back through the ceiling, no doubt to check
on Melissa again now that she had decided it was her mission in . . . eternity.

"It's great to hear your voice, too," I said in return. I
don't follow all the rules of decorum—okay, I follow two
of the rules of decorum—but one of them I believe in is
the need for meaningless conversational boilerplate.

Phyllis, of course, has no such compunction. "The
deceased is a Maurice DuBois," she began, probably reading off a sheet of notes she'd taken or a copy of the police
report. "Shot twice, one in the leg and one in the head,
execution-style."

"This part I know already." When you're talking to my
friend the journalist, it's sometimes important to remind
her that, one, you're not a complete and total idiot and,
two, you're still included in the conversation.

Paul moved closer, no doubt wanting me to put Phyllis
on speakerphone, but I was in a cantankerous mood and
didn't want to have to explain to the journalist why I was
making her voice echo around the room when I was supposed to be alone.

"Okay, you've spoken to Anita." Phyllis likes to show
off how well entrenched with sources she is by referring
to them by first name only. Luckily I knew McElone's first

name. "So, here's what you don't know: Mr. DuBois was from Santa Monica, California. He was forty-eight years old, not married, no children. Flew here night before last on a ticket that was purchased that evening ten minutes before the plane left the gate. He's listed as being in the import/export business, which means he's a career crook. Didn't find a murder weapon, which is no surprise. No doubt the gunshots are the cause of death. But nobody heard the shots and there's not as much blood as you might think, so he might have been killed somewhere else and then dumped in the alley, likely from the trunk of the killer's car, except probably not because he wasn't light and there are no drag marks. How much of that did you already know?"

"Some," I admitted. I had known Overcoat was from the Los Angeles area and flew in the same night as Melissa and Steven. That was about it. "But what I don't get is what he could have done in such a short time here to get someone that mad at him." That was a test balloon; I wanted to see how much Phyllis knew.

There was a certain ironic lilt in her voice. "Why don't you ask your ex?" she asked. "I hear he's back in town and the police are very interested in discussing this shooting with him. That what you wanted me to say?"

Okay, she knew enough. "I'd sort of have preferred not," I allowed. "What do you think the best course of action for me would be under these circumstances?"

"You want to cover the story for me?" Phyllis asked.

"No!"

"Just checking."

There was a pause while Phyllis considered my question seriously. During that time, Paul actually put his ear into my phone, which meant putting his head into mine. I got that he wanted to hear what was being said, but it was a little too surreal for me, so I took a step back and shook my head. Paul, looking surprised at my squeamishness, remained motionless.

"If I'm you," Phyllis answered, "I'm doing my very best to convince your ex to tell his whole story. It might not be the one you want to hear, but once you know the truth you'll be able to act responsibly. And by 'responsibly,' I mean—"

"You mean telling you exactly what he said so you can publish it in the paper," I finished for her.

"You are wasting your talents in the hotel business," Phyllis suggested.

"You'd be amazed how many people agree with you," I told her.

The kitchen door opened on cue and Melissa, hair unbrushed, pajamas still on, shuffled in and headed for the coffeepot, not the lovely hot chocolate (okay, at this point let's call it *warm* chocolate) I extended toward her. She poured herself a cup and put in only a fraction of the half cup of milk she usually used. She sat down at the center island and sat there drinking it while looking as tortured as Humphrey Bogart after Ingrid Bergman has walked into his gin joint in *Casablanca*.

"I'm not telling you anything about what Steven might say to me," I informed Phyllis. Liss turned to look at me, the dazed expression still on her face. "And that's not only because I have no idea where he might be at this moment in time." Liss turned back to face forward and sip her hot cup of joe.

"Then you'd better find him," Phyllis answered. "The cops find him first and your options are all about paying attorneys and finding ways to reduce the charges. You find him first and maybe you can sort something out."

Paul was close enough to parse some of that out, and he nodded in agreement.

"Sort what out?" I asked. "You're making it sound like it's a foregone conclusion that Steven actually killed this guy." Melissa's shoulders shuddered, but she did not look back.

"He was the only contact your DuBois guy had in Jersey," Phyllis said. "He owed the guy's boss a *lot* of money. He couldn't pay that money no matter what he promised. The only person on this coast who actually benefits from DuBois being dead is your ex. Who else should the cops suspect?"

"You're not helping," I sighed.

"Yes, I am. You just don't want to see it yet. Look, you had enough issues with the guy to divorce him."

"Half the marriages in this country end in divorce," I pointed out. "How many of those people blow a thug's brains out in an alley?"

"Or possibly somewhere else," she reminded me. "We haven't ruled that out yet."

"Thanks. That's a huge weight off my shoulders. The fact that I divorced Steven doesn't have a logical conclusion in my believing he's a murderer, Phyllis. The guy has never lifted a finger against another human being in my presence. The Steven you're describing is not a guy I would recognize."

"Okay, let's say he didn't kill DuBois. Who did?"

I closed my eyes because it felt better. "How would I know that?" I asked.

"You have an investigator's license. Find out." Phyllis, with a flair for the dramatic and a real instinct for a great exit line, disconnected the call.

I put the phone down on the counter next to me without opening my eyes and just stood for a few seconds. I heard Paul say, "What did she say?" and heard Melissa slurp some coffee at the same time. Through the wall—which I really should not have heard—I heard Yoko chanting something. I even heard Maxie, no doubt coming back down from the attic, asking in a clear, loud voice, "What the heck is wrong with *her*?"

There was no choice. No matter how much I wanted to keep things as they were, no matter how much I wanted to deny the situation around me, it was too clear. I was not being given any option, so I did exactly what I did not want to do.

I opened my eyes.

Sure enough, Maxie was hovering over near Liss but not engaging her. Paul was squinting in my direction, his brow so furrowed a family of moles could have taken up residence in it. My daughter, back to me, did not appear to have moved, not even when Maxie had asked what was wrong with me.

"Okay," I said aloud. "We have work to do."

Paul's eyes gave up squinting, but they still seemed to be boring into me. "Do you mean what I think?" he asked. People ask you that without telling you what they're thinking. They do it because what they're thinking is so in-your-face that they're showing off exactly how foolish they are by asking such a ridiculous question.

I chose, diplomatically, to ignore that because I was going to need Paul very badly for the foreseeable future.

"Yes," I said. "We're going to investigate Maurice DuBois's murder and try to prove that Steven didn't kill him."

My daughter stood up, walked over to me and gave me a hug.

Sometimes there are benefits to be had even from stupid decisions you make.

Ten

"I haven't heard from Steven and I wouldn't tell you if I had."

My ex-mother-in-law, Constance Rendell, has eyes like those in a shark. They're black and emotionless. Stare just at her eyes and you can easily see her eating Robert Shaw in *Jaws*. Concentrate on the rest of her face and you'll think she's just lovely.

I'll tell you what happened and you can judge her character yourself.

For the record, I didn't really think Steven would come home to his mother for cover after finding out Maurice DuBois had been killed, or after finding out the cops were after him for killing Maurice DuBois. Either way, it seemed unlikely he'd go to the Edison home in which he'd grown up, where his parents still lived.

The place was not the least bit run-down or shabby-looking. Constance would allow for no such thing. She ran a tight ship and probably would have made an excellent commandant. She had always disdained my housekeeping, which I thought was perfectly adequate even before I started asking people to stay in the house I was maintaining. She once told Steven—and he relayed it to me as if an amusing anecdote—that she thought I should hire someone to clean after I had finished cleaning just to point out all the things I'd missed. No doubt she would have applied for the job and then stolen from my liquor cabinet.

Steven's father, Harry Rendell, was nowhere to be seen when I arrived on the family doorstep. The sun reflected off the front windows, making it impossible to see inside. Constance, whom I had not called ahead because I didn't want to give The Swine any notice in the extremely unlikely event that he was lying low in the compound (a split-level on a quiet street leading to Route 27, which I was counting on to take me back to the Garden State Parkway and my shore home), said her husband was out running errands. Apparently that ran in the family. Harry had retired from almost four decades of work for a local car dealer in the service department, doing endless oil changes and tune-ups mostly because staying home with his wife was a considerably less pleasant prospect.

I liked Harry. He had treated me like the daughter he'd never had despite having a daughter, Steven's sister, Melba (you think I'm making that up, but I'm not), who had caused considerable consternation during her teenage years, which had only gotten worse once she hit her twenties. She had been through four rehabs by my last count and I had divorced The Swine some years earlier, so my news updates had been sparse. Melba now lived in Arizona. But it's a dry heat.

So it was my luck to get Constance and not Harry when I'd rung the doorbell. Mentally I cursed Paul for making me drive up here on a fool's errand. Guess who was the fool.

"I was just asking because Melissa wanted to see her father and I didn't know where he was," I told my ex-mother-in-law, who had arrived at the door at nine on a frigid Sunday morning wearing a short-sleeved pantsuit and in full makeup. I was still in the jeans and snow pants from having "shoveled" my front walk.

"You are not," Constance said. I'd like to point out that she had not yet asked me in. We stood on the front step and even with my jacket and her in short sleeves, I was the one whose teeth were chattering. It helps if, like Constance, you don't have a nervous system. "Melissa just spent almost a week with Steven in California. It's not like she's pining away for her daddy."

Constance treats my daughter like the mistake she clearly believes Melissa to be. That's enough for me, but there's so much more to enjoy in her personality. Sarcasm. The National Language of New Jersey.

"She has something she wants to tell him about their trip and Steven isn't answering his phone," I countered. "Is there some reason he doesn't want his daughter to get in touch with him?" I was operating on the assumption that Constance had heard from my ex-husband. When we were first married he used to call her every time we went out to dinner. Just in case she called the apartment and didn't get an answer. And he had a cell phone.

"I have no idea why he wouldn't want to hear from her." Constance sniffed. "Maybe he's finally realized how you turned that girl against him." It was not a new refrain.

I wasn't taking the bait. "Do you know where he is, Constance? It's important and I'm cold."

"It's because you don't eat right," my ex-mother-in-law pronounced. Constance is great at making pronouncements.

She's like the Queen of England, only without the total lack of real power.

"Steven won't get in touch with Melissa because I don't eat right?"

"You're cold because you don't eat right," she snorted.

"No, I'm cold because this side of the Earth is turned away from the sun this time of year. We humans call it 'winter.' Now, why don't you tell me where my daughter's father is so I can get into my car and turn on the heater?" Like that heater would do any good. There was a block of coffee-flavored ice in a cup sitting on my dashboard as we spoke.

"I don't know where he is and I don't understand why you drove up here instead of calling me first." Constance's eyes darted suddenly to the left, then back at me. Could Steven have been hiding in the house after all?

"May I come in, Constance? I'd like to get the feeling back in my toes before April."

She waved a hand dismissively. "If you'd take in a little more fiber you wouldn't have that problem."

"I don't really have time for a pot of beans while I stand here. Can I come in?"

"You're rude and uncouth."

"That doesn't answer the question," I pointed out. "Not to mention, 'rude' and 'uncouth' mean the same thing." They don't, really, but I needed to get back a little of my own.

"Oh, fine." Constance stepped to the side, allowing me a path into the house. It was not what I'd expected and it probably meant Steven was not, in fact, here.

I stepped inside and was immediately struck with the lack of warmth. Not in temperature; the absence of a sub-zero wind was the very definition of relief. But as I'd noted every other time I'd stepped into Constance Rendell's house, this could have been a model home for the developer

of this neighborhood. Nothing out of place, no family photographs in evidence, no sign that anyone other than Mr.
and Mrs. Generic had ever lived here. The furniture was
clean and arranged tastefully. The carpet had been vacuumed, probably within the last hour. There were books on
the shelves that probably had never been opened. There
was no television. The coffee table had not a crumb on it,
just a very attractive arrangement of flowers that were in
all likelihood fabric.

My first thought was to look to the right, which was the
direction in which Constance had stolen her giveaway glance.
There was nothing but domestic perfection there, either. The
dining room, in which I had never dined, was immaculate. I
had often wondered if this was just the house the Rendells
showed people and perhaps they had another more ramshackle
one on the next block where they really lived.

"Thanks," I said, although Constance hadn't done anything but take a step to her left. "That feels better." I rubbed
my gloved hands on my arms just to illustrate exactly how
cold I had been outdoors.

"Fiber," she muttered.

As welcome as the indoor environment was, my fervent
goal was still to get the hell out of here as quickly as possible and try to coax a tiny bit of warmth out of the Volvo's
alleged heater on my way back to Harbor Haven. We had
a Sunday spook show scheduled for eleven, and even
though Liss could certainly handle my end of it if I wasn't
there, she'd had enough to deal with for the past day or so
and I felt it best to make it back in time.

"Look, Constance," I began. "Steven's gotten himself
in trouble again. It's going to be worse for him if I don't
find him than if I do. So if you have any idea where he
might be hiding out, your best bet is at the very least to tell
him to get in touch with me so we can work this out. Okay?"

"What do you mean, he's gotten himself in trouble

again?" my ex's mother asked. "Has he married someone else?" That was her version of the worst thing her son could do—entangle himself with someone like me.

I didn't ask to sit down. Part of it was that I wanted to bolt for the Volvo. Part of it was that I was actually unsure whether Constance would allow me to park myself on one of her wrinkle-free sofa cushions and didn't want to find out. "I mean he's made yet another in a series of shady business deals, he's gotten called on it and now a man has been found dead in an alley next to a bar and Steven is currently the prime suspect. *That's* what I mean by trouble. So where is he, Constance?"

I have on rare occasions met people meaner than Constance Rendell. I've met people who are actually more rigid, although not many. I've even run into one or two who might have been more disapproving. Maybe one, anyway. My third-grade teacher was kind of harsh.

But never in my life have I encountered anyone as absolutely unmovable as my ex-mother-in-law. "I have no idea," she said. Her voice didn't even quaver, not a tiny bit.

I hadn't slept much in the past two nights. I was worried about my daughter's state of mind. I had concerns about my business bouncing back from a truly awful winter season. My ex-husband was on the same side of the continent as I am, and that's never a good thing. Not to mention the guy in the alley with the bullet in his head. I just wasn't in the mood for Constance.

"Yes, you do," I said. "You know exactly where he is. You didn't look the tiniest bit surprised when I told you what was going on. You didn't flinch when I showed up at your door unannounced and unexpected." I started to circle back toward the dining room, where I'd noticed a floor-to-ceiling drape that was fluttering just a bit when I could be sure the windows weren't open. "And you took a quick glance over in this direction when I asked you where your son might be hiding."

I had backed Constance up away from the dining room entrance just by placing myself in her way. She saw where I was going and suddenly her face tensed even more than usual. "Don't," she began.

"I don't have a choice," I said, and strode purposefully into the dining room. Once there I rushed to the wall with the quivering drape and headed for the pull cord on the right side.

"You mustn't," Constance said, her voice actually cracking in something like terror as she followed me into the room. "You don't understand."

"No, *you* don't understand," I told her. It was fun being self-righteous; maybe I should try it more often. "This is a matter of life and death!" And I pulled hard on the cord that opened the very tasteful heavy green drapery and flung it open.

Standing behind the drape was a man in his sixties with thinning gray hair parted in a conspicuous comb-over that was fooling nobody. He was thin, with a white mustache and skinny legs, wearing socks with actual garters.

I know that last part because the man was wearing no trousers. He was, and I am grateful to this day, wearing plaid boxer shorts. It's not the plaid part I'm grateful for.

"Oh, hello," he said.

Speechless, I turned back to face Constance.

"I can explain," she said.

"Oh, I would love to hear you try," I told her. "Truly I would."

"The reverend came to discuss some church business—" she began.

This just kept getting better. "The *reverend*!" I said. I turned toward the man inside the drapes, who was no longer inside the drapes. *On Sunday?* "Tell me, Reverend, do you always conduct church business without your pants?"

"Alison!" Constance would never be too mortified to resist scolding me. "You're talking to a man of the cloth."

"From the waist up, anyway."

Constance, who has made a part-time career of ignoring anything I say, continued to do so. "The reverend came to discuss church business and we were having a cup of coffee. He spilled some on his trousers, so I offered to put them in my dryer for a few minutes."

There were holes in this story large enough to pilot the starship *Enterprise* through. Not the least of them was the fact that the man had found his pants behind a dining room chair and was now putting them back on.

"Uh-huh," I said. "So he decided to hide behind the drapes when the doorbell rang because he was afraid his coffee stains weren't properly dried yet?" I turned toward the reverend again. "You know your butt was facing right into that window the whole time you were back there, right?" He looked behind where he was standing, and his hands went to his face. He hadn't buttoned his trousers, so they fell to the floor again.

Constance looked away. "Don't tell Harry," she said quietly. "Please. If you have any decency in you, don't tell Harry."

I had very little interest in getting involved with The Swine's parents' marital issues. But for the first time possibly in my life, I had some leverage over Constance Rendell and I was going to use it.

"Fine," I said. "If my phone rings in the next two hours and your son is on the other end, I won't be making a phone call to your husband. If it doesn't, I won't be held responsible. How's that?"

I headed toward the door. Even then, Constance was doing her level best not to ever break character.

"I don't know where he is," she said. Her voice was aiming at defiant and coming down somewhere around whimpering.

"Find out," I said, and left.

It was still unbelievably cold outside, but somehow I didn't feel it as I walked to the Volvo. Maybe I wouldn't need the heater on the way home after all.

All right, you have the facts. Now I ask you: Was I wrong about my ex-mother-in-law?

Eleven

My phone actually rang before I made it back to the Garden State Parkway (and I'm giving you the whole name now because you might be from out of state—we just call it "The Parkway"). Luckily I have installed a Bluetooth device on my sun visor to keep from being pulled over by the New Jersey State Police ("Troopers") so I could answer hands free.

"What did you say to my mother?" The Swine.

"Since you called me back, I don't have to tell you," I answered. The logic was convoluted, I'll grant you, but then I really wasn't interested in telling him anything. I needed him to tell me something. "Where are you?"

He chuckled. "Like I'd tell you."

"I'm the best person for you to tell. The cops are after you. I'm guessing Lou Maroni is still after you, only now he's mad. If I decide to report how often you've paid child support in the past six months, I can probably get the

Ocean County Sheriff after you. So I'm the person you want to talk to because maybe I can help you figure a way out of this mess."

The guy in the monstrous SUV in front of me clearly believed the road was his and his alone; he was wobbling between lanes like a child at Toys R Us trying to decide between the action figures ("dolls") and a video game. Nah, the video game would always win. Never mind. I stayed back because even though it was just past ten on a Sunday morning there was no guarantee SUV Guy was not drunk.

"I don't need your help," Steven answered. "I've got it all figured out."

"You had it figured out when Maurice DuBois showed up at my door yesterday morning," I reminded him. "You were going to get me to sell my house so you could get six hundred thousand dollars when you only needed to pay Maroni back four."

"You knew about that? That was just something I told Maurice. I didn't really think . . . You knew about that?"

"Yeah. Maybe you're not the slick operator you think you are, Steven. I know the detective on the case. Lieutenant McElone is reasonable and she's good. She'll find out what happened. Come back and we'll go there together. You can tell her your story."

The SUV cut across two lanes to get to a right turn, causing me to hit my brakes with some authority. I couldn't even blame SUV Guy, because when it went by I could see the stupid thing was being driven by a woman. Some days just don't go the way you want them to.

"You think I'm going to the cops?" my ex snorted at me through my sun visor. "That's your plan?"

"Why? What's yours? Arrange for Melissa to come see you on visiting day? You know orange was never a good color for you." Glad as I was to be rid of my SUV nemesis, the thrill of having caught Constance in . . . what I'd caught her in had worn off and the reality of the Volvo's terrible heating system was reasserting itself on my consciousness. In other words, my feet were freezing.

"I'm not going to jail, Alison, and I'm not going to the cops. Thanks for getting in touch by threatening my mother, but I've fulfilled my obligation now, so I think I'll be hanging up." But no click followed. The Swine was waiting for my next move.

That almost convinced me not to make one, but then I pictured Melissa's dazed expression the night before and reminded myself that this wasn't about me. Totally.

"You're bluffing, Steven. I know your voice. You've got nothing. You're in over your head and you've decided, as usual, that you can just pretend there's a plan and that's the same thing as having one. It doesn't work that way. This time you have to deal with reality and you have to come to grips with the idea that someone depends on you. Since you just spent almost a week with her, I think maybe you understand that a little. Now, do you care about your daughter or not?" It was mean, playing the Melissa card, but sometimes one has to be cruel to be kind, in the right measure. It's a Nick Lowe song; look it up.

I'd made it onto the Parkway now, and since the Volvo had warmed up in the fifteen minutes that had taken, it was blowing something other than frigid air onto my feet. It wasn't much, but it was something. Meanwhile, I was having an argument with the thing that's supposed to keep the sun out of my eyes and it was just a touch surreal, frankly.

It took a long moment for The Swine to digest what I'd said. I decided that the quaver in his voice when he spoke again was genuine, because while he might be a swine, he does love his daughter. "I'm not going to the cops, Alison. You show me another way to get out of this mess and not hurt Melissa, and I'll be happy to go along. But I'm not going to the cops."

Okay, that was probably the best I could have hoped for. I wished Paul were here to suggest a plan of action, but even Maxie had begged off this trip, saying she was going to visit her boyfriend, Everett, at the gas station he haunts. I took a cleansing breath, which just made my lungs cold.

"Okay, you don't have to go to the police," I told my ex. "But we do need to sit down and plan strategy. Come to the guesthouse this afternoon and be prepared to do something you've never done before in your life."

"What's that?" The Swine asked.

"Tell me the truth."

He moaned in what I was sure he believed was justified exasperation. "You've got to learn to trust me," he said.

"I will the very first time you do something trustworthy. Now, are you coming to my house today or do I drop a dime on your mom?"

"What have you got against my mother?" he actually asked me.

"It's only a one-hour drive, Steven. We don't have that kind of time. Will I see you later?"

He was stalling because he needed a better angle; I knew the way his mind worked. "Okay, but not at your house."

It's all about power and control with the Rendells. "Why not?" I asked.

"Because you know the cop and the cop knows you. She's probably got somebody watching the house in case I come back. I'm not coming back."

"You could just tell me your whole story now," I suggested. "Save you the trip." I reached for the voice recorder I use when I'm doing private investigator stuff. I keep it to record interviews so I can take them back to Paul and he can tell me how I messed up.

"Not on the phone." Why do people say that? How is talking on the phone different from talking in person? Did he think my cell phone was tapped?

"All right, you want to meet but not at the house. So where?"

I expected him to take time to think and was unnerved when he came right back with an answer. "You remember that coffeehouse in Point Pleasant? The dark one where we used to meet when your parents were telling you not to see me anymore?" Another area in which I should have listened to my parents, but then there'd be no Melissa. One must sacrifice for the greater good.

"The Old Bean? Yeah."

"Is it still there?" It had been sixteen years.

"Amazingly I think it is," I answered. "Why do you want to meet there?" It would have been so much easier at the house, where Paul could observe and advise and I know where all the sharp objects are kept.

"Because I don't want it to be in Harbor Haven. The cops may not be looking for me everywhere yet. Because I know the area and I know the place. And because, as I might have mentioned before, it's dark. Right now that's a good thing for me."

All that made sense, which caused me to think it was a setup of some kind. That's how you have to think when you're dealing with my ex-husband. I know; gives you a lot of confidence in my judgment, doesn't it?

"What if it's not there? What if I check when I get home and I find out the Old Bean went out of business? Are you going to start answering the phone when I call you?" I was arguing just because I felt that doing exactly what Steven wanted was somehow a mistake. I can't imagine where I got that idea.

"I just checked on Google. It's open until eight tonight. I'll see you there at two."

And he hung up.

So I did the only logical thing under the circumstances. I made a decision to go see Detective Lieutenant Anita McElone right after the spook show.

The show, it should be noted, was something of a lackluster affair. With three guests in the house, only two of whom (Anne and Yoko) were in attendance, the ghosts were hardly inspired. Maxie complained of having to leave Everett "just for this."

Melissa, who was scheduled to do her "flying girl" bit (Paul or Maxie carries her down the stairs in a horizontal position facing forward), did not appear from her room. That was troubling. She loved the looks on the guests' faces when she soared over their heads and had never missed a chance to do so before.

I needed to get Steven's troubles worked out, and quickly. It was three hours until we were to meet. I was going to confer with Paul about strategy as soon as the show was over.

He "juggled" some apples by simply moving them around in a circular motion. Maxie took some rubber cement from her sleeve and made the walls "ooze." I took a few questions from the guests for the ghosts ("What does it feel like to be dead?" "I don't recommend it."), and Paul did his power interruption thing by sticking his finger into an electrical socket, which made the lights flicker. The audience couldn't see the finger, so it lost some of its wow factor, but we were giving it the old college try, and both Anne and Yoko were smiling when they left the den after we declared the performance complete.

I flopped back into an easy chair and considered my options. I didn't have any. My daughter hated me, my ex-husband was going to try to con me, my supply of guests was dwindling and I didn't even have a reason to convert the basement into living space. It was barely worth getting up in the morning.

Eyes closed, I couldn't see if the ghosts were still there. Maxie might very well have fled the second the show was over—she was starting to complain about "being your dancing monkey"—but Paul would stick around, no doubt eager to discuss the case.

"I know what you're going to say, but I'm exhausted," I told him, resting my eyes because it actually felt good. "I don't think I can persuade Steven to turn himself in to McElone. I'm going to go over to the police station in a minute and tell her where I'm meeting him so she can pick him up. Melissa will resent me forever because I'm getting her father imprisoned, but there's no other way. So don't try to talk me out of it, Paul."

"He's not here," Maxie said. "He went into the basement as soon as we were done. But it was a nice speech."

My eyes flew open. Maxie was floating near the ceiling doing her Cleopatra-on-a-barge thing, not moving very fast, which meant she wasn't terribly agitated. "What are you doing here?" I asked.

"I'm here all the time."

"You're here and Paul left? What alternate universe is this?" I stood up. This was the time I was supposed to be unburdening myself to Paul and he was supposed to listen and offer sage advice. That was his job. Didn't he know that?

"I dunno. He said something interesting was going on with the energy stuff and he wanted to go try something out." She picked at her fingernail as if it was chipped and she needed to polish it. She could easily change the color anytime she wanted through the power of . . . ghostiness, or something.

"That's weird." Maybe I should go into the basement and talk to him. I looked toward the kitchen, where the basement door was located. Paul was serious about this energy theory of his and thought it could get him to another plane of existence, but turning his back on a case? That couldn't ever happen.

"Don't you want to know what *I* think?" Maxie asked. She did one quick revolution around the perimeter of the den ceiling, which was not small. Her energy level, at least, was on the rise.

"About what?" On the other hand, Paul could be cranky when you distracted him from something he had focused upon; if I went downstairs and he was in that kind of mood, it wouldn't help and he might be snippy for the rest of the day. I had a feeling I'd be needing him after the meeting with Steven, especially if I went through with my McElone plan. Maybe it was best to leave him alone now. I looked at Maxie. Ghosts can be such drama queens.

"About your little plan to rat out your ex-husband to the lady cop," Maxie said. People think there is a "Jersey accent," and Maxie was exaggerating her tones to make it sound like that. The inflection is closer to Brooklyn than New Brunswick and besides, there are at least three accents from New Jersey, largely depending on the speaker's proximity to New York or Philadelphia.

Oh, right, she had heard me spill my guts—presumably to Paul—about my guilt over planning to talk to McElone. If she went blabbing about that to Melissa, it was close to a guarantee that my daughter would not speak to me again for at least a year. It was clearly best to placate the dizzy spirit now.

"Okay. What do you think?" I braced myself for the five-minute lecture I was about to receive on loyalty, decency and never talking to the police, but I was still glancing toward the basement door.

"I think it's the right thing to do," Maxie said. She maneuvered herself into a vertical position and drifted down a little from the ceiling. "It's practical and it protects Melissa. You can't let some goon come around here looking for your ex and put your daughter in trouble, right?"

This *was* an alternate universe. Maxie was agreeing with me, basically parroting my words back to me. Paul was cutting out early after a spook show to work on his exit from my house and perhaps my dimension. Melissa was upstairs, having missed her first spook show because her father was looking at a murder charge.

Could I depend on my usual rule of thumb, which was that if Maxie thought something was a good idea I should never do that? Did I need a second opinion from Paul, or Mom, or Dad, or Murray Feldner, the guy who plows my walk when *real* snow happens? Probably not Murray. We went to high school together. He used to copy off me on tests.

"You think I should go talk to McElone?" I said, to Maxie but really not. "Don't you usually say to avoid the cops at all costs?"

Maxie gave a half nod. "I used to be scared of the military, too. Then I met Everett and he's taught me stuff." Her boyfriend, Everett, was in the army for the better part of his life and now appeared as a ghost in his fatigues most of the time.

This was really unsettling: Maxie was making sense.

"I have to get out of here," I said.

Twelve

My ex-husband has more faults than could fit into the San Fernando Valley. But one thing that has never been a point of irritation is Steven's punctuality. He's always on time.

In fact, he was already seated at a table in the Old Bean—which wasn't nearly as adorable a coffeehouse as it thought it was—when I arrived, and I was ten minutes early. He was sitting casually, a man without a care in the world, with a large mug of cinnamon-infused Colombian, black, steaming in front of him. When I showed up he was reading a copy of the *Wall Street Journal*. He was wearing a pair of dark khakis and a pressed denim work shirt that I could only assume he had bought the day before, in between leaving my house and either killing or not killing Maurice DuBois.

He was going to be a big hit in prison.

The Swine stood and smiled ingratiatingly when he saw me approach. I recognized the smile; it was the very one he had flashed on our first date. Which led to our second date. Which, if you wanted to trace a timeline past a number of other dates, led to Melissa.

I knew now not to trust that smile, so I sat down in the chair opposite the one Steven was holding out for me. He could always be a gentleman when he wanted something from you.

"So," he said with an odd humor, "what shall we talk about?"

A waitress came to take my order, which was for another hot chocolate. Coffee is a drug, a medication, for me. Hot chocolate is a recreational beverage. This time I even got whipped cream. Hang the expense! (It was no extra charge.)

Once Monica—the waitress told us her name and that she'd be taking care of us, which was a comfort—walked away, I turned back toward The Swine. "Oh, I don't know," I answered. "How about those Mets?"

"It's basketball season," my ex countered. Even when being sarcastic he could never turn down a chance to correct me on something. But he was always on time, and I needed to remind myself of that. "Why don't we discuss Maurice DuBois?"

That seemed like a decent idea, given that I didn't want to talk to him about anything else, ever again. "What can you tell me that I can pass on to the police?" I asked.

Steven looked amused. "That you can pass on to the police?" he echoed. "Nothing. I prefer to stay out of jail, thanks."

Wait. What? Did that mean what I thought it meant? The Swine *had* killed DuBois? Monica brought my hot chocolate and I wasn't even sure I wanted it anymore— though I did eat the whipped cream. I mean, it wasn't like I hadn't fantasized about him going away for a long time. I tried not to consider Melissa for a moment.

"Well, that's not encouraging," I said.

"Look, you were there. You knew there was someone demanding I give him money I couldn't possibly get in time." He sipped his coffee and sat back. "It was going to be him or me. I prefer it not to be me."

"That was the only option?" I definitely didn't want the hot chocolate now. Just one small sip. Wow, that was good. "There was no way to negotiate?"

"You don't negotiate with those guys, Ally," he said.

I couldn't muster enough energy to look annoyed at him; my mind was racing too fast.

"They come after you. It's the Wild West with these dudes. I don't have a lot of options."

"Well, what are you going to do now?" I said. "DuBois was just the messenger. Lou Maroni is the one who wants four hundred grand from you, and he's not going to give up because you got rid of poor old Maurice."

"I have to keep running. That's why I agreed to see you here. I'm saying good-bye, Alison. You won't see me again."

Those were words I'd longed to hear (although to be fair I'd heard them once before when I wasn't prepared for them and spent a year in therapy afterward), and now I was horribly alarmed. "Steven. You can say good-bye to me whenever you want, but you can't disappear from your daughter's life. What are you going to tell Melissa?"

"I'm not going to tell her anything. Leaving that little girl is the hardest thing I'll ever do. I'm not sure I could ever explain it to her in a way that wouldn't guarantee she'd hate me forever. So I won't. I'll let someone who's much better at explaining the hard parts of life tell her, someone who's done it for Melissa before."

There were bars going up around me, iron bars that wouldn't possibly be movable or bendable. There was a door in front of me, but it was locked and it was just as heavy as the bars. I knew a trap when I heard one.

"You can't leave this to me," I said in a voice barely more than a whisper. "You can't always be the fun parent and ask me to deliver the bad news when this is your screwup. You can't possibly make me look that girl in the face and tell her that her father isn't ever going to be in touch with her again. She'll associate it with me for the rest of her life."

"Better you than me," The Swine said. And he was never more a swine than in that moment. He stood up, grabbed his coat from the back of his chair, pulled a scarf from its sleeve and put it on as he walked toward the door of the coffeehouse. He was completely suited up for the cold, gloves and all, when he opened the door.

There he found Detective Lieutenant McElone.

I didn't see Steven's face, but I saw the lieutenant's. She was not smiling. "Steven Rendell," she said. "You are being held for questioning in connection with the homicide of Maurice DuBois." Behind McElone were two uniformed officers who took over the handcuffing of my ex-husband and turned him around while McElone explained to Steven that this was not an arrest. Yet. When they did that, he was looking directly at me.

I'd never seen Steven look quite that angry. His face was a combination of astonishment, pain and rage that almost distorted it beyond recognition as the man to whom I'd once been married. He stared me down to the point that having half stood, I sat back down at the table, speechless.

But he was not. "You," he said. "You called the cops and set me up. You're the last person I would have expected to betray me like this, Alison. And you're going to have to tell Melissa what you did. She can associate *that* with you for the rest of her life."

McElone did not acknowledge me as the uniforms took Steven to the waiting cruiser and the door closed again, no doubt to the relief of the other three stunned patrons of the Old Bean who had been watching and shivering as the drama played itself out. Just before she closed the door, however, the lieutenant did look in my direction.

"I'll be in touch," she said.

Thirteen

"Dad is in jail?" Melissa said.

She was sitting on a barstool in the kitchen with a tur-
key sandwich in front of her on a plate. It was untouched,
but her cell phone wasn't; she was getting texted by her
friends about every twenty seconds. She was not paying
much attention to the phone and more to me, but I was not
getting the nightmare reaction to the news that I had been
dreading the whole way back in my freeze-dried Volvo. I
was getting something much worse.

She was being reasonable and results-driven. My
daughter looked at me without a tear in either eye, hands
in a pyramid under her nose, listening intently and pursing
her lips in thought. She was all strategy and necessity. It
was chilling.

"Well, not exactly, honey. Not yet. Right now he's being
questioned by Lieutenant McElone and an investigator
from the county prosecutor's office. If they think they have

enough evidence to hold him, he'll be kept at least until Monday morning, when they can arrange an arraignment and possibly a bail hearing in front of a judge."

Paul, floating over the stove, studied Melissa closely like a really interesting work of art, but one that might move or change at some point. He didn't want to miss anything. That didn't stop him from lighting one of the front burners with his foot just to see if the energy worked on gas. It did.

"So the lieutenant hasn't charged him yet." Melissa had been studying civics in school and there had been a section on the criminal justice system she found fascinating. That might have been because Jared was in that class, and she absolutely didn't have a crush on him at all. "That means they can't hold him longer than forty-eight hours, but that still takes us into Tuesday." She nodded as if agreeing with herself. "There's time for us to clear him."

Whoa! "Us? What can we do?" I asked. "We're not lawyers."

"No," Paul jumped in. "We're investigators. There are a number of things we can do to find out who actually murdered Maurice DuBois."

Oh boy. Apparently they had Kool-Aid in whatever dimension he was inhabiting and he had drunk it. "The police believe Steven had some involvement," I said between clenched teeth, trying to be subtle in my head fake toward Melissa.

"You don't have to shield me, Mom," my daughter said. Apparently subtlety was not my strong suit. "The police think Dad killed Mr. DuBois. But we know he didn't, so we can explore areas that they won't bother to check." She looked toward Paul. "What should we do first?" Her phone buzzed again. She glanced at it and her face registered something other than pleasure, but she looked up again. No doubt she was being reminded of homework she was supposed to have done over her vacation.

"The key is to determine who else will benefit from DuBois being dead," he started. "Murder isn't something anyone does lightly. There has to be a motive. In this case, we have no other suspects yet, so we can't possibly determine motive. We need to know who was aware of DuBois's presence here in New Jersey. He probably didn't even know he was coming here until your dad got on the flight Thursday night, Melissa. So we need to get to DuBois's cell phone and see who he contacted, where he was staying and who called him."

"Will Lieutenant McElone give you Maurice DuBois's cell phone, Mom?" Melissa looked at me as if she were conducting a board meeting of the corporation she will no doubt own one day and wanted me to find out whether a rival company was going to compete with us in an emerging market.

This was going on too long. "Wait. Let's stop and think about this for a moment," I said. It's what I say when I don't know what comes next. There had to be some way to avoid this.

"Think about what?" Liss asked.

"The lieutenant isn't just guessing, honey," I said. "You know her. She's not going to bring in your father if she doesn't have some type of proof."

Melissa is a very intelligent girl. Normally she gets to the gist of something faster than I do, but when she doesn't want to confront something, she can find pathways around it that aren't on any map. "The lieutenant doesn't need proof to question Dad," she said. "She knows the man is dead. She wants to know what Dad can tell her about it. We need to give her more information about who killed the man in the alley."

"Liss . . ." I started. How to do this? I mentally cursed both The Swine and McElone for placing me in this position. "The lieutenant isn't just asking Dad for information about the man who was shot. She wants to know what connection he has to it." Okay, so I chickened out at the last minute and didn't say McElone considered Steven her best suspect. You didn't have to look into Melissa's eyes and tell her she might never see her father again without bulletproof glass between them.

Even with my gutless evasion, Liss got the message. Paul watched her intently. Paul is big into people's reactions to things whether they are suspects in a case or not. He has a heart—at least figuratively—but his mind gets in its way pretty regularly. He'll think about the other person's feelings, but he'll do it later.

"Lieutenant McElone thinks Dad killed this man." Liss looked terribly concerned; I got that. But her eyes narrowed as she put it all together. "And you *agree* with her?"

I wasn't going to cop to that even if it was true. "I'm not saying that," I began.

But I didn't get a chance to continue, because Maxie was floating down from the ceiling. Maxie likes nothing better than to get credit for having an idea I'll accept, so in a triumph of awful timing she caught a glimpse of me and said without even trying to read the room, "So, did you go see the lady cop like you said you would?"

Melissa's face favors her father no matter what the circumstances. But when she heard that, her expression was a dead ringer for Steven's when he'd been turned around and faced me at the Old Bean. "You went to see Lieutenant McElone?" she demanded. "*Before* Dad got arrested?"

There wasn't any way on this planet this situation would turn out well for me. I knew that, but I had to at least offer a defense. Unfortunately the best I could do on such short notice was "He didn't exactly get *arrested* . . ."

Melissa did not wait for me to finish. She picked up her phone, put her plate back in the fridge (that girl is well mannered) and left the kitchen. I tried; I did. I said, "Liss, you know that I—"

That was as far as I got. My daughter turned, standing in the kitchen doorway, and glared at me. "I know that you have a gripe with Dad. Of course you do. He went out to California and moved in with Amee. But you need to get over that. He's not The Swine, Mom. He's my dad, and I'm telling you he would never kill somebody. Stop being so mad at him and face the facts." And in a self-righteous manner only a thirteen-year-old girl could possibly make work, she turned and pushed the kitchen door open, then vanished into . . . the den.

I stood, stunned, in the middle of my kitchen, trying to remember what I was supposed to do next. I had a very strong urge to call my mother. As I reached for the phone in my pocket, I wondered what I'd say when she picked up the phone. "Your granddaughter's being mean to me?" My own grandfather once told me that grandparents and grandchildren get along so well because they have a common enemy. I didn't think that ploy would work well with my mother.

"What'd I miss?" Maxie asked.

Paul looked at her, then at the kitchen door, which was still swinging, then back at Maxie, then at me.

"I think we have a case to investigate," he said.

In the end, I did call my mother. She and Dad were in the next Dodge Viper (Mom looks like a badass and drives below the speed limit) to my house, where she was surprisingly sympathetic to this madwoman who was complaining about the behavior of her saintly granddaughter. Paul, half in the boiler, had felt it best to retreat to an area where we would most likely be undisturbed.

We convened in the basement, where Dad, who was ankle-deep in floor, could assess the space that I had now decided was going to stay unfinished because I was done with this house and probably should have sold it when

Steven wanted me to. Maybe I could have kept him out of jail. I could do guilt with the best of them.

My father was not, however, envisioning a cozy new guest room in my basement. Instead he was trying to figure out what Paul was constructing down there.

The late private investigator had gone all Doc Brown on us, amassing electrical and electronic equipment in one corner as if he were expecting energy to be a precious commodity that no one would have access to very soon so he needed to horde as much of it as possible. I had not called him on it yet, simply because I was afraid he'd explain, and what good was that going to do?

Mom, who had unpacked the makings for a lavish dinner from her little backpack—on no notice at all, she just had it around the house ready to go—was not thrilled with being in a dusty spot like this, but she would indeed follow my father anywhere and this was where he wanted to be.

"I talked to Steven's mother and she didn't know anything except how to reach him, which was probably just to call his cell because he'd answer her," I told them. "I don't know who else to talk to."

"How about his father?" Mom asked.

I thought about talking to Harry Rendell after what I'd seen at his house. "I'd rather not," I said.

"It would be more likely that a business associate would be involved," Paul suggested, although he was busy gathering extension cords and piling them in the corner where I'd once thought a spare guest room would go. "Do you know any of the people your ex-husband worked with when he lived on the East Coast?"

"Not really," I said. There was an old CD player in one corner and Paul was giving it the lean and hungry look. "I didn't get involved with his work much, and he tended not to bring it home because he was in Manhattan all day. I heard names, but I only met actual people a couple of times, and it was years ago. Paul—" I waved my hands to distract him from the thrilling obsolete technology he was ogling. "Have you tried reaching Maurice DuBois on the Ghosternet?"

Paul can communicate with other ghosts with a kind of telepathy/sensitivity hybrid I call the Ghosternet because I am hilarious. Paul did not agree with that assessment, but he had not asked me to stop.

"It's still very soon after he died," Paul reminded me. "It usually takes at least three or four days before someone's spirit might become cognizant of the change. We don't know if DuBois will surface at all, but if he does, it probably won't be until tomorrow at the earliest." He picked up the CD player and moved it into the corner with the rest of Mt. St. Sony.

Dad couldn't stand it anymore. "What are you doing?" he asked Paul.

"He's making a pile of junk," Maxie said. "Can't you tell?" Maxie thought she was being amusing. Maxie, unlike me, is not hilarious.

"I am collecting equipment that can channel electrical energy," Paul told Dad, wisely choosing not to engage Maxie at all. "I am planning a very serious experiment and it will require routing electricity from the roof to the basement."

A fairly long silence followed that. "In *my* house?" I asked finally.

Paul looked a little surprised. "I would have asked permission before trying it, of course, Alison," he said. "But I assure you there will be no danger of damage to anyone or anything in the house."

I shook my head in wonder. "The case, Paul. What should we do about Steven? Is there any chance he *didn't* kill Maurice DuBois?"

Paul diverted his attention again to look at me. "Of

course there's a chance, and a fairly strong one, I would say. He has a motive, to be sure, but the timing is probably off, since Josh can confirm your ex-husband's whereabouts for at least part of the time in question. Can you verify the medical examiner's estimate of DuBois's time of death?"

"I'll ask Phyllis. She has an . . . arrangement with the ME's office in the county." Phyllis knew a guy who worked for the ME, and she got information in a way that I preferred not to think about when I'd eaten in the past forty-eight hours. "If she knows anything—and she will—I can get her to tell me."

"Good. Then go to the police station. See if they have indeed jailed your ex-husband. If not, try to contact him and get some names of previous associates. If they have, ask where he's being held so you can go visit him there."

I took a step back involuntarily. "You want me to go see Steven?" The look on his face at the coffeehouse was imprinted on my cerebral cortex. It was not something I cared to see again. "Um . . . would they let Melissa see him?"

"Alison," my mother said. "Is that what you want?"

She had me. It wasn't what I wanted. I shook my head and tried to notice something on my feet I could focus on.

"You should have thought of that when you went and ratted your ex out to the lady cop," Maxie volunteered.

My father's eyes widened a little. "Alison," he said. "You gave up your ex to the police?" He grinned. "I'm proud of you." Dad was probably the most vocal critic when Steven and I had announced our engagement.

"Jack," my mother admonished. Lightly.

"No, as a matter of fact, I didn't," I told the gathering. "I decided against going to see McElone, got halfway to the police station and then just turned and drove to Point Pleasant to meet Steven after I thought it over in the car for a while."

"What!" Maxie was appalled. "The first time we agree on a plan and you didn't go through with it?"

"You were just scolding me for turning him in and now you're scolding me for *not* turning him in," I pointed out. "Make up your mind."

"Girls," Mom admonished. Lightly.

"She started it," Maxie said, and swooped into the upper floors.

"Sure," I said to the ceiling. "It's easy to win all the arguments when you can just fly out of the room."

Then I heard footsteps above, which would have been in the kitchen. The guests generally don't go in there, although there are sometimes snacks they keep in the fridge and they're welcome to take what they like anytime. Because I don't serve food, they usually have no reason to patronize my kitchen.

"Melissa?" I wondered aloud. I headed for the stairs as Dad simply rose to check.

"No," I heard him call from upstairs a moment later. "Worse."

It couldn't be.

But there he was, in all his "glory." Once Mom and I got upstairs—Mom takes a little longer than I do—we found The Swine in my kitchen, with Dad, Paul and Maxie hovering over his head like United Airlines flights stacked up over Newark Airport. "Ally!" he said, the fake charm practically washing over me. "And Loretta." He moved to hug Mom, who looked positively nauseated at the prospect. "So good to see you."

Mom stood stock-still while Steven put his arms around her, making it look like he was hugging a very small tree. She endured the embrace and then exhaled when he let go. "Steven," she said, her voice freezing as it reached him. "I'm surprised you're here."

"So am I," I told the Swine. "How'd you make bail?"

"I didn't," he said. "They didn't charge me because I didn't do anything wrong and they know it." He stood with his arms folded, daring me to disprove his statement. I couldn't and didn't necessarily want to, although I didn't believe him simply out of habit. "Your Lieutenant McElone figured that out pretty quick and let me go."

"She's not *my* Lieutenant McElone," I said. Defensiveness is my go-to posture when The Swine is in the house. "We know each other a little bit."

"You told her how to find me."

"I thought you said you didn't tell her how to find him," Maxie said.

"I *didn't*," I told both of them. "I don't know how McElone found out you were going to be at the Old Bean, but it wasn't from me."

"Okay," The Swine said. His tone indicated that it wasn't okay at all.

Paul, busying himself with turning the ceiling fan on and off, was creating two problems: One, he was distracting The Swine, who asked why the fan was taking on a mind of its own; and two, he was cooling off a room when it was nineteen degrees outside. I gave him a look that hopefully my ex did not see and Paul, duly chastised, stopped touching the fan mechanism. "Sorry, Alison," he said.

"What is that?" Steven asked.

Luckily the kitchen door swung open and Melissa walked in. Her face was turned toward her phone—naturally—but Steven did not let the opportunity pass to show us all how much she adored him. "Lissie!" he said.

Liss looked up, startled. "Dad!" she said. She wasn't as over-the-top as I might have expected, but walked over to hug her father and smiled. "Are you okay?"

"I'm fine, baby. It was all a misunderstanding." You know, like Watergate.

"What happened?" Melissa asked.

"Yeah," Mom said. The Swine has a way of bringing out the tough-as-nails dame she thinks she is. "Exactly what did happen? How did that man looking for you end up dead in an alley?" And they wonder where I got my demure personality.

"I have no idea," The Swine lied. "But for the moment it's not my problem. The cops have to find somebody else to blame."

There was something he wasn't saying. I could hear that in his voice. "How exactly did you convince Lieutenant McElone she shouldn't hold you?" I asked. "I know her, and she's pretty hard to convince." It was true—McElone still wouldn't come into the house when she knew the ghosts were around, which in Paul's case was always.

"I told her I was innocent." That was the best he could do? The man who had once gotten seven Orthodox Jews to invest in a casino by convincing them the Sioux Nation was one of the lost tribes of Israel?

"Everybody tells her they're innocent," I answered. "I know at least three people still in jail who told her they were innocent. How come she believed you?"

"Because I am innocent," The Swine said. He had so much nothing it was a little sad.

"Dad." Melissa could get to Steven in ways I would never dream about. "Tell us for real. What evidence did you give the lieutenant that made her let you go?"

"I gave her my alibi for the time the man died, honey," her father said. Right to her face. "Once that checked out, she had to release me."

"*What* alibi?" Dad demanded. "We don't even know what time the guy was shot."

I passed that along to The Swine as my own observation. "I told them I was with your boyfriend, Alison," he crooned. "They called him and he confirmed it."

"You told them—" My phone was out of my pocket faster than Wyatt Earp could have drawn his Colt .45, assuming that was what Wyatt was packing. What do I know about guns? I pushed the button for Josh and waited for him to pick up.

"Hey, I was going to call you," he began. "I got this call from—"

"From Lieutenant McElone," I finished for him. "She wanted you to confirm The . . . Steven's alibi?" Melissa frowned. Her father didn't appear to have caught my near slip.

"Yeah. I didn't even know he was in custody. But I guess he didn't do it, right? Because he was with me at the time the lieutenant asked about."

"He was?"

"Sure. You remember. He was there at your house when I got there, and I brought him back here, however briefly." Josh seemed to think I didn't recall the situation. What he didn't realize was that I remembered it, but I didn't believe it had happened the way it appeared to have happened. They're two different things, and they often collide when The Swine is in town.

"That I get. What time did she ask you about?" I didn't like the cat-versus-canary grin on my ex-husband's face. He had played the system and gained some sort of temporary get-out-of-jail-free pass.

"About ten o'clock," Josh answered, sounding just a little confused. "So he was at your house when it happened."

That made no sense. "Then why didn't she call me to confirm it?" I wondered aloud.

The Swine held up a hand. "They asked for one name of a person I was with. I gave them one name. No sense to bring this into the family."

I made a mental note to send him a Christmas card with cyanide in it this year.

Luckily Josh hadn't heard him. "I have no idea," he

said. "We still on for dinner tonight?" We rarely went out for dinner while I had guests, but this was the lowest-maintenance group since the time I had a grand total of one guest during a hurricane one year. So we'd made plans before Steven showed up to have what Melissa called "Date Night" this evening.

"I don't see why not," I answered. After the age of twelve it is legal to leave a child alone in the house. There is no provision in the law—I checked—for leaving a child with two ghosts and her unreliable father. I figured Liss could handle it. Then I remembered. "But my mom brought a whole load of food."

My mother waved her hand. "That's for tomorrow," she said. "I just brought it today because we were coming for an emergency."

Steven looked "concerned." He tries. "What emergency?" he asked.

"You." Mom, Dad and I pointed at him. He didn't see Dad, but I think he got the point.

The Swine laughed. "You people don't give me enough credit."

Melissa looked up from her phone before I could make a comment on how much credit her father might be due, and how getting credit had led to his current troubles to begin with. "Let's go up to my room, Dad," she said. "I have some pictures I found from when I was little." She and Steven walked out while I was trying to decide if she really liked him better than me or was just attempting to get her father out of harm's way. Because my mother did not look happy.

"That guy." Maxie shook her head. "There's something about him."

"Yeah. It's called acid reflux," I said. I reached into a cabinet for a container of Tums I kept there. Orange is best.

Josh, blissfully unaware of most of what was going on

in my house, said he'd come by to get me around seven, when the guests were often out getting dinner for themselves. I cooed a little discreetly at him and we ended the call.

Paul looked down at me with a look of true consideration and deep thought. I looked up hopefully. Paul has a way of clarifying a situation and creating a plan of action that makes me optimistic in a crisis.

"Do you think you could do without this?" he asked. He pointed to the microwave oven sitting on a countertop and looked positively avaricious.

The microwave? I used that to heat up coffee and thaw out frozen . . . Wait. "No!" I shouted at him. "You can't have my microwave. What is this all about?"

"Are we staying with Melissa tonight?" my father interjected. "I saw a loose piece of molding in the library and thought I might be able to shore that up for you." Dad was a handyman in life and really hasn't given it up despite dying seven years ago.

"We're happy to," Mom chimed in. She was still looking at the door as if wondering whether that awful man who had left with Melissa could be trusted.

He couldn't, except with Melissa.

"If you want," I said. "Check with Liss and see if you'll be intruding on a father/daughter moment." Far be it from me to break up that burgeoning friendship. I was just the mother, after all.

Dad flew up through the ceiling, but Mom said she wanted to go up there anyway—probably to check on The Swine—and started for the stairs, which I knew wasn't easy for her.

My mother doesn't care much for my ex-husband, in case you were wondering.

Maxie looked at Paul, then at me, said something about looking for Everett and hightailed it out through the back

wall toward the beach. Paul scowled a little. It always bothers him that Maxie has free run of the planet and he's stuck
within my property lines.

"Okay, what's going on?" I said as he drifted slowly
down toward my eye level. "I get that you're looking into
your theory of energy and I get that it's a little dull around
here sometimes so you need to do your experiments. But
we have what you'd call a case to investigate now, one that
could impact me and my daughter, and you're distracted
by things like my microwave oven. What's all that electrical stuff in the basement? What are you planning to do
that's so important? Specifically, please."

Paul stopped and considered. He looked me right in the
eye. "I'm trying to move on to the next level of existence,"
he said.

Fourteen

Josh looked over his menu at me. "Paul thinks he can go to heaven or something if he electrocutes himself?" He shook his head. "Why?"

I was deciding between the fettucine Alfredo and the gnocchi Bolognese. "That's not exactly it, but you're close," I said. Bolognese. I put down the menu and looked at Josh. "What he said was that he thought a surge in the amount of energy that flowed through him might nudge him into the next level of existence. He thinks maybe he's made of energy, but his level is just too low to get where he wants to go. With this great big surge he might be able to move on."

Josh scanned the menu, but I knew he was getting the chicken marsala and so did he. "And where does he think all this extra energy is going to come from?" he asked.

"Um . . ." This was the tricky part I'd have preferred not to discuss. "Paul says he can harvest the energy—that's his word, 'harvest'—by attaching this contraption he's building to a lightning rod on the roof."

Josh put down his menu. "A lightning rod. On your roof."

"Pretty much."

"And how does this not end with your house being without power and/or burning down?"

"Paul is sure it's safe," I reported. He had actually said "*fairly* sure," but why quibble?

"And you're okay with this?" Josh looked at me. I usually love the way he looks at me, but this level of concern was stirring up my own unsure feelings about Paul's nutty crusade.

"Well, *okay* might be going a little too far," I admitted. "But how can I deny him after all this time the chance to move to another plane of existence? It's all he thinks about and it's . . ." I was going to say "It's killing him to stay like this," but that would have been an obvious misstatement. "It's really important to him. The man has probably saved my life more than once. How can I tell him no?"

Josh is not a didactic boyfriend. He's not threatened by the presence of my ex-husband, at least not nearly as much as that threatens me when Steven spends time with Melissa. He hasn't raised an issue about me living with two dead people in my house. He doesn't complain that I can't take vacations or even frequent nights off like this one. He is amazingly understanding. So it didn't surprise me when he said, "I understand," nodding just a little bit. "How about this: Can Tony and I be there when he tries this, so we can help you deal with it if something goes wrong?"

I exhaled. "I was hoping you'd say that. I'll buy some extra fire extinguishers."

The server, who was careful to tell us her name was Julia, took our orders, gave us a smile to indicate we had done well (do people order badly at restaurants, drawing snarls from the waitstaff?) and took our menus back with her. I felt so validated by her approval of my Bolognese that I was emboldened to look my boyfriend in the eye. I could see by his expression he was still mulling over the logistics of Paul's scheme in his head.

"When is he planning on trying this?" he asked. He looked at his watch, as if it might be any minute.

"Probably not for a while. There has to be lightning, see, and we are in the middle of winter."

Josh smiled. "Yeah. I heard about that on Twitter. Cold, right? And snow?"

"You're so up-to-date." I reached my hand over and placed it on his. I don't know what I was doing right the day we re-met, but someone somewhere had been smiling on me.

"That's me, Mr. Tech. I own a paint store." Josh looked at his watch again. It was thirty seconds later than the last time. He didn't seem especially nervous, but I was starting to wonder if he had a late appointment with his hypnotherapist or something. (He doesn't really have a hypnotherapist.) "So, what's the latest on your ex's legal issues?"

I filled him in on The Swine Saga as well as I understood it. "He's up to something, but I can't figure out what," I concluded. "With Steven there's always an angle. To get released from custody when McElone was certain enough to bring him in must have taken some pretty serious tap dancing. She's not easily convinced. Of anything. Ever."

"Maybe he's really innocent," Josh suggested. He managed to do so without checking the time again, but I could tell he wanted to.

"He might not be guilty, but he's far from innocent," I answered. "I don't really think Steven killed this DuBois guy, but I do think he's involved in something that resulted in the man being shot, and he's probably in over his head, which is his natural state. There's no question in my mind he's hiding something."

Josh put up his hands in a pyramid and rested them under his chin. "Well, if this was an investigation, what would you do with a suspect like him?"

It was a good question. "Probably stakeout," I said. "Watch and see who he's associating with, that sort of thing. But I can't do that with Steven."

"Why not?"

I gave him a look. "He does sort of know what I look like."

He twisted his lips around in a "thinking" face. "I suppose he does. But you know people he won't recognize. Or even see."

My boyfriend is down with the ghosts. "Hey, that's not bad. I can get Dad to tail him and report back on his movements. You're a genius."

"Yeah, but I don't like to brag." Josh checked his watch again.

I couldn't let that one go by. "Okay, what's going on?"

His expression was trying for surprise but landed on mild panic. "What do you mean?"

"You're looking at your watch like you're trying to time the contractions. Do you need to be somewhere else?" Julia brought our drinks, which killed the conversation for a short time.

"No, of course not. I don't know what you're talking about." This time he conspicuously avoided looking at his watch but did glance toward the restaurant's entrance, which was behind me.

"You do so. I'm a licensed detective, Josh. I know when something is up." I'm a *bad* licensed detective, but there was no need to mention that just now.

"Well, your Spidey sense is off this time, Sherlock. Nothing's going on."

"Something sure is. You're mixing your pop culture metaphors."

But this time he was smiling and before I knew it, there was a man in a suit standing next to our table. He didn't exactly look formal, but professional, and he was carrying an envelope.

"Are you Alison Kerby?" he asked. Me.

Josh was grinning like the Cheshire Cat, so this couldn't be an awful thing, but his smile had a tense pull at its corners.

I admitted to being myself, and the man offered me the envelope.

"Telegram," he said.

Telegram? Was I living in some alternative 1954? Weren't telegrams always bad news? I looked up at the man in the suit. "For me?" I asked. It was a stupid question, but a placeholder while I thought.

"If you're Alison Kerby."

I was undeniably Alison Kerby, so I took the envelope from his hand. I didn't know telegrams came in envelopes. In the movies they're always just free sheets of paper that are snatched from the kid in a uniform with a cap at the door who, depending on what the screenwriter wants us to think about the recipient of the message, does or doesn't get a tip. This, apparently, was no longer how such things were done.

Josh still had that odd look on his face that made me think he was going to either bust out laughing or curl into the fetal position under the table. I figured it had something to do with the telegram, which he somehow had known was coming, so the best way to end this surreal scene was to read the wire and deal with what it said.

I extracted the paper inside, which was yellow not because it was old but because that was the color it was intended to be by the company sending the telegram. I read the words and let them sink in:

LET'S PLAY COLOR QUIZ FOREVER. STOP (It actually said

STOP. I thought that had gone the way of the delivery boy with the cap.) WILL YOU PLEASE MARRY ME? STOP.

Underneath it read JOSH.

Whoa.

Instinctively I looked up from the paper and saw Josh's gleeful/tense face and now I understood why it looked that way. He was wondering if I was going to say yes or no.

A thousand thoughts flashed through my mind in a millisecond. Shouldn't he know what I was feeling, and so not be worried? Would he move to the guesthouse, because I couldn't live anywhere else and keep my business? Should I sell the house and move in with him? Was it necessary to ask Melissa's permission if I said yes? Who sends a telegram to propose? Was it a way of asking without asking? Did that mean Josh was torn on the subject? What did WILL YOU PLEASE MARRY ME? STOP mean, anyway? Sort of sending a mixed message, wasn't it?

"Yes," I said.

Josh grinned with relief, I think, and stood up. I stood up, too, so that by the time he got to me, we could embrace and kiss without the awkward one-person-in-a-chair scenario. I was vaguely aware of other people in the restaurant applauding as Josh kissed me, which meant they must have known what happened. It was sort of like when people get engaged on the Jumbotron at a sports arena, but less horrifying. A little less horrifying.

But I felt his arms around me and I knew it was the right decision. This was the guy.

We didn't spend a huge amount of time kissing because of the whole Jumbotron analogy, so once we were finished, Josh looked at me and said, "You're sure?"

I understood. I'd hesitated. A guy doesn't want to see that when proposing. "I'm sure," I said. "It was just so out of the blue."

"You have no idea. I've been trying to figure out when

to do this for months." He did not reach into his pocket. "I didn't get a ring. I figured you would want to help pick it out. Was I wrong?"

And that reminded me once again that I definitely had the right guy. I hugged him close. "You're never wrong," I said.

"Can I get that in writing?"

I didn't remember much about the rest of the dinner. No, let me be clear—I didn't remember *anything* about the rest of the dinner. I did recall telling Josh the only way my acceptance was revocable would be if Melissa disapproved, and I estimated a less than one percent chance of that happening. Especially after I texted her and asked, "Is it okay if I marry Josh?" and she texted back, "YAY!!!"

I was pretty sure that was not disapproval.

Josh and I talked about plans. Not a big wedding, we agreed. He'd move into the guesthouse and give up his Asbury Park apartment. It would be something of a commute to his store, but he didn't mind getting up even earlier in the morning to make it work.

I offered to sell the guesthouse and give up my business. Josh looked at me as if I had suggested I would sprout wings and fly to Jupiter. "I really don't think that's a good idea," was what he said.

And the fettucine Alfredo was delicious. I changed my order because it was a special occasion.

On second thought, maybe I *did* remember a few things about the rest of the dinner.

I didn't think about Steven and the dead body in the alley at all until well after we got back to the guesthouse. Melissa and my parents had shown great wisdom by not telling Steven my news, but asking him instead if he could find a particular kind of hinge Dad had suggested that he said Home Depot would never have. Steven had been gone for more than an hour already in search of an all-night hardware store, and had never even asked why that hinge was necessary. That was good, because Dad couldn't think of a reason.

They had also hung up some bunting in the den and the "HAPPY BIRTHDAY" sign I hung up on Liss's birthday and when a guest might be celebrating while at my house. Mom had gone out for a bottle of sparkling wine (they don't let you call it champagne unless it comes from that region of France, and this definitely didn't), and all three guests, Paul and Maxie joined my family and my fiancé (*that* was new!) in the den for a toast.

Dad, who knew Josh from Madison Paints when he was alive and Josh was a toddler, raised a glass with nothing in it because, let's face it, what would be the point? Yoko, Mel and Anne were now used to having objects float around.

Melissa repeated Dad's words as he spoke so Josh and the guests (but mostly Josh) could hear them. "I've known Josh almost as long as I've known Alison, so I'm really tickled to see this day," he said despite the fact that he wasn't actually alive to see it; why quibble over the details? "Josh was a fine boy and is now a fine man. He's honest, he's reliable, he's loyal. He came back to Alison after years apart, when she was going through a couple of phases." (There I got the parental look of "what did you put me through?" no doubt recalling the Swine Years.) "And we're so glad he did."

Then my father swooped down to be close to me and even the non-ghost-seers in the room saw how our perspectives changed—their eyes went to the spot where Dad was hovering. His voice got softer and his words caught a little here and there. "And my Alison." He looked at Mom. "*Our* Alison. What a wonderful woman you've become. A terrific mother, a devoted daughter. A good friend. We're so proud of you. And your mother and I are thrilled to see how happy you are now. We're glad you're going to make that permanent."

I confess to wiping away a tear. Most girls don't get to hear that from their dead fathers.

Dad rose again toward the ceiling, feeling his role as toastmaster and wanting to address the group as a whole. He raised his glass higher. "So here is to my baby girl and her new husband. May they always—"

He was interrupted by a voice from the doorway. "What is *that* all about?" it called. "How do you get that glass to float around like that?"

Everybody turned to look. At the door to the den stood three men I'd never seen before. They were dressed almost identically in khakis and long-sleeved polo shirts with woolen overcoats—exactly like the one I'd seen on Maurice DuBois the morning he came to the house looking for Steven.

The morning of the day he was shot and killed.

"It's a convention of magicians," I said. Dad dropped the glass onto the rug just to reinforce my point. "This is my guesthouse. I'm Alison Kerby. How can I help you gentlemen?" But I knew the next thing he was going to say before he even started to move his lips.

"Where's Steven Rendell?" he asked, although it sounded more like a demand.

I did my best to look surprised. "Steven Rendell is my ex-husband," I informed the man, who I was sure knew that already. "He's not here."

I saw Melissa's arms tense up a little.

"I'll get something to hit them with," Maxie said with a weary air, and in a flash she was through the ceiling.

"Is this part of the celebration?" Anne Kaminsky asked.

"Well, if he's not here, where is he?" the man said, as if Anne had not spoken.

"I couldn't tell you," I said. It was an evasion, but a pretty transparent one. I was trying to buy time to think.

Paul looked the men up and down from very close up. He floated through one of them. "Concealed weapons in shoulder holsters," he said. "That's why the coats are open, for faster access." Thanks a heap, Paul.

Before the man who had spoken could respond, I asked, "May I ask why you're looking for my ex-husband?"

"He owes me money," the man said. "My name is Lou Maroni. Does that ring a bell?"

Fifteen

The dynamic of the evening had changed in an eyeblink.
Now there were a number of priorities to consider. One, I
had to get these guys out of my house before Steven
returned. Or did I? Maybe it would be a better idea to have
The Swine confront the consequences of his actions. Nah.
That wasn't going to happen.

Two, I had really wanted to celebrate our engagement.
It was a surprise, but it wasn't a shock, because Josh and
I had been together for a couple of years now and while
we had not actually discussed marriage, we had talked
about changing our (read: his) living arrangements. So
getting these guys out of the house was important on a
personal as well as safety-related level.

Three. I wondered if there was a way to alert Lieutenant
McElone to the presence of our guests, and if so, whether
that was even a thing you could do. I mean, they technically hadn't committed any crime yet. Do you call the

police when people enter your house without knocking first? Is that trespass?

Four, Melissa looked scared. That trumped all others and jumped to the front of the line.

"I don't know anything about any money, Mr. Maroni, and I don't know where Steven is," I said. "I'm sorry, but I'll have to ask you to leave. We were having a private celebration."

"They got engaged!" Yoko announced to the three armed men.

One of the brutes behind Maroni squinted as if she'd said something in a language other than the one he understood. "Then how come it says Happy Birthday?" he asked, pointing to the sign hung on the wall over the fireplace.

"I guess they didn't have a sign that said Happy Engagement," Yoko allowed, finger to her lower lip.

"Seriously," I said, trying to steer the conversation back to the topic at hand and glancing anxiously at the door for the impending Swine infestation. "I can't help you gentlemen, so would you please let us have some privacy?"

Maxie dropped through the ceiling wearing her trench coat, which she quickly vanished to reveal a rather large sledgehammer in her arms. I thought I'd left that out in the shed. I probably had.

The second henchman (I decided that was what they were) behind Maroni said, "How do they make *that* float around in the air?"

Oops.

Behind my back I gestured for Maxie to get rid of the hammer. She huffed in frustration, but the trench coat reappeared and the offending object became invisible to the non-Kerby mortals in the room.

"That's a good trick," the first henchman said.

Maroni chose not to marvel at the astounding miracle

he had seen before him. "We're not leaving until we see Rendell," he said convincingly.

"He's not here," Melissa said, stepping forward and facing her adversary directly. "You won't find him here, so saying it like that isn't going to get you anywhere. We don't know where he is. He was here yesterday, but we haven't heard from my dad since then."

She even had the good sense not to punch the words *my dad* too much. That girl could act professionally. If I sold the guesthouse, maybe her Hollywood salaries would pay her college tuition bills. But perhaps that was beside the point.

Maroni studied my daughter carefully. Melissa commanded respect in people of all ages. He was not going to dismiss her as a silly little girl.

"Why should I believe you?" he asked.

Liss did her best to stare him down. "Because it's the truth and you don't want to have to intimidate a thirteen-year-old," she said.

The man in the overcoat considered that, then nodded once. "Good enough. But I'll be back tomorrow if we don't find him first. And that time I'm going through the house from top to bottom because your father owes me a lot of money and I'm also not going to let a thirteen-year-old get in my way. Is that fair?"

"If she says he's not here, he's not here," my mother volunteered. It wasn't the whole threatening-The-Swine thing that was bothering her; it was the audacity that anyone could possibly mistrust her granddaughter, who was at least mostly lying.

"That wasn't the question," Maroni said without taking his gaze off Liss. "Fair?"

"Fair," she agreed.

"Good." Maroni buttoned up his overcoat and the two

slabs of beef behind him did the same. "I hope we won't see you tomorrow."

"I hope so, too," I said, simply to reaffirm that I was in fact the mother here.

The three men turned, adjusted their scarves almost in unison and walked out of the house. I could hear the collective sigh of relief float around the room like Paul and Maxie, who weren't breathing but made a noise like a sigh anyway. Just to be sociable or something, I guess.

Josh looked at me. "Does this kind of thing happen all the time around here? I mean, once I move in, should I expect that?"

"Pretty much," I said, and hugged him around the waist.

"She's kidding," my mother told my fiancé for fear he didn't actually know me well enough to understand. "This is the first time I've seen gangsters here."

I heard Maroni's car start up in the driveway and pull out—how had I missed that before? That helped me relax a little bit. I looked up at Paul but didn't have time to speak.

"I think I'm going up to my room," Yoko said to me. "After that I need to meditate." She walked out, serene but with an edge, if such a thing is possible.

Mel and Anne looked at each other. They were holding hands, which I saw as a good sign for their marriage. Then they went separately back to the rooms they were renting, which I did not see as such a great omen. People aren't consistent and that bothers me.

"I didn't get to finish my toast," Dad said.

I wished I could hug him. The ghosts can deal with us as they can with inanimate objects, but when I reach for one of them my hand goes through and I get a varying sensation depending on the ghost. I reached out a hand and Dad took it, which gave me the comforting sense of sawdust and Aqua Velva that he emitted. "It's okay," I told him. "It was a lovely toast."

My gaze gave Josh a direction in which to look, which was helpful when he wanted to talk to Dad. "I can't thank you enough for the kind words, Jack."

"This is getting mushy," Maxie complained. "I wanted to hit somebody with the sledgehammer."

"Maybe tomorrow." Paul looked distracted and concerned. Melissa looked up at him.

"What kind words?" I closed my eyes. It's a visceral reaction I get when I'm not primed to hear The Swine's voice. He was behind me. "And who's Jack?"

To be fair, Steven knew my father from when he was alive. He had no reason to expect that Dad was in the room now. So it was, in its own way, a reasonable question. I just wasn't in the mood.

I blew past it. "We just got rid of three of your friends," I told Steven as I turned to face him. "Mostly it was your daughter who saved your hide."

Liss gave me an "oh, Mother" look, but I'm impervious to those now. She'd have to do better. After all, it's my job to embarrass her, and if she started dating Jared, she'd have to get used to that. Not that she had a crush on him.

"What are you talking about?" The Swine was slick, but he was never quick on the uptake. "And whose birthday is it?"

"I could hit *him* with the sledgehammer," Maxie offered. It was tempting but would require too much explanation afterward.

"Mom and Josh got engaged," Melissa told him. That might have been retribution for the remark about saving The Swine's hide. "Just tonight."

My ex-husband's face lit up in the most sincere fake smile you've ever seen in your life. "No kidding!" He reached out a hand to Josh, because why talk to me? "Congratulations!"

Josh took his hand but looked like he hoped there was some Purell handy for afterward. "Thanks," he said, almost completely out loud.

"So, how did this happen?" The Swine went on, as if it were some magical process attainable only through the spells of wizards on a night the moon was full.

"You're missing the point, Steven," I said. "There were three men here looking for you, and one of them told us he was Lou Maroni."

My ex stopped in mid-glad-handing and turned to stare at me. I thought my mother might take Maxie up on her sledgehammer offer based strictly on The Swine's expression, which bordered on homicidal.

"Lou Maroni was here?" he said, advancing on me. I saw Josh close ranks and place himself between us. "Are you serious?" Why did he look like that?

"Yeah. But we made him go away."

"Why would you do that?" The Swine demanded. "How could you let him get away?"

Melissa and I passed a look that questioned Steven's sanity.

"They were coming for you because you owe him all kinds of money," I reminded him. "We thought it best to get them out of here. How is that—"

"How many times have I told you, Alison?" The Swine shouted. "Keep out of my business!" He turned on his heel and stomped out of the house while all of us—dead and alive—stared at each other in wonder.

"That went well," Maxie said finally.

The rest of the celebration was, let's say, subdued. Liss reminded me she had school in the morning, the first time she'd done that since second grade. I released her from any further revelry and she went up to her room. That was just about the time Mom and Dad decided to take off for Mom's house. Josh stuck around, but Paul and Maxie did, too, and that put something of a crimp in our celebrating. The ghosts weren't about to leave us alone tonight.

Maybe living here after we were married wasn't the best idea after all.

We sat on the sofa in the den, Paul hovering just over the side table, not pacing but sort of swaying back and forth, shimmying in the center of his body. It was like watching smoke try to make a decision.

Maxie said she was going to get Everett in case we needed military protection against the mob. Maxie has an interesting view of . . . everything. She zipped through the side wall at her top speed, which was fairly impressive. If she could find a car going slowly enough on the road, she could hitch a ride part of the way to Everett's home base at the Fuel Pit. Odds were she would not be back soon.

One down, one to go.

"The way I see it," Paul began, "we need to identify possible suspects in the murder of Maurice DuBois. In order to do so, it's necessary to determine the people with whom your ex-husband has been associating, both here and in California."

Josh took note of the direction in which I was looking and put his index finger gently under my chin, stroking gently. "Is one of them talking?" he asked.

I looked down to take in my fiancé. I was going to have to get used to calling him that. "Paul's the only one left," I said.

"Ah. So investigation stuff." The stroking became a caress, which was better. I got a little closer to Josh.

"Yeah. Something about identifying suspects," I said.

"Ooh."

Josh's arms sort of engulfed me, but not in a rough way. I snuggled up next to him.

"Alison," Paul said, looking away. "We have business to discuss."

"Uh-huh," I answered.

Josh leaned over and kissed me quite expertly. The man had a talent. I responded in kind.

"Alison," Paul said again.

I didn't answer him.

"The investigation."

We broke the clinch for a moment. "Tomorrow," I said. Then I kissed Josh again.

"I don't think this can wait," the ghost insisted. "Your ex-husband's life could be in the balance."

This time we didn't even come up for air.

"Oh, fine," Paul huffed. "I can prepare for my energy experiment."

My eyes were closed, but I was fairly sure he was already descending into his basement lair.

"Is he gone?" Josh asked.

I held close to him. "Uh-huh," I said again.

"So it worked."

"Yeah. Paul hates the gushy stuff."

"Good," Josh said. "Want to go upstairs?"

That seemed like a good idea.

Sixteen

"So, where's the ring?" Jeannie Rodgers scanned my left hand with some degree of disappointment.

"We're going to go get it next week," I told her. "Josh didn't want to pick one out that I wouldn't like."

We were sitting in Jeannie's minivan, the vehicle of choice for the suburban parent of young children. Personally I'd rather drive the world's oldest Volvo wagon with a suspect heating system—which I did—than wobble around in one of these paddy wagons, but it was a better bet to use Jeannie's car today because as large and lumbering as it was, it had a distinct advantage.

The Swine didn't know what Jeannie drove, so he wouldn't notice us doing surveillance on him as he went about his day.

Finding Steven's whereabouts had been a trick to begin with. While the original plan had been to have Maxie or Dad follow Steven from my house, he had stormed out the night before, but as it turned out Maxie had spotted him when she left to find Everett and was looking for a ride. She hitched one with The Swine despite his not going toward the Fuel Pit, and reported back early this morning that he'd been staying with a friend from high school, Bobby Bertowski, in Avon-By-The-Sea, which we locals called Avon. Luckily Jeannie was available this morning because my father was too far away to get to Avon in time and Maxie would have required a ride as well.

In fact, she was in the farthest reaches of the minivan, sticking her feet out the rear hatch as we sat outside a coffee shop in Belmar. We'd followed The Swine here from his temporary digs at ten thirty a.m. Steven was not an early riser when he wasn't required to be.

"You sure you're engaged?" Jeannie asked. "I don't know if it's official if you don't have a ring."

"It's official," I said. "As official as it can get. I mean, nothing's *legally* official until you're actually married."

"No ring?" Maxie marveled from the back. "I bet he's just leaving his options open."

I made a face, which Jeannie thought was aimed at her. "I was just asking," she said.

"I'm not mad at you. How long has he been in there?" If Jeannie weren't present I could ask Maxie to go into the coffee place and see who Steven was talking to, listen in on the conversation. But of course Maxie had shown up in Jeannie's car five minutes after she picked me up at the house, so talking to her would be problematic. The fact was, I could probably do that anyway and Jeannie would think I was being hilarious.

"Thirteen minutes by my watch," Jeannie answered. "What are we looking for? I mean, does his taste in muffins really have much to do with whether he killed somebody?" There was a snort from behind me, which I had naturally assumed was Maxie being a pain, but instead it turned out to be Oliver waking up from what for him must have been a surprise nap.

Most days Jeannie drops her children off at day care, something that would have seemed impossible to imagine before Molly was born. Let's just say Jeannie was a little less relaxed when she had one small child than she is now with two. Mostly because that level of micromanagement aimed at two little ones probably would have killed Jeannie. Or Tony would have.

But today the day care center was closed because of an infestation of bedbugs that required some serious insecticides, and that meant no children in the building. It was about forty degrees too cold to keep the kids outside, so Ollie and Molly were in the backseat of the minivan in car seats, Molly sleeping and Oliver, until a moment ago, following her lead. Now he was announcing his intention to become awake and impatient.

"We want to see if he's meeting anybody," I said. I pulled a pair of binoculars from the tote bag I carry and tried to zero in on The Swine. The coffee shop, which was imaginatively called the Coffee House, had a plate-glass window in the front, but he had chosen to position himself somewhere else in the establishment. I made a head gesture toward Maxie, who didn't notice because she was trying to tickle a baby who clearly didn't know she was there.

Oliver, on the other hand, was showing something approaching interest in the ghost behind him. His eyes followed her finger as she attempted to tickle Molly. Molly did not react at all, but Oliver laughed loudly.

"What's funny?" Jeannie asked him.

"The lady."

I figured I'd cover up for him, although I'll admit sometimes I wonder why it's necessary. Oliver had shown signs of seeing the ghosts before, but was never as clear about it as he was being now. "He's not visible from here," I said to Jeannie. "Can you get closer?"

She gestured with her right hand. "Do you see another parking space?"

It was true: Even on a weekday morning in winter, you can't find a place to park in a town on the Jersey Shore. The place was packed to the gills and I had only three guests at home and a mortgage payment due in a week.

I chose not to focus on that issue and did another sweep of the coffee shop for The Swine. He appeared after a moment, carrying a large mug toward a table. There was a woman next to him—of course—whose skirt was showing off her legs even in this weather, but it wasn't clear whether she was with Steven. "I wish we had somebody inside," I said, hoping Maxie would take the bait.

She had noticed Oliver's attention and was now trying to engage him in a game of peekaboo, something so two weeks ago for him (literally) that it was frankly embarrassing she'd even make the attempt.

"Well, he'll notice either of us and I don't think Oliver is old enough to order a latte just yet," Jeannie answered.

"Maybe I can just get out of the van and get closer enough that I can see inside better," I suggested.

"Yeah, because a person out in the street in twenty-degree weather watching a coffee shop with binoculars isn't the least bit conspicuous," my best friend pointed out.

"Fine. Be logical."

Maxie was now contenting herself with moving her hand up and down like a flapping bird and reveling in Oliver's gaze following it wherever it went. She was giggling like a two-year-old herself while the actual toddler was wearing a serious expression, watching her with rapt concentration.

Just then The Swine showed up in the front window again, this time with his obviously borrowed leather jacket zipped up. He was heading for the door.

The woman whose legs I'd caught a glimpse of before—and which he had no doubt caught more than a glimpse of himself—was walking out with him. "Wait," I told Jeannie, as if she had indicated she was going to do anything but that. "He's on the move."

Molly chose that moment to wake up and start moving toward the crying stage. Babies are very good at that, and especially proficient at being inconvenient. Jeannie turned around to look at her daughter.

"Aw, you okay, pumpkin?" she cooed. "Just wake up?" She caught a glimpse of Oliver, his head going up and down following Maxie's finger. "What's with you, little boy?" she asked.

"The lady," he repeated.

Jeannie looked at him with an expression she usually reserves for me. "Uh-huh," she said.

I barely caught any of that because I was keeping my enhanced gaze on The Swine. He had just reached the door to the Coffee House and was about to walk outside. He pulled on a pair of gloves and was definitely talking to Legs McShowoff next to him. Should I have been this judgmental about my ex the day after I got engaged to another man? A question for a quieter moment.

"If they stay together we can follow them," I said to Jeannie.

But of course that was not in the cards. Steven opened the door, let his high-heeled friend out ahead of him and then stepped out into the bracing air. Molly was working up to a full cry, but Jeannie, ever stalwart, held on to the steering wheel waiting for instructions.

"Okay, now, Molly," she said. I didn't know what that meant, but Molly, upon hearing her name, calmed a little.

Meanwhile, Steven was giving his leggy friend a kiss on the cheek and they were separating, walking in exactly opposite directions. Just what I didn't want. I opened the passenger door of the minivan and Molly, hit by a burst of frigid air, started to cry again.

"I'm going to follow the woman," I told Jeannie. "The Swine is headed for his car, I'll bet. You follow him and then text me and let me know where he goes and what he does." I got out of the van.

"What if he goes to six different places now?" Jeannie wanted to know.

I watched Ms. Legs as she headed up the street. No time to wait.

"Just stick with him," I said. "Make a note of everywhere he stops and anybody he talks to." I closed the door of the minivan just as Jeannie started to pull away.

The woman wasn't all that far away, but I still had to walk pretty swiftly to stay a reasonable distance behind her. If she got into a car I'd lose her.

Wait. I just lost my ride home, too. I'd have to call Mom or Josh.

"Which one are we following?" Maxie, who could have done this job herself, had naturally waited for me to get out of the only warm vehicle to which I had current access to phase through the wall of the van and join me. I figured Ollie had started crying in Jeannie's minivan and she didn't know why.

I reached into my coat pocket and pulled out the Bluetooth device I use to look like I'm having a conversation with a living person. You'd be amazed how it keeps me from being committed to a mental institution. "Now you're helping?" I asked Maxie. "Where were you when I needed you?"

"When did you need me?" It was perhaps the best question she'd ever asked me.

"I could have stayed in the van and you could have followed this woman," I said. "I'm freezing and don't have a ride home. I got out of the van and now here you are."

Maxie, now to my left, had three separate people pass

through her as she floated through. She nodded. "Yeah. I was wondering why you did that."

There was no point to arguing and besides, Gams McStilts was turning a corner. We were about fifty yards behind. "Go up and make sure she doesn't get into a car or duck into a store someplace," I told Maxie. "We need to keep her in sight."

For once she didn't ask questions and zoomed ahead to the corner, which she reached about a half minute before I did. When I got there, Maxie was just in front of me. The blonde we were following was fixing the heel on her shoe (yeah, she was really trying to get guys to look at her legs) by leaning her foot on the base of a lamppost. "She's been doing that pretty much the whole time," Maxie reported.

"What's the matter with her shoe?" I asked.

"Nothing I can see."

Uh-oh. "She's onto us," I said.

"What's the *us* stuff? She can't see me."

I ignored that because . . . what was the point, and decided to keep walking as if I were in a hurry to get to my incredibly important destination, which I was now hoping had a hot chocolate included in it. I power-walked up the street until I was about six feet from Stretch Mc— Oh, you get the idea. She had long legs.

"Why are you following me?" she asked as soon as I was abreast with her.

I didn't even have the wherewithal to act as if she must be talking to someone else. "What do you mean?" I shot back, sharp as a tack. An old tack. One that had been pushed into solid brick.

The woman put down her foot and turned to face me. She was tall, but not basketball-player tall. The four-inch heels were adding to the illusion. So she could look down at me with a gaze that was intended to drive fear deep into my heart.

I felt nothing. It was too cold.

"I *mean*, you've been right behind me since I left the coffee shop and you stopped when you turned the corner and saw me standing here. You were trying to decide what to do. So you're here. You caught me. What do you want?"

"I don't want anything. I don't know what you're talking about." I looked quickly at Maxie, who was rolling her eyes.

"She's not going to believe you," she said.

"I don't believe you," the woman said.

"See?" Maxie. Ever helpful.

"Why not?" I demanded. I didn't actually care about the answer to the question, but it bought me time to think. Which I wasn't doing, but the time was there. It's a process.

"Because you're not walking away now," the blonde told me. "You don't want me to get away. So who sent you?"

Short of breaking down in tears, something I would never do in front of someone who had just had coffee with The Swine, I had no other option. I pulled the PI license out of my tote bag. "I'm a private investigator," I said. "I'm looking into a murder." Let her think she was a suspect. Let her be the one to break down in tears on a public street.

"Seriously?" the blonde asked. "You want me to believe you're a detective?"

"The state of New Jersey believes it. I don't care whether you do. You can do what you like, but I'm trying to find out who killed a man, and I think you have a connection. Would you like to talk about it? I'm not a cop, so you're in no danger of being arrested."

The woman pursed her lips, trying to decide something. "Okay," she said. "What do you want to know?" She wasn't questioning anything about there being a murder, which was sort of interesting.

"I'd really like to know if there's a warm space where we can continue this conversation," I answered.

"Well, I just had coffee. What do you have in mind?"

"*Me* having coffee," I said.

"Good one," Maxie said. Maxie is a huge help in situations like this.

Blond Woman rolled her eyes. "Fiiiiiiiine," she moaned. "Can we at least go somewhere else?"

We ended up in a Dunkin' Donuts three blocks away, which was three blocks more than I wanted to walk but was the best possible option. The wind had picked up a little, never good news in a New Jersey winter, and was blowing directly into our faces, which was a serious annoyance for everyone but Maxie, who kept floating ahead of us wondering aloud what was keeping two healthy adult women from keeping pace.

I ordered a hot chocolate but eschewed the whipped cream because, hey, there was a wedding somewhere in my future. I had priorities. Blond Woman, who told me her name was Susannah Nesbit, sat opposite me at the table, aggressively not having anything.

Maxie enjoys nothing more than rearranging the donuts on the racks behind the counter, but she was controlling herself as much as I'd ever seen her do, which was commendable in a twisted sort of way. She did keep glancing at the racks as she hovered over us, listening in on the conversation.

Before we began I got a text message from Paul. Ghosts can't be heard over phone lines, but he had the capacity to press buttons and I'd gotten him a rudimentary phone for exactly this purpose. The text read, "No luck contacting DuBois. Ask Lt. McE about what caliber gun."

Great. Now I had to talk to McElone again, but only after I somehow found a ride home. Neither of those was the pressing issue at this moment.

"You met a man in the coffee shop just now," I told Susannah, who probably knew that already. "How did you know him?"

"Steven?" She seemed not in the least concerned about giving away the name of the man I'd just mentioned in connection with a murder investigation. I was starting to like her. "He's a friend of a friend."

"Who's the friend?" I asked, wondering which friend I meant. I mean, was the friend of the friend or the friend him- or herself? This was getting confusing.

"Actually he's my friend's son," Susannah said. "Harry Rendell."

The Swine's father was setting him up with random incredibly leggy women in coffeehouses? "How do you know Mr. Rendell?" I asked.

"Which one?" Susannah and Maxie said that one in unison, except just one of them knew it.

"Harry," I said.

"Oh, I know Harry from way back," Susannah said, alone this time. "He's a pal of my dad's from the Elks, or something." That didn't tell me much.

"Why did he want you to meet his son?" I asked. Okay, so I was getting married to a guy whom I'd met through my father at Josh's grandfather's store when we were twelve, but that was a whole different story. Wasn't it?

"Harry said Steven might be able to help me out with an investment plan," she said. "Steven is a financial adviser."

Oh, is that what we're calling it these days? "And so you met in the coffee shop to talk business?"

Susannah smiled vaguely and looked away.

"It ain't about business anymore," Maxie noted.

Another text from Paul: "No luck finding DuBois on Ghosternet." That wasn't helpful.

"You're dating him?" I asked Susannah, although I felt sure Maxie was right.

"We hit it off when we met the first time," she said, voice not quite defensive but flirting with it.

Steven had been in the state for two days. "When did you meet for the first time?" I asked.

"Oh, a couple of months ago. I see him whenever he's in town."

That took a moment to sink in. "You met him a couple of months ago and you see him whenever he's in town?" I heard my voice rising but couldn't do anything to stop it. Susannah looked startled and Maxie looked amused. "How often has he been in town over the past couple of months?"

Susannah's eyes were wide and she leaned back, away from me. It took her a moment to respond and when she did, her voice was low and tentative. "Three times?" she said, as if there were a correct answer to the math problem on the board and she was hoping she'd gotten it right.

"Son of a—" I had to get myself under control. I took a deep cleansing breath. I remembered that—and only that—from Lamaze training. And then I'd had a C-section. "Okay." So The Swine had been in New Jersey three times in the past two months or so and had never let his daughter know he was here. He'd paid for airfares and possibly hotels and was now three months behind in child support. That train of thought wasn't helping me concentrate on the murder of Maurice DuBois, which seemed somehow less significant right at the moment.

"Let me start again," I suggested to Susannah. "You met this man two months ago and you've seen him three times since then." And yet he was not staying with her on this trip, which in Swine terms was unexpectedly ethical. "Why did he want to meet today?"

Just then a text came in from Jeannie. "I think he might have a girlfriend." This was just getting better and better. I did not respond.

"I wasn't expecting to hear from him, but Steven said he had to make an emergency trip in to see his daughter."

Her voice dropped to a theatrical whisper. "You know, his ex-wife almost never lets him see her."

The only murder on my mind right now was not Maurice DuBois's, but I had to soldier on. I could figure out just how to kill The Swine and get away with it later after I got home. Still, I did note that my teeth did not wish to part when I squeezed "All that aside, why here today?" through them.

"She's talking about you," Maxie reminded me. She was eyeing the racks again and I almost told her to go ahead just to get her out of the way, but the thought of the poor kids working the counter dealing with flying donuts and having to reorganize everything won over my desire to make Maxie go away.

"Well, I didn't know at first." Susannah clearly thought she was telling a fascinating story, natural-born raconteur that she was, but all I wanted was an answer to my question. "But it turned out when I got to the other coffee place that what he wanted was to give me something."

I'd bet he wanted to give her something, I thought, but was it something she could bring with her? "What did he give you?" I said. Without wincing. I thought that was something of a triumph.

"I'm not sure I should tell you." Susannah was clearly a tease. If she'd really wanted to keep the information between herself and The Swine, she wouldn't have mentioned this mysterious gift at all. I used the sit-there-and-wait strategy and it paid off as it often did. "But you're a PI and everything, so I guess it's all right." Interesting logic, but who was I to argue?

She reached down to the floor for her very professional briefcase and pulled it up onto the table. It was a small table—Dunkin' Donuts is not built for luxury—so I had to do some fancy maneuvers with my hot chocolate to keep it from spilling (mostly drinking all that was left), but I managed.

Susannah worked the latches on the briefcase and opened it toward herself. That didn't do much for me, but I assumed she was going to show me what was there. Except she took a long moment to admire it. "Isn't it a beautiful briefcase?" she asked.

The briefcase? That was the big surprise? "Um . . . yes, it's absolutely lovely," I said. Hardly the gift that says *you're the one*, but according to Jeannie, one wasn't the number The Swine had in mind anyway.

New text from Jeannie: "He stopped at a movie theater. Can't go in with the kids. R-rated."

"You know," Susannah went on. "Originally Steven wanted me to throw the briefcase in the Shark River."

I was midway through a text to Jeannie asking for a ride home when that registered. "He gave you a briefcase and wanted you to throw it in a river?" Even for The Swine that was weird behavior.

Susannah laughed. "I know, right? But I convinced him to let me keep it. I just have to throw what's *in* the case into the river."

It wasn't a question I really wanted to ask at this point, but Paul would certainly insist. "What's in the briefcase?"

Maxie, who had maneuvered herself to a station above Susannah's head, put her hand to her mouth. "Wow," she said. It took a lot to impress Maxie to that level of noneloquence.

Susannah turned the briefcase around and showed me its interior.

It was a completely standard, ordinary briefcase except for its lining, which appeared to have been stuffed in crudely, perhaps in a hurry. The lining was made of foam rubber and filled the interior of the case from edge to edge, making it impossible for anything to rattle inside when the case was being moved around. At the center of the lining was a cutout, again seemingly done in a hurry, perhaps with a sharp knife. It cradled the real contents of the briefcase snugly, again to prevent any noisy rattling or other accident.

That was a handgun.

"Steven said if I threw the gun into the Shark River, I could keep the case," Susannah said.

My eyes must have been the size of hubcaps. My voice was suddenly hoarse. "Did you . . ." I cleared my throat. "Did you touch this?"

"I touched the case. Not the gun. I'm not stupid."

That was clearly open for debate, but it simplified matters. I looked Susannah in the eye. "Can you give me a ride?" I asked. "I need to see a friend."

Seventeen

"You didn't tell me your friend was a cop," Susannah Nesbit said.

That was true; I figured if I mentioned a desire to see Lieutenant McElone in the Harbor Haven Police Station, Susannah might decide I didn't need the ride so much and bolt for the door. Jeannie could have picked me up, but I was certain the lieutenant would want to test the gun and, if it was relevant, talk to Susannah.

I wasn't paying much attention because I was texting Jeannie to send me the address of the theater where The Swine had stopped for his curious matinee, and which movie he was seeing. That last part was just for my own amusement.

Yes, I knew that the gun we'd brought McElone could possibly implicate The Swine in Maurice DuBois's murder. I also knew that if it was relevant and I helped Susannah lose it in the Shark River, I would be an accomplice to the crime of destroying evidence and besides, The Swine had said I wouldn't let him see his daughter and he deserved to go to jail just for that.

"Would you have brought me here if I'd told you that?" I asked.

"Of course not," Susannah replied. "It's just awfully dishonest of you."

"Pah!" That was Maxie's version of a laugh. She was lying on her back in the middle of a heavily trafficked corridor in the police station. Maxie likes to have people walk through her as long as she's the one coordinating it. When the living, in their blissful ignorance of the ghosts around them, pass through her unexpectedly, she tends to knock hats off heads and untie shoelaces. She looked toward the window. "I'm gonna wait outside," she said. "Cops scare me." And she was gone.

Lieutenant McElone walked out of the bull pen where she worked and looked Susannah and me up and down as if deciding whether we would comfortably fit in the trunk of her police cruiser. "Come in here," she said, pointing inside. I'd been there a number of times before, so I walked straight to McElone's cubicle. Susannah followed me.

But when I sat down, I saw a man behind the desk, looking at me with some consternation. From behind me I heard McElone say, "I don't work there anymore. Come this way." She didn't sound amused, but then, she never does.

I got up, apologizing to whoever that cop was sitting at McElone's old desk, and followed Susannah and the lieutenant to a separate office off the bull pen. The door bore the nameplate "Anita McElone, Chief of Detectives."

She ushered us into the small office, which held a bookshelf, a desk and two uncomfortable chairs (government issue). She sat behind the desk and Susannah and I dealt with the molded plastic chairs.

"Chief of detectives!" I said. "Wow!"

"We have three detectives and I'm one of them," McElone said as she settled behind her pathologically neat desk. "All it means is that I'm reading two more cops' paperwork."

"Still," I tried. "Are you a captain now?"

McElone regarded me with some sharpness. "There is no change in rank with the position," she said.

"So you're a lieutenant?" Susannah, clearly imbued with the ability to read, pointed to the nameplate on McElone's desk.

The lieutenant—since she was still that—sighed lightly. "Yes," she said. "Now, can we please move on to something other than my rank?"

"I take it you got back a ballistics test on the gun we brought in," I said.

McElone shook her head. "Just something very preliminary. A full ballistics workup will take time, but we have concluded that this gun is definitely the same caliber as the one that shot and killed Maurice DuBois outside Hanrahan's."

I didn't even ask what caliber as Paul had suggested. What was the point?

"The thing is, the weapon's serial number has been filed off and there are no fingerprints on it. It's not traceable at the moment and it could take weeks to find out who the registered owner is, and that's probably not the person who committed the murder because this is likely a stolen gun."

That wasn't terribly unexpected, at least not to me and probably not to McElone. Susannah, on the other hand, appeared stunned. Her nostrils flared.

"That gun *killed* somebody?" she coughed.

McElone seemed confused by her amazement. "Yeah," she said. "Why did you think he gave you a gun and asked you to throw it in the Shark River?"

"I thought it was his way of decreasing the number of

guns available in New Jersey," Susannah said. No, really. She said that.

The lieutenant chose not to respond, which I thought showed the kind of wisdom that had gotten her promoted to chief of detectives. "What exactly did Mr. Rendell tell you when he gave you the gun?" she asked.

Susannah, perhaps believing there was some implication of complicity in what McElone was asking, sat back and put up her hands, palms out. "He didn't give me the *gun*," she protested. "He gave me the *case*."

"Okay." McElone could be reasonable, especially when she clearly thought this woman wasn't sharp enough to be conspiring with a murderer. "When he gave you the case. What did he tell you he was giving it to you for, and why did he ask you to throw it in the river?"

Susannah put down her hands and took a breath. "Steven said the case was a gift, but he wanted me to throw it in the river because it was made of organic materials and it would nourish the fish."

Wow. Was I this gullible when I agreed to marry The Swine? (Don't answer that.)

McElone glanced at a form in front of her, which I recognized as the statement I had given her earlier. "But then you said you wanted to keep the case, so he told you to throw the gun into the river, right?"

"That's right."

McElone looked up into her eyes. "You know the gun's not made of organic materials, don't you?"

"Of course not!" Susannah scoffed. "Guns are made of metal."

Give the little girl a lollipop.

"That's right," McElone said with a straight face. "So what was the rationale for throwing it into the river?"

"Well, like I said, I thought he wanted to keep a gun out of the hands of criminals." Susannah was actually going to stick to that one, even given a full minute to think of something less ridiculous, like that Steven wanted to see if the gun would shoot fish outside a barrel. Susannah seemed to vacillate between a cutthroat businesswoman type and a complete and utter airhead. It was possible both were true.

"He could have thrown it in himself," McElone pointed out. "Why ask you to do it?"

"It's the kind of relationship we have," she answered proudly. "We don't question each other's motives. It's one of the things that drove him from his ex-wife, from what I hear."

McElone looked at me briefly and must have read my eyes. "Do you think the ex-wife is someone we should look at for the murder?" she asked. That is McElone being hilarious. She thinks.

"That jerk isn't smart enough to kill somebody," Susannah replied. "Look at the husband she threw away."

I don't have a blood pressure problem, which is good all the time but especially at that moment. "I'm sure she had her reasons," I said. Like the blonde in the bikini in Malibu.

"Ha! Don't get me started on her!" Susannah had "met" my ex-husband four times including today and wanted to offer her dissertation on exactly what a lunatic I must have been, fueled by the information she'd gotten from The Swine himself. I scoured my mind for incriminating evidence I could possibly offer to get him jailed faster.

"Better if we focus on the murder," McElone said, no longer being hilarious. "Did he mention the name Maurice DuBois at any time?"

Susannah made a "thinking" face and actually put the tip of her index finger to her chin. "No, I'd remember that one."

"Anyone else he's been in business with since he got

back to Jersey?" McElone asked. "Any other . . . friends he might be visiting?"

Susannah had caught the implications in that last pause. "He doesn't have any other *friends* like me," she said sharply. That wasn't true according to Jeannie, but Susannah apparently didn't know that.

"Anyone else he mentioned?" the lieutenant asked, not taking the bait.

"He said he had a cousin Richie he was going to see today in Marlboro, but that's all I know," Susannah answered. "I don't know what that was about."

I didn't know about a cousin Richie, but the movie theater was in Marlboro. I cocked an eyebrow at McElone, who noticed but did not acknowledge it.

"Why didn't you question him about the gun?" the lieutenant asked our prime witness. "Why he had it? Why he wanted to get rid of it? Why *you* had to be the one to do that? Why in the river?"

"I told you, we have a relationship based on trust." The kind of trust one can cultivate in four meetings, most of which I was guessing involved little conversation. "I didn't want to ruin that with a lot of questions."

McElone sat back in her chair and regarded Susannah with something resembling a light snarl. "Well, consider this," she said. "You might very well be an accomplice to a capital crime. A man is dead. It's not a real stretch to believe he was shot with the gun you were going to dispose of in the Shark River. You didn't even bother to ask why that might be necessary, which some prosecutors would say indicates you already knew the answer. That could put you into the case *before* Maurice DuBois was shot, and that makes you an accessory before the fact. You could be looking at conspiracy, possibly manslaughter if not murder charges, unless you give me a reason to believe that you really didn't have anything to do with the killing and were just trying to do a favor for a friend. So what can you tell me that will do that for you?"

"Ooh, she has a mean side. I've never seen that before." I hadn't even seen Maxie come into the room, but there she was to my left, watching McElone with a delighted smile on her face.

Susannah, who had entered the room either oblivious or confident—it was hard to tell—now looked downright terrified. And I'd be lying if I said I didn't get just a little satisfaction out of that. A bit of sympathy, sure, but also just a tad of vindication. Go around talking about *me* behind my back (just because you didn't know who I was) and see what's coming to ya, lady.

"I don't know anything," she said, not quite crying but not quite *not* crying. "Steven gave me the case and told me to throw it in the river. Honest. That's all I've got. I'm not hiding anything. You've gotta let me go."

McElone, who I was sure had never intended for one second to hold Susannah in custody, stood up. She is tall and powerfully built and can look very intimidating when she wants to. And right now she wanted to.

"Give me something I can use," she said quietly but with authority. "Tell me something that will help me find out who killed Maurice DuBois. If it wasn't Steven Rendell, who was it?"

"I never *heard* of Maurice DuBois!" Susannah had crossed the line into crying and she was doing it with a pent-up vehemence I wouldn't have expected when she stopped me on the street in Belmar. "How can I tell you who killed a guy I never even met?"

"What do you know about Steven Rendell's debts and how he was going to pay them?" McElone said. She leaned a little onto her desk, supporting herself with her fists on the surface. "He owed a lot of money. He didn't have time to pay it. What did he tell you he was going to do?"

Susannah brightened because she could answer this question and hoped the teacher would pass her on the test based on what she had. "He was going to get his ex-wife to sell her house and use the money to pay off the guy who was after him," she said. "He can talk that dope into anything."

If Maxie had actually owned a gut, she'd have split it laughing. She couldn't speak for an actual minute. That's a long time. Take out your watch and look at the second hand for a whole minute. See?

McElone, however, just closed her eyes for a moment and pushed up on her closed fists to retake a standing position. "You can go," she said. "I have your contact information. I'd request that you not leave the state until we get in touch."

"I'm not leaving the state," Susannah said, leaping up and grabbing her purse, her coat and her expensive scarf. She hightailed it out of the office before McElone could change her mind.

I stood up after her. "That didn't really yield much," I said to the lieutenant. "Sorry about that."

"It's not your fault. You did the right thing." Since I saved her life, sort of, McElone has been almost frighteningly polite with me. I sort of yearned for her scorn like in the old days. "But let me give you a word of advice, okay? And just this one time, maybe you could take it." That was more like it.

I was picking up my tote bag as Maxie regained her breath and hovered into a vertical position. "Advice for me?" I asked. Maybe McElone was going to tell me something that would help discover if The Swine was a murderer—which was unlikely, no matter how much I'd have liked to see him behind bars right now—or more specifically, who had shot Maurice DuBois.

"Yeah." McElone's voice dropped to an urgent whisper. "You don't want to be anywhere near this case right now. For your own good. Just stay away."

Maxie's eyebrows rose almost to the ceiling, but they had a head start. The top of her head was already sticking through the tiles. "For your own good?" she echoed.

"I'm not sure I can do that," I told the lieutenant.

"*I'm* telling you. You really have to," she said.

"Whoa," Maxie said. "The lady cop never said *that* to you before." That was true, but I didn't actually need Maxie's reminder. That's the time you can most count on Maxie, when you don't really need her.

(In the interest of full disclosure: Maxie has been there more than once at crucial times for me. And she never, *ever* lets me forget it.)

"You're serious," I said to McElone.

"You bet." I always appreciate when someone doesn't say, "Serious as a heart attack," because it takes me five minutes to stop monitoring my chest for unexplained pains after that and I lose the thread of the conversation. "You don't want to have anything to do with it. Leave it to me."

"Is it all right if I ask you one question before I leave?" I said.

McElone looked at me for a moment. "One question."

"Can you give me a ride home? Susannah just left with the car."

Eighteen

"This is very encouraging." Paul was hovering a little over the floor in the basement, stringing together the extension cords, surge suppression strips and electrical devices he had confiscated from my house and trying to keep all the cords straight.

"I don't see how," I told him. "The lieutenant practically ordered me off any inquiries about Maurice DuBois's murder. She wants me to just sit back and let her railroad Steven more efficiently."

Paul stroked his goatee, a sign he was thinking deeply. "I meant the electrical experiment," he said, never taking his eyes off the pile of prongs and extenders. "But you must know Lieutenant McElone has no legal authority to keep you from asking questions and following leads."

I insinuated myself between Paul and the snaky objects of his undying affection. "Paul. It's February. There isn't going to be a thunderstorm for at least two months. You can obsess about your plans to electrify the basement and burn down my house then. I'm just trying to figure out how to tell the insurance company a ghost was trying to move to another plane of existence so they should pay for all the damages."

"Nothing is going to happen to your house," he assured me. I was less than totally convinced, as even his tone was a little shaky. "But the message here is that we can still investigate the DuBois killing whether the lieutenant tells you to stop or not. Besides, you know her well enough to have confidence she would never jail your ex-husband if she did not have solid evidence he did the shooting, and we can be fairly sure he didn't."

I was about to explain to the ghost how I knew The Swine *much* better than he did and considered it less than certain he hadn't actually stepped over the last line of polite behavior, but the basement door opened and Melissa appeared at the top of the stairs.

"Are we having a strategy session?" she asked. "Nobody told me."

I hadn't wanted to include her but figured I could deflect the blame. "Where's Maxie?" I asked.

"On the beach with Everett. They like to go out there and drive seagulls crazy." Animals can sometimes sense the ghosts without seeing or hearing anything unusual. It leads to anxious behavior, which Maxie finds riotous.

Speaking of animals, Lester the ghost dog floated down from where Liss was standing, and she followed him to the basement. Lester got there first and kept going, so his feet vanished in concrete by the time she made it down. Lester doesn't care about perceptions but he does like to be around humans. I mentally thanked myself for taking my allergy medications this morning or Lester would make me sneeze like it was flu season. Which it was, but luckily we'd all been vaccinated. Those of us who were alive.

"Well, we don't have much to go on," I said, since it seemed Melissa was going to be part of . . . whatever this was going to be, anyway. "There's this cousin Richie I've never heard of before, but there's also Lou Maroni and his posse, whom your father seemed to be upset about missing last night. If we could find them, I'll bet we could find him."

"We've found him," Melissa said. "We've found him more than once. He'll answer me if I call him right now."

"Melissa is correct," Paul said, wrapping extension cords on an old garden hose caddy. "There seems to be little advantage to searching for your ex-husband right now. He is accessible enough and the police no longer seem to be looking for him. Did the lieutenant explain why she let him leave after he was in custody?"

I shook my head. "She wouldn't answer any questions about that. I got the feeling she was not happy about letting Steven out but didn't have any choice."

"This woman you met said Dad has a cousin Richie?" Melissa asked. "I've never heard about any relatives in New Jersey except Grandma and Grandpa Rendell."

"Neither have I," I said. "And frankly that's weirder. Liss, get in touch with your grandfather and ask him if there's a cousin Richie we don't know about." I still wasn't all that crazy about the idea of contacting Harry Rendell if I didn't have to. Liss nodded and got out her phone. There was no point in texting Harry—he was a twentieth-century kind of guy who grudgingly owned a flip phone—so she dialed his number looking slightly on edge. The Rendells have never really cultivated much of a relationship with Melissa, although I always took that as Constance's doing. Liss walked to the other side of the basement putting her finger to her ear.

"Hello, Grandpa Harry?" My father was always "Grampa." No distinction necessary, even years after he'd died. He still loved it.

Melissa walked toward the window and Paul took the opportunity to link two of the extension cords together and roll them up on the hose caddy. I had a quick flash of what it would have looked like to a guest if someone had wandered down at this moment. You get that sometimes, picturing the hose caddy loading cords onto itself with no visible help. My house is an interesting place to live. But for Paul, it isn't an interesting place to be dead, hence the electricity experiment.

I tried not to take it personally.

"What I don't understand," Paul said without diverting his attention from his task, "is why the lieutenant seems to be concentrating her investigation on your ex-husband but did not hold him even for twenty-four hours for questioning when she had the opportunity."

I was busy texting The Swine: "Who's this Cousin Richie I never heard of before?"

"It doesn't make sense," I said to Paul. "I think now that she knows Lou Maroni and his large entourage are in town, she'd be busy looking for them. Seems to me they're the most logical suspects. They knew DuBois better than The Swine did."

Almost immediately, a responding text: "Who have you been talking to?"

I could practically hear the accusatory, tense tone of voice. The dilemma then became: Should I reassure or irritate? It wasn't much of a dilemma. "That doesn't answer the question. Who's Cousin Richie?"

"Perhaps the lieutenant is allowing your ex-husband to roam freely so he can lead her to the more likely suspects," Paul suggested.

The Swine texted, "That's not funny, Alison." Which didn't bother me at all.

"It wasn't intended to be. Cousin Richie. Who?"

Melissa ended her call and walked back over to us. "Grandpa Harry never heard of a cousin named Richie," she said.

"Did he wish you a happy birthday?" It had been two weeks previous.

"It didn't come up." Her grandparents hadn't gotten in touch, then. I thought they'd sent a card.

"Don't let it bother you, honey," I said. "It's how they are."

Liss shrugged.

"Did your grandfather tell you anything useful?" I asked.

"He said Dad was there yesterday, but everybody was acting funny. He did say Dad had a meeting with a guy in the garage." She knew exactly what she was saying and looked at Paul and me for reaction.

"In the garage? In this weather?" I asked.

"Is it cold out?" Paul was brought up in Canada and no longer had an operating nervous system, so it was hard to tell whether he thought he was being amusing.

"Yeah. I pumped Grandpa Harry for some information on the man Dad was meeting and he said he was kind of stocky and wore a hat the whole time. Not a knitted hat, like a hat men wear in old movies."

Lou Maroni was not someone you'd describe as "stocky." He wasn't large at all, in any direction, and relied on his henchmen (for lack of a better term) for the muscle, I was guessing. "Could it be one of the men who came here with Maroni?" I asked.

Liss made a face that indicated she didn't think so. "They all seemed to be in, like, a uniform, and none of them had hats," she said. "Besides, they weren't, you know, fat. They were more like bodybuilder guys."

"So there's someone else involved," Paul said, stroking the goatee. This time he was clearly engaged. Not like Josh and I were engaged. You know, engaged in the discussion.

This whole getting-married thing was going to take some getting used to.

"You think it's someone new?" I asked Paul.

"We don't have enough facts to make a determination," he said. He always says that. It gets annoying, but he's a nice guy, so I give him some slack. "But based on the people we've seen so far, that is certainly one way to interpret the information Melissa just brought us."

"There is no Cousin Richie." It had taken The Swine long enough to answer. "Who told you there was?" Ball in my court.

"If there's no such person it doesn't matter." Fight annoying with annoying, I always say.

I looked up at Paul. "How do we find out who this person is?" I asked.

Paul actually looked away from his amazing creation. Whatever it was. "I think it's time for us to ask Maxie to do what she does best," he said.

The thing about Maxie is that she really hates being asked to do something when she'd rather do anything else, and she'd always rather do anything else. But as we had discovered since this thrill ride began, Maxie has a real talent for Internet research. And the one surefire way to convince her to work on a case is to appeal to her ego, which is the size of Montana, only bigger.

"You know you're the only one who can get this right," Melissa was telling her. The other surefire way to get

Maxie to do something is to have Liss be the one to ask. She adores my daughter and will pretty much cave in to any request she gets that comes from that direction. "We're trying to keep my dad out of jail for maybe the rest of his life." With most people that would be overkill. When talking to Maxie it was understatement.

We had adjourned to the library. Yoko and Ann were out doing some souvenir shopping, something considerably more challenging on the Jersey Shore in February than in July. Mel was in his room, probably staring out the window and looking stunned. It had become his routine, and I didn't blame him. Ann's quick turnaround and inconsistent (in my eyes) behavior must have been awfully confusing.

"We were going to go down to the miniature golf course," Maxie said. "We like to move the balls around while people are putting." She held out a hand and Everett Sandheim, her ghost boyfriend, took it.

"It's February. There's nobody there," Everett pointed out. He's a steadying influence on Maxie with his military background. It's interesting because I had first known him as a homeless man with some mental illness, but he had reverted to an earlier time in his life after he became a ghost. "Besides, we are more useful here. You should do what you can to help, and so should I." Having settled that—and it seemed to work, since Maxie will usually follow Everett's lead—he turned toward me. "What can I do, Ghost Lady?" The name is a long story.

Actually it was a helpful question. "The thing is, my ex-husband is going to come here soon," I said. "We're going to have a brief conversation, after which he'll storm out of here in a huff. I want you to get into his car when he leaves so you can tell me where he went and who he met with later today. Would that be okay?"

Everett probably wanted to salute. His military training was strong in this version of him, but Maxie had taught him that he was no longer actually in the service. So instead he nodded briskly and said, "I'm happy to help."

Maxie, staring out the window at the snow-covered beach, sighed. "Okay," she said. "What do you need me to do?"

This was Paul's realm, so he took charge, pacing about a foot and a half off the floor. "First, we need to know as much about Lou Maroni and Maurice DuBois as possible. Business dealings, associates—that's especially important—and personal details."

Maxie had produced a pad and pencil and was wearing her favorite green visor, which she thinks makes her look businesslike when in fact it makes her look like the world's strangest pit boss. "What kind of personal details?" she asked with a certain wariness.

"Marriages, children, family ties," Paul ticked off. "Anything that might indicate a pattern. Unusual hobbies. Things like that."

Maxie scribbled in her book, although I was certain she probably had absorbed what Paul said and was already planning her work. "Anything else?"

"Yes. Look into a type of computer software called SafT. It's a start-up that's supposed to—"

"It protects your personal data, passwords and all that," Maxie said. "I was there."

"No, you weren't," I said. Maxie had come in only to ask about dinner and then left.

"I can hear way better than you think I can." That was a terrifying thought. "What do you want to know about it?" Maxie asked Paul.

"The Internet is full of chatter on such innovations," the goateed ghost answered. "See what you can pick up. Whether the program was actually considered viable. What its current stage of development might be. If there are serious competitors. Anything that would make it more or less valuable a property."

"Gotcha." Maxie pretended to be chewing gum and "shot" at Paul with her finger. For some reason, when she's working, Maxie seems to think she's a brassy gal in a nineteen forties Warner Brothers movie. Paul says if that works for her we should just indulge the fantasy, so I said nothing, although my mind was racing with possibilities. I stored them for another occasion.

"That's it for now," Paul said, giving Maxie her marching orders. "Get back to us with results as soon as you can."

Maxie was already gone (probably into Melissa's room, which is her first choice for work, followed by my roof), but Everett hung back awaiting his assignment tailing The Swine.

He didn't have to wait long. Steven barreled into the house less than ten minutes later, frenetic energy driving his movements and the cold New Jersey wind—something he'd successfully avoided the past five winters—adding to the already enhanced redness in his face.

"What are you doing?" he said by way of greeting. Our daughter, sitting in an easy chair and in plain view of her father, did not so much as merit a quick hello. She noticed that and it registered on her face.

"I'm sitting in a room with our *daughter* trying to figure out how to keep you out of jail for the rest of your life," I answered, unsuccessfully trying to keep the irritation out of my voice. "What are *you* doing?"

The Swine stopped his peripatetic advance. He looked directly at Melissa, remembered who she was and put on Smile #53, the paternal one that was meant to melt his little girl's heart. I could tell with a quick glance that it wasn't working.

"I'm sorry, Lissie," Steven said. "I should have said hi when I came in. I'm not mad at you." He even managed not to emphasize the word *you*, so as to better indicate his displeasure with me. Melissa's gaze didn't waver.

"Don't call me 'Lissie,' remember?" she said. "I'm not six anymore."

"Very good, Melissa," Paul said. "Keep him on the defensive."

Liss looked a little annoyed at that; she was ticked off at her father, not plotting strategies, but she didn't look at Paul or Everett. She took out her phone. It is the current thirteen-year-old way to avoid adults.

"Of course not. I'm sorry. Melissa, your mom and I need to have a conversation right now. Would you mind?" He gestured toward the door.

"Yes, I would," she answered. That was my daughter. "I'm involved in the investigation Mom is doing and I need to be included in any *conversations* that have some importance involving that." She looked over at me, and I picked up the ball and ran with it.

"She's right," I told my ex-husband. "Melissa is a valuable partner in the work I do and she deserves to be included. So, what were you saying?" I did not bat my eyelids. Much.

To his credit—and it pains me to say that—Steven managed to regroup. He took a breath, nodded (probably to himself) and looked first at me and then at Liss. "Okay, you're right. You two are trying to help me and I need to respect that. Sometimes I forget." Like, for example, always except when we were standing right in front of him. Sometimes then, too.

"All right, then," I said. "You were fuming about something. Let's have it."

Everett, with his military training, was not relaxed. Everett was *never* relaxed, but his manner was not intense. He stood—floated—toward the back door, watching for signals that might give him information he could share later. But he'd never met The Swine before and couldn't know what to expect like Liss and I did.

Steven's eyes didn't make it to slits, but they had

ambitions. "You spoke to . . . someone about my situation and I'd like to know who," he said. He was trying to get that smooth tone back in his voice, but he was too angry at my having found out something he didn't want me to know. I'd had that experience before, so I knew how he was going to handle it.

"And I'd like to know who Cousin Richie is and why I've never heard of him before. So since you want to know something from me and I want to know something from you, I have a compromise to propose." Melissa was watching me closely and I wanted to make sure I played this right. It couldn't just be about beating The Swine at a game; it had to include some amount of actual progress in clearing him of the Maurice DuBois murder.

"What's the compromise?" he asked.

"You go first." I sat back and folded my arms. He knew I wasn't going to budge off that position and he was smart enough not to go through the motions of trying to persuade me.

"I don't have a cousin Richie and you know that," he said. He was stalling, so I sat and waited. Liss, still intent on me and not paying attention visually to her father, could see what I was doing and let the silence stand. "So whoever told you that was clearly mistaken or lying. Now please tell me who it was so I can set that person straight."

"You mean the person I spoke to today hasn't called you yet asking about the conversation?" I countered. Something about the best defense equals good offense and other sports axioms I don't care about.

That really seemed to perplex The Swine. "I haven't heard from anyone today," he said, suddenly fidgeting with his sleeves. "Maybe my phone is dead."

"You got my text well enough," I said.

"Maybe there's a voice mail I haven't checked. Who should I be looking for in my contacts?"

I sighed audibly. That was for effect. I stood up from my barstool and put my hands on my hips in a gesture of frustration. "After all these years, Steven, isn't it time for you to talk honestly to me and Liss? Just once? You're up to your neck in this one and we are actually trying to help you. How about telling us the truth so we can deal with it? Did you kill Maurice DuBois?"

Melissa drew in a sharp intake of breath. She didn't expect me to be that direct. That surprised me; I thought she would have anticipated exactly the tactic I would use even if she didn't know her father's moves nearly as well.

"No," he said, but his face was oddly jolly. He was still hiding something; it was his favorite thing. "It wasn't physically possible for me to have done that, and your Lieutenant McElone knows that, which is why she let me go."

"So what's this Cousin Richie thing? Who were you meeting with at your parents' house yesterday? At the movie theater today? Was it him?"

I'll give this to my ex-husband: He doesn't show you his panic. He clearly didn't have a response and didn't want to come clean because that's against his religion or something, so he did what I had indeed predicted before he arrived. He looked profoundly insulted.

"I don't have to put up with this kind of browbeating," he said. He marched to the kitchen door and walked out of the house, heading for his car in the driveway on the north side. I didn't even get the chance to ask him what kind of browbeating he *would* have to put up with; that's how fast he was.

Paul, equally quick on the uptake, pulled the cell phone I'd given him for messages out of his pocket and tossed it to Everett, who was already heading for the north wall. "Use this to text anything relevant," Paul said.

"Yes, sir," Everett answered as he phased through the wall, giving him a head start on Steven. He'd make it to the car first and wouldn't have to worry about incidentals like keys and doors. Or the arctic winds.

"You were right," Melissa said. "He went running as soon as he had to answer a question. Good work, Mom."

This wasn't turning out to be such a bad day after all.

Nineteen

Bobby Bertowski was a short man. Not munchkin short, but below average height. This was not especially important, but Bobby seemed to think it had some bearing on everything that had happened in his whole life.

"That's what got me," he told Melissa and me in his apartment in Avon-By-The-Sea, pronounced like the people who used to come to your door and try to sell you skin cream. He had said it was "Aa-von," and was now regaling us with tales of shortness. "If I'd been three inches taller, I could have been a big wheel like Steven."

I wasn't really interested in debating the size of my ex-husband's wheel, but Paul had suggested we see Bobby, reasoning that "He's the only other person we know for sure your ex-husband has sought out since he arrived here."

At the moment we hadn't even really been discussing Bobby or his perceived lack of height. But once I had mentioned that I was Steven's ex-wife and Melissa had identified herself as his daughter, somehow the subject had arisen. So to speak.

If Liss had not been in the room, I might have suggested that perhaps The Swine was not quite the wolf of Wall Street that Bobby might have thought. I asked what he did for a living.

"I manage an Enterprise Rent-A-Car in Eatontown," he answered, and while that seemed like an adequate job if not a thrill-packed one, Bobby said it as if he was confessing a terrible secret that I should certainly know should be kept confidential.

"That sounds nice," Melissa said. I didn't think she was being ironic.

Bobby huffed but did not contradict her. I didn't see how his shortness or his low (if you want to put it that way) station in life was relevant to what had been going on with Steven, so I tried again—this was the third time—to steer the conversation back in its intended direction.

"So, when Steven came here the other night, did he say why he needed a place to stay?" I asked. It seemed the right way to dip a toe in the water.

But Bobby looked at me as if I'd asked him how many arms he had. "I would think you'd know," he said. "I thought you threw him out of the house."

Okay, maybe that was the wrong toe. "I meant, did he tell you why he was here in New Jersey, and what kind of problems he was having?" I would have asked why Steven hadn't informed his daughter he'd been here at least three times in the past two months, but I had avoided telling Melissa that part.

Bobby stood up without a clear purpose and started to sort of wander around his living room, which was spare but neat enough. There was the inevitable TV, which in this case did not dominate the space because it wasn't that big (this was no doubt a theme) and the love seat on which Melissa and I were sitting. Bobby had been in an over-stuffed armchair that at least didn't have a drink holder in its arm, but now he was seemingly desperate to pose lean-ing against a fireplace mantel. The problem was, he had no fireplace and therefore no corresponding mantel. So he leaned against a fake swordfish mounted on a piece of fake wood. The effect was not especially evocative.

"Why don't you ask him yourself?" he said, his face a vision of simulated thought.

"I have. Now I'm asking you. I need to know, specifi-cally, if he has met with anyone while he's been staying here. I need to know if he's been discussing any business deals that went wrong and what he might be doing about them."

"Is this a divorce thing?" Bobby asked.

Melissa squared her shoulders. "No, it's not about their divorce," she told Bobby. "My dad has gotten into a lot of trouble and my mom is a private investigator. We're trying to help him. So you should know that anything you tell us is only going to be used to make things better for him and that nobody—including my dad—will ever know where we got any information you give us."

That girl was good.

Bobby absorbed all she'd told him and did exactly what I would not have expected of him: He stopped treating her like a child and took her seriously. Points for Bobby. "He hasn't met with anybody here that I know about," he said, talking directly to Melissa. "Of course, I work during the day, even on Saturdays, so I haven't been around all the time. He might have seen somebody while I was out."

Knowing a good thing when I saw it, I let Liss take over the questioning. "Did he tell you anything about a business deal he was working on?" she asked.

"He said there was something called SafT that I could

invest in if I wanted to," Bobby told her. "But I don't have that much squirreled away. I couldn't give him anything." It was more a lamentation than a statement; clearly Bobby had seen Steven's cockamamie software start-up as his ticket to the big time.

"How do you know my dad?" Liss asked, trying to draw him out of the mood he was displaying. Her tone was friendly and curious. Mine had been, I was beginning to realize, sort of accusatory when I started the conversation with Bobby. I was getting the master class in questioning that I might have expected from Paul, but I was getting it from my thirteen-year-old daughter. I couldn't decide whether to be ashamed or proud.

"We went to high school together," Bobby said, moving past the nonfishing trophy and migrating to a trunk on the floor that was supposed to look like something a pirate would bring back with booty in it. Instead it looked like something you'd buy at Kmart. He put his foot up on it like Captain Morgan and looked more like Angelina Jolie showing off her high-slit dress at the Oscars. "He kind of took me under his wing. I was his wingman." He seemed to have just hit on that thought, and it pleased him. "When he got a new girlfriend, I'd go along to act as lookout."

Time for me to step in before Steven's daughter had to hear more of that. "Did Steven say anything about people looking for him?" I asked Bobby. "What to do if anybody asked, something like that?"

"In high school? I was just looking out for her parents, mostly."

It took every ounce of willpower I owned to avoid rolling my eyes. "No, Bobby. Not in high school. Since he's been staying here. Did he say anything about people coming to look for him, or give you instructions on what to tell them?"

I could practically see the gears turning in Bobby's mind. Should he tell us something Steven had expressly informed him was absolutely not for public consumption? Would he be a wingman betraying his best pal or a guy saving the day and moving up in status? Was it better to—

"Please," Melissa said.

Bobby looked up. His eyes met Liss's and for once he didn't look away or walk around his living room looking for something to pose near. That was a good thing, since there was precious little living room left and I was afraid he'd try to lean on me.

"He said there were going to be people looking for him, but they never came," Bobby said. "He said I shouldn't lie to them about where he was, but that he wasn't ever going to tell me where he was going, so if they came at a time he wasn't here, I really wouldn't know what to say. But there was one guy I was always supposed to let in and who I should text Steven if he ever came. That guy seemed to be central to whatever was going on."

Finally a promising lead. I'd have to compliment Melissa on her excellent interrogation skills. "Who was that?" I asked Bobby.

"Steven said his name was Maurice DuBois."

Lieutenant McElone had stated in no uncertain terms that I should not have anything to do with Steven's situation, and for once I was in no mood to let her know I hadn't done as she'd, you know, ordered. So I did the next best thing and went to see Phyllis.

Melissa was more than familiar with the *Harbor Haven Chronicle* offices, since Phyllis is a dear friend and I'd consulted—that's the word I like to use—with her on pretty much every investigation I've ever undertaken. I served as a paper delivery girl for Phyllis when I was exactly the age Liss was now, and my daughter wasted no time in pointing that out.

Melissa sat casually on a pile of old newspapers in one corner, which led to thoughts (mine) of having to have her parka dry-cleaned. She looked the *Chronicle* publisher in the eye and said, "Hey, Phyllis. I turned thirteen two weeks ago. Am I old enough to deliver papers for you now?"

Phyllis smiled, but it was a sad smile. "Afraid I don't actually have the need for that service anymore, honey," she answered. "I have only fifty subscribers who get the hard copy these days. You wouldn't make enough to justify the air in your bike tires." Most of the *Chronicle*'s current readers found it online, where Phyllis sold advertising and actually made more money per view than she used to per copy. Very little in the way of printing costs these days. It had taken a while, but Phyllis was not one to stick with the old ways just because they're the old ways. She wanted to keep the business alive. "I'll tell you what, though," she added before Liss's disappointed expression could register. "I'm going to need an assistant editor here pretty soon. I can't do this all myself. Would you be interested in that?"

My daughter's face did the quickest change from frustrated to elated I'd ever seen. "Sure!" she said. "When can I start?" You'll notice she didn't ask what the job paid, and neither of them had consulted with me to see if it was all right.

"Well." Phyllis's eyes had a slight twinkle of mischief. "The state of New Jersey won't let a person get working papers until she's fourteen, so only one more year until you can start training to take over the whole operation from me when I retire. What do you think?"

Melissa looked skeptical, like she'd been set up. "You knew I couldn't work for another year. Are you just putting me off?" She doesn't kid around, my daughter. Except when she does.

"No! I think you'd make a great publisher, but I have to abide by the laws of the state and so does your mom if she wants to keep both her licenses." That's innkeeper and

SPOUSE ON HAUNTED HILL   195

private investigator. One pays more than the other. Because I'm pretty sure I've never been paid as a PI. Most of my clients were dead people.

Liss looked at me. "Are you in on this?"

I held up my hands defensively. "First I'm hearing about it, but I'm happy someone is consulting with me about your new career."

Liss narrowed her eyes and looked sideways at Phyllis. "Can I let you know?" she asked.

"I'll hold the job open until you're fourteen. How's that?" She held out a hand.

Melissa took it. "Deal."

"Great," I said. "Now that the publishing empire is secure again, can I find out about what I asked?"

Phyllis put on a pair of half-glasses and picked up a paper from one of the many piles on her desk, her filing cabinets, her shelves and the floor in her office. "The identification from fingerprint matches at the FBI are confirmed," she said. "The guy with the bullets in him at Hanrahan's is Maurice DuBois. There's no way your ex is still hearing from him."

"Can there be two Maurice DuBoises?" Melissa asked in wonder.

A text arrived from Paul's phone, which meant it was from Everett. "He's stopping at a strip mall in Brick Township. Getting slice of pizza. No contact." I texted back to follow The Swine inside and see what happened. Seconds later came "Yes, ma'am."

Before we left the house Maxie had delivered an extremely early report on her initial Internet research, and the only definite result had been the fact that a local news anchor in New York City was named Maurice DuBois. He was definitely not the man shot in the alley, but that was all we knew.

"There are, but probably not involved with your father,"

I told her. "What's more likely is that someone else is using this guy's name, but what would be the motive for doing that? Obviously someone disliked this DuBois enough to kill him. Why become the guy you shot?"

"Could be he's the one who killed DuBois and figures nobody else is that mad at him," Phyllis suggested. "There must be some value in the name. If he has good enough fake IDs or the real ones with his face on them, he can have access to insurance policies, bank accounts, credit accounts and properties owned, and that's just for starters."

"What about his wallet?" I asked, pointing to the paper she held. "Does it say?"

New text from Everett: "Stopping in Asbury Park." That was quick, and then I realized his first text had been sent a half hour ago and I'd just seen it. The pizza must have been to go. I saw no need to tell Everett anything else.

"Nothing missing," Phyllis said after scanning the sheet. "All ID was intact, which led to the fingerprint search confirming it was DuBois. There was even two hundred and sixty dollars in cash and nobody touched that."

"In an alley outside Hanrahan's?" The place didn't necessarily have the most genteel reputation in town. "You'd think they'd steal his money just out of habit."

"Well, we never thought this was a robbery," Melissa pointed out. "We figured he got shot because of some business deal that went bad, didn't we?"

I didn't want to point out that her father was involved in just such a business deal with Lou Maroni, so I simply nodded. Phyllis took off her reading glasses and twisted her mouth to one side, thinking.

"The wallet was in his inside coat pocket," she reported. That didn't seem especially curious. "He was lying on his right side in the alley and the wallet was in his inside pocket, on the left side. His right arm was up, extended over his head, but his left was down."

She was getting at something. "And?" I asked. It speeds up the process.

"I wonder if he was right-handed," Phyllis said. "Because if he was, he might have been aiming his own gun when he was shot."

Melissa looked sideways at Phyllis. "Did they find a gun next to him?" she asked.

"No. That doesn't mean he didn't have one."

"Was he wearing a holster?" I asked.

"Not according to this."

"What are we talking about?"

"Two possibilities," Phyllis said, somehow finding her office chair amid the clutter and sitting on it. "Either the killer took his gun or somehow DuBois was shot with his own gun."

"Three possibilities," I said. "DuBois didn't have a gun and I'll ask again, what are we talking about?"

The phone buzzed again and the text came from Everett with the address at which The Swine was stopping in Asbury Park. I stopped, read it twice, shook my head and looked at Melissa. "Come on," I said. "We have to go."

"What about the gun?" Melissa asked.

"Phyllis will figure out why she thinks there was another gun. Get your stuff. We have to leave."

"Why?"

"Your father just stopped off at Madison Paints," I told her.

"He's with Josh?" Melissa asked.

I was out of Phyllis's office and already halfway to the door. "We have to go," I said.

Twenty

"We're missing the afternoon spook show," Melissa said.

"I don't care," I told her. "Maxie and Paul can handle it if any guests show up. But they might not. This isn't a huge ghost crowd. Besides, finding out what's going on is much more important right now."

We were braving the brutal climate of the inside of my Volvo wagon on our way to Josh's store in Asbury Park. I had no idea if Steven was going there as a subtle reminder to me that he could be dangerous if he felt like it or . . .

Or he and Josh were doing business together. I really didn't want to think about that. Could I be blind enough to think Josh was different and then find out he was The Swine II?

No. I'd known Josh for years, and then years again. That simply couldn't be the case.

"I get that we have to find out what's going on, but why can't you just call Josh and ask him?" Liss said, sitting back and hugging herself for a little warmth. I made a mental note to get the Volvo's "heater" looked at. Hang the cost! My daughter was freezing.

"Because if I ask your father I can't trust the answer, and if I ask Josh he's going to try to be diplomatic. That means I can't trust his answer, either, and that's not good enough right now."

"You don't trust Josh?" Melissa sounded shocked.

"I *do* trust Josh, but he gets funny when your dad is involved," I explained. "He doesn't want to say bad things about Dad too much and he doesn't want to compete. So sometimes he just doesn't do anything, which would have been better this time, but it seems that Dad is getting him involved in what's going on. I need to know how and I need to know why."

Liss nodded. A lot of girls would be devastated by an analysis like the one I'd just given her. She seemed to be analyzing it for herself.

"You're not thinking about yourself," she said finally. I could see the steam from her breath. Maybe if she tethered herself to the roof and sat outside, she'd be warmer. "You are going to change the situation when you get there. You should let Everett tell you what they're talking about and decide what you're going to do after you have the information."

My first impulse was to tell her six different ways in which that was wrong. I'd need to observe the interaction for myself; Everett wouldn't catch the nuances in the two men's behavior that I would; it would be more immediate to talk to them while the meeting was still going on; and . . . three more ways. But I've learned over the last thirteen years that my daughter is often more sensible and intelligent than I am, and have been badly burned by not following her reasoning in the past.

I pulled the car over to the side of the road, parking in

a Burger King lot to get us out of the way. I started to think of reasons to go inside without buying any food just to get out of the cold, and I was in my car. That was it, I was calling Marv Winderbrook tomorrow about a heater for the Volvo. Because thinking warm thoughts wasn't cutting it right now.

So I turned toward Melissa. "You're saying I'd be more of a problem than a solution?" I asked.

"Well . . ." She studied my face for a mood; no sense in going the wrong route here. "Sort of. You wouldn't do anything wrong, but just being there would make them act different, and that wouldn't help."

"You don't have to worry about insulting me, honey."

"I wasn't. I just wanted the fastest way to get out of the car and into a warm house." Eminently practical, among all the other amazing things my daughter manages to be. "But I still think all of that is true."

"Come on," I said. "Let's go into the Burger King and get a hot chocolate."

"Can I have coffee?"

While having various hot—and they're not kidding about the *hot*—beverages, we debated the wisdom of texting Everett and decided it was too risky. If we weren't hearing from him, that meant they were still inside Madison Paints. If he was there with Josh and The Swine discussing whatever they could possibly have to talk about, pulling out his phone to text or hearing it beep with a message from me would draw attention. Steven might dismiss it, but if Josh saw a flying cell phone he'd know I'd sent a spy. He can't see the ghosts, but he knows they're there.

In fact, there were three ghosts in the Burger King as we decided to wait until Everett could report back. One was dressed in clothing from the nineteen forties, which put him here before the King had decided to start grilling patties; the other two were a couple in their seventies, I'd say, watching the manager of the place give orders. She must have been their daughter, from the delighted beaming expressions on their faces. Liss and I opted not to let them know we were aware of their presence, finished our drinks and braved the car once more.

As it turned out, there was no reason to rush home, either. None of the guests had decided to attend the afternoon spook show, which was both a relief and a worry. If nobody wanted to see the spirits in action, would my guest-house still be special enough to attract visitors when the weather broke?

Still, there was plenty of activity. Maxie wanted to take a bow over having manipulated her laptop—a newer model than mine and she'd been dead for five years—into divulging some information on the topics Paul had assigned. We met in the movie room, where I could recline in a chair made for exactly that purpose and Melissa could lounge on a sofa in front of a coffee table on which she put her feet.

"What've you got?" I asked Maxie. She twitched a bit at being treated like an employee.

"Your Maurice DuBois was an interesting guy," she said, green visor and black T-shirt (bearing the legend "Dude, You Got a Dell") presenting a contrast to her busi-nesslike manner, although Maxie would have disputed that. "But the most stuff came from this software, SafT."

Paul, idly turning a space heater on and off from ten feet away with his finger, had clearly heard some of Max-ie's information before we arrived. "That's not the biggest thing," he noted.

Maxie looked annoyed. "Maybe not, but it's the most."

I asked Paul to leave the heater on, as Liss and I were still recovering from a nice ride home and he looked embarrassed. "Go on, then," he said, instructing Maxie. Paul likes to pretend we're a real detective agency and he's the boss who sends all his operatives out into the field. We all have our delusions.

"I was *going* to. Anyway, this SafT thing. Turns out your ex was actually onto something there. Some of the tech sites, the ones for people with more than an eighth-grade education, were all excited about this thing. Said it would revolutionize the Internet because nobody could hack anything it touched. You wouldn't have to worry about your data. Some of them thought even governments would be interested in it because the threat of some foreign power or terrorists or somebody hacking into their computers is what keeps them up nights."

Melissa, who had been listening intently, sat forward, putting her feet down (which made me feel better about the coffee table) and leaning her elbows on her knees. "So I bet that would make it really valuable," she said.

Maxie beamed at her. "You're right," she said. "The speculation was this thing was going to go in the billions."

That made *me* sit up and take notice. "The *billions*?" I said. It seemed impossible The Swine could possibly have mixed himself up with something that good.

"So, why was Steven having trouble finding investors for it?" I asked. "If it was worth billions, it seems something with that kind of potential would have them lining up around any number of blocks."

Maxie leaned a bit. That's her way of saying she's thinking. "Well, I had to dig pretty deep to find anything about it. I think your ex was trying to keep it quiet, maybe so nobody could find out how much there was to be made."

"That doesn't make sense," Melissa said. "Dad would want people to know it was really big so they'd want to give their money, wouldn't he?"

"Only if it was real," came a male voice from the hallway. In walked Lou Maroni and his two attendants. "That was the question, after all."

"You guys really have to learn how to knock," I said. "I mean, is that really too much to ask? Hang on. I'm going to get Steven for you." Out came my phone.

But Maroni held up his hand like Diana Ross singing "Stop! In the Name of Love." "I'm not looking for him right now," he said. "I'm looking for you."

That couldn't possibly be a good thing. "Me?" My voice had dropped half an octave.

"I'm getting the shovel," Maxie said.

"Hang on," Paul told her. "We might not need it. I can electrocute him if necessary."

"Yes, you," Maroni said, not having been privy to the discussion of how to immobilize him. "You might have something I'm looking for."

I'd once had a similar situation involving a deed to George Washington's old shore home, but that hadn't been fun and I doubted this would take a better path. "I don't see how that's possible," I said. "The only person in this family who's ever met you before is Steven, and he hasn't left anything for you."

I felt Melissa standing on my right side. She would not hesitate to close ranks if there was going to be trouble, but I didn't want her in harm's way. "Go sit down," I told her under my breath.

"Make me."

Go raise children.

"It's very simple," Maroni said, not advancing on us at all. I did not take that for a good sign; a man with a firearm doesn't need close proximity. "When we were walking in, I heard you talking about a software program called SafT that could be worth billions of dollars. That was what you said, wasn't it?"

"I did a little research about it on the Internet," I said. "Because Steven said you were investing in it and he said that's what everybody was all excited about. So I found out what you would find out if you did the same searches."

"*I* did the research." Maxie sniffed.

"Yeah," Maroni said. "I know all that stuff already. What I don't know is where your pal Steven might have left the patent application and other documents for that software, because right now they're technically mine and I'd like them back."

I wasn't crazy about the direction this conversation seemed to be taking, but I couldn't say it was a surprise at all. I consciously took a step away from Melissa, ostensibly to get a better angle to face Maroni head-on, and said, "Okay, first: I have no clue where those papers would be. Nobody's ever even mentioned them to me before. Steven never brought them up and neither did you when you were here last. So I couldn't begin to tell you where to look except that it would be somewhere that's not in my house. But I'm wondering exactly why you think those documents belong to you. Wouldn't they belong to the person who created the software to begin with?"

Maroni looked amused more than anything else, and that wasn't pleasant to see. "Technically you're right. That's exactly who should have the papers in question. But in this case that's not possible, so I'm guessing Mr. Rendell has them with him or left them here, and I'm afraid I'm going to have to ask you if I can take a look at the room he was staying in. Would that be your bedroom?"

Melissa almost took a step toward him, but Maxie said, "Don't. Let me handle it." Liss stopped, but Maxie didn't do anything.

"It so wouldn't," I said. "And *I'm* afraid I'm not letting you search any of the rooms in my house, because this is my business and if word gets around that I am not protecting the privacy of my guests, I could lose this house. So you're just going to have to take my word for it, because as it happens, I'm telling you the truth. I've never heard of any patent documents before the moment you brought them up."

Maroni held up his hands on both sides, gesturing toward but not to his two lovely assistants. "And if we insist?"

"I'll have to call a friend of mine at the police department and report that you are trespassing and making terroristic threats," I said. "But you can trust me, whatever it is you're looking for isn't here. Now, Steven was very upset that he missed you the last time you came. Would you like me to call him? You can ask him where these papers you're looking for might be."

"No need," Paul said. I turned to look at him and saw he was pointing toward the hallway, where I could now hear footsteps approaching.

Maroni and his men, however, were staring at a space in the air over my head and looking confused. "What are you looking at?" he asked.

The Swine strutted into the room like he'd just invented ego and wanted to take it out for a test spin. Chest out, arms back, head held high, he was a dazzling example of someone who had much more confidence than an objective perspective would encourage. "So! How is every—"

He stopped dead in his tracks as if someone had put up one of those invisible walls mimes keep running into right in his path. He actually said, "Oof!"

Maroni and his traveling muscle show turned. I couldn't see their faces, but I could hear the evil grin in his voice. "So, Steven Rendell," he said. "I was hoping to see you again."

"Shovel?" Maxie asked.

"Shovel," Paul said.

Before she could leave, Maxie was shouting, "Everett!" Her boyfriend had just phased through the side wall and was making his way toward her, seemingly distracted by the three unfamiliar men, because he twisted his body toward them as he floated.

"Who are they?" he asked.

"Enemy combatants," Maxie told him. She's picked up a little military lingo since they've been together. "We were just saying I should get a shovel to hit them with."

I wanted to ask Everett about Steven's visit to Madison Paints, but there were far too many people in the room now.

"Lou," Steven said. He wasn't even trying to do his "happy to see you" voice. "What's up?"

"I think you know. You've been doing your very best to avoid seeing me. You even flew all the way to New Jersey from L.A. only a couple of days ago just so you wouldn't have to see me." Maroni turned a bit so I could see his profile, which was not exactly a treat. "I've been spending a little time with your beautiful family." And three ghosts, but why tell him that?

"Don't get anything yet," Everett told Maxie. "Let's see what happens. It's best not to be the first to fire."

"They're not involved," Steven told his "investor." "You don't have to bring them in on it."

"They're already in," Maroni insisted. "They're in because I couldn't find you. So I was asking your wife where to find the SafT patent papers."

"Ex-wife," I pointed out.

"Of course," Maroni said. "*Ex*-wife. Shows good taste."

"Thank you," I said.

"Patent papers?" Steven said. You could hear the sweat in his voice and he was a Californian who had just come in from temperatures in the teens while wearing an inadequate coat. "I don't know anything about patent papers. Can't you get them online?"

"Let's find out," Maxie said, and "put on" her trench coat, then zipped up through the ceiling, where she could work on her laptop without being obvious to the civilians in the room. "Keep me informed, Everett."

"Will do." Everett is excellent at taking orders, which is probably why he gets along with Maxie so well.

"Yes, I could, but you know perfectly well that the originals are going to be required to cash in on the patent once this thing hits." Maroni was speaking slowly as if to a somewhat dim-witted child. "You're stalling, Steve. You know where they are and you don't want to give them to me. So maybe I should take something of yours and we can swap."

He looked creepily toward Melissa.

"Shovel," I said. "Definitely shovel."

"It's not snowing," The Swine told me, clearly sure that I had gone completely mad. "You don't have to shovel anything."

"Try to stand clear of him," Paul ordered. "I can get a good charge into one thrust, I think." He held out his hands as if he were about to try flying back to Krypton.

"Wait." The last person I expected to speak took a step forward when I wanted her to take several steps back, like to another state. Melissa looked Maroni right in the eye. "Why do you need those papers, and how come the original owner can't have them?" she asked. "It doesn't make any sense. The person who created the product gets the patent."

Maroni nodded. "Very good, young lady. But in this case we have a problem, don't we, Steven?"

Everyone turned their attention to The Swine. He looked for a sympathetic face and didn't even get one from the people he couldn't see. "See, the patent is held by Maurice DuBois."

Twenty-one

"Oh, Stevie!" Lou Maroni scolded The Swine in an exaggerated tone. "You didn't tell your wi—*ex*-wife—that little detail? That the guy who made this thing everybody thinks is going to make them rich is the guy who ended up with a few too many pieces of metal in his body in an alley?" He made the "tsk, tsk" sound and wagged a finger at Steven. "Shame on you."

It was the closest I'd come to feeling sorry for my ex-husband in years. I still didn't get there, but it was close.

Part of the reason I couldn't react was that I was still stunned. "Maurice DuBois was your inventor?" I said to Steven. "He was the guy you were investing all that money from other people in? And when he ended up dead you didn't bother to tell anybody?"

As always happens at such times, my phone buzzed. A text from Josh: "There for dinner in an hour?" Was it that late already? Wait, I needed to find out about Josh and The

Swine meeting behind my back and in front of my ghost spy. Too many things were happening at the same time, and I didn't understand any of them. I didn't text back just yet.

"How was I supposed to know he was going to get shot?" The Swine answered, but I noticed he wasn't looking at Maroni or at me—he was talking directly to Melissa. "Believe me, I didn't see this coming. Not any of it. I wouldn't have put you in any danger, baby. I promise."

My daughter, in case you haven't noticed yet, is a much better person than I am. She looked over at the father, who had pretty much abandoned her, lied to her on multiple occasions, ignored her when he didn't want anything and rarely paid her child support, and said, "It's okay, Dad. Really. I'm not mad."

"But we are," Maroni told him. "About those patent papers."

Steven closed his eyes tight as if something had hurt him sharply. "I honestly don't know anything about them, Lou. I don't. I didn't know Maurice was going to fly out here or I wouldn't have come myself. What he did with his documentation is a complete mystery to me."

"Well, then." Maroni settled himself into one of the armchairs I wasn't currently occupying. "I guess we're going to be here awhile."

I texted back to Josh: "Yeah. Please bring enough for more people."

Instead my mother and father showed up and Mom was, as ever, carrying most of a Thanksgiving dinner in her backpack. But she was somewhat puzzled at the presence of the three extra men in my movie room, still not unbuttoning their overcoats and not taking off their identical fedoras.

"What's with those guys?" she asked me in the kitchen.

"They in some kind of cult that makes you dress like Peter Lawford?"

I gave her the *Reader's Digest* version of current events. "The thing is, I don't know who to believe," I told her finally. "The three guys who seem to be holding us hostage just by not leaving, or the guy I lived with who never told me the truth for a half hour for years?"

"You know where I stand," Mom said, still unpacking various courses of something Melissa and she were going to cook. "Your ex-husband is not to be trusted."

Paul, hovering over Mom's head, was stroking his goatee. Something was up. "Keep in mind, Loretta, that the three men sitting in the movie room are armed. They came here with a purpose and they indirectly threatened Melissa. They are not trustworthy, either."

Mom stopped talking. It's what she does when she knows she's wrong but she still doesn't like The Swine.

"We need a plan of action," I said quietly to Paul. You never knew who was outside the kitchen door. "Does Maxie's shovel strategy fit here?"

Paul shook his head. "She and Everett are monitoring the situation in the movie room. From what I can tell, your ex-husband is sitting there looking uncomfortable while the three men are silent, intimidating through their presence alone."

"What about Liss?" I asked.

"She's turned on the television and is watching *Young Frankenstein*," Paul said.

Ooh. One of my favorites. Wait. Men. With guns. In the same room as my daughter. "We should get her out of there," Mom said.

"I gather Maroni and his two associates are going to make a move at some point," Paul said. "I do not think it will involve Melissa, but we can't rule that out. The best strategy is to find the paperwork they want and give it to them."

I took in a deep breath and let it out. I didn't want to accede to Maroni's mean tactics, but I also didn't see how The Swine was entitled to anything that belonged Maurice DuBois, either. "Let's go search Steven's room," I said.

"Let's?" Mom asked. "You want me to go search through his underwear and stuff?"

"He didn't bring anything with him, Mom. Whatever he's got is on his back now."

Mom looked at me. "That's worse."

"Besides, he hasn't been staying here. He's been at Bobby's apartment. If he stashed the papers in his room, they won't be hard to find because there won't be anything else there distracting us."

Paul held up a hand. "Perhaps it's best if I go in first by myself," he said. "No one can see me and that will cast no suspicions." He made sense, but then, he usually does. Then he stopped and turned his head. "Did you hear that?"

I hadn't heard anything unusual. My stomach turned over. "Liss?" I asked.

"No. Thunder."

"It's February, Paul. You're not doing your electricity thing today. Go search Steven's room."

He nodded and swooped out. Mom glanced over at me. "Do you think he'll really shock himself into the next level?"

"How would I know? I don't get the Dead Guy Newsletter." I stopped helping Mom put groceries away—in my kitchen—and bit my lower lip. "The thing is, finding or not finding these papers isn't going to tell us who killed Maurice DuBois. We still need a plan."

Mom sniffed. She's not crazy about killers, for reasons that don't at all escape me. "You don't think it's those three men in the Mafia suits?"

"If it was them they would have found what they needed. They wouldn't have shot him if he could still lead them to billions. No. I think it was someone else."

"Who?"

"That's the question of the day." I took my phone out of my pocket and started scrolling through numbers.

"They let you keep your phone?" Mom asked. "Aren't they worried you'll call the police?"

"That's the thing. They haven't done anything illegal. I could call McElone and she could come and not arrest them. But . . ." I found the people I was looking for and created a text chain. "How many people can you and Liss cook for tonight?" I asked Mom.

"How many do you need us to cook for?"

I gave my mother a hug.

It's not hard to sound urgent in a text message. They're sort of like telegrams (and I had some recent experience with telegrams, so I knew what I was talking about)—the form itself seems somehow immediate and necessary. So when I texted a select group of people and insisted they arrive at the guesthouse immediately, I got no argument from any of them. It wielded a sort of power I had never realized I could command.

The other thing was to be sure I sounded like I was demanding, not requesting, each person's presence. The most confused reply I got was from Tony, who asked if he and Jeannie should bring the kids or get a sitter. I told him the choice was his but we were trying to unmask a killer. I guessed the sitter was the option to be used but never got a reply.

That was what it had come to: my best friends were used to me calling and asking if they wanted to come over to catch a murderer.

My fiancé—I just like saying that—showed up first because he had been planning on coming anyway and was probably on his way when I'd contacted the others. Josh got the short version of our current situation and volunteered immediately to go into the movie room and watch out for Melissa. I did not ask him about meeting with The Swine, because I didn't want to have that conversation in front of my mother.

Paul arrived from the room I'd given Steven the one night he'd stayed here and he was shaking his head. "Nothing," he reported. "And I mean nothing. You've cleaned up since your ex-husband was staying there, Alison. So you know there isn't any paperwork out in the open. I checked even inside walls but didn't find anything."

I reported that to Josh, who was standing in the kitchen because I had told him Dad was making sure Melissa was fine despite the presence of three possibly violent men and her father. Josh knew my own father in life and so trusts him as anyone who knew him would, but he wasn't happy about the situation, which meant he was, you know, sane.

"If Paul can't find anything, that means it's not in the room. But Steven might have hid them in the house if he knew people were going to come looking," Josh said.

"He's so smart," Mom said. Already treating Josh like her own son. Which would no doubt come as a surprise to his parents. That was it! In-laws!

"He spent some time at his parents' house yesterday and the day before," I said. "And he met with someone in their garage. I'm assuming it wasn't Steve Wozniak and they weren't reinventing all of electronics for the twenty-first century, so he might have done something with those papers there, assuming he ever had them at all."

"It's a good thought," Paul said, but it was at the same time Josh was wondering aloud why I didn't just ask Steven himself, so I answered Josh first.

"Because I can't trust that any answer he gives me will be true," I said. "I don't think he's said one true word to me since he's been back on this coast, and maybe not for the past ten years at least."

"Look, I'm not going to defend Steven to you," Josh said. When people start like that, it usually means they're going to do exactly what they say they're not going to do. "But I don't think he's as shifty as you make him out to be, at least not all the time." See?

Mom looked at him with some puzzlement in her eyes. "Maybe you just haven't gotten to know him well enough," she suggested. That, coming from my mother, was practically like saying the man was a serial killer, a public menace and a person of poor hygiene. And that he didn't like puppies.

Josh shrugged. "Obviously not as well as either of you. I'm going to check on the movie room." And he walked out.

I stared after him a moment wondering what could possibly have transpired between him and Steven that would cause such a shift in attitude. I looked at my mother. "Before I married Steven, you wanted to tell me not to go through with it, didn't you?" I asked.

She thought for a moment. It's hard for Mom to admit that she ever had bad feelings about anything I've done in my life. The ashtray I made out of flammable Popsicle sticks in second grade and brought home to a nonsmoking family she considered an admirable work of imagination and ingenuity and it stayed on our coffee table until it was "accidentally" destroyed while the rug was being vacuumed. Twenty years later.

But this time I'd backed her up against a wall. She nodded, finally. "I sort of wish I had, but then there's Melissa," she said.

"Would you tell me if you felt that way this time?" I asked quietly.

Mom walked over and gave me a hug. "I have no reason to do that this time," she told me. "He's a wonderful man. Marry him."

"How are we going to find out about the documents possibly being in your ex-husband's family garage?" Paul said. He was looking away from Mom and me out of his discomfort with the emotions on display. Paul is uncomfortable with any emotions on display. I think it's his British side.

"If I give you the address, can you find someone on the Ghosternet who might be able to take a look?" I asked. "I won't be able to get there until tomorrow, and I have all these possible murderers coming for dinner. Besides, I can pretty much guarantee there won't be anyone home there tonight."

Mom and I had let go of each other and stood looking at our resident investigator ghost, who was still averting his eyes. "I've made contact with a few trustworthy people," he said. "Please give me the information and I will ask if anyone in the area can check." Then his head turned suddenly again. "Sure you didn't hear thunder that time?"

I rolled my eyes. "I'm sure, Dr. Franklin," I said. "No need to get out the kite and the key until the weather breaks, at least two months from now."

Paul gratefully dropped through the floor without a sound, no doubt thrilled to be out of the room with these two gushy women. Mom looked at me and smiled.

"Tell Melissa I need her in here," she said. "She's a better cook than I am."

On my way to the movie room I heard a knock at the front door and found Bobby Bertowski standing there looking sheepish. "Why am I here?" he demanded by way of greeting.

"Why are any of us here, Bobby?" I showed him the coatrack and he hung up the parka he was wearing, putting his gloves in the pockets. "The others are inside. I'm sure you'll be happy to see at least one of them."

He followed me to the movie room, where I passed on Mom's message to Melissa. She was slightly put off but only because one of her favorite scenes in *Young Frankenstein* was about to begin and she wanted to see Gene Hackman pour hot soup in Peter Boyle's lap. But she understood about responsibility and besides, nobody was going to eat until she got to work. She left after I looked at Lou Maroni and said, "She's cooking. Deal with it."

Maroni shrugged. "Did I ever say she couldn't leave the room?"

Bobby walked directly to Steven in true toady fashion and smiled as he sat down next to his role model. "What are you doing here?" my charming ex asked.

Bobby pointed at me. "She said I had to come."

Nobody else so much as looked up. And when I say "nobody else," I'm talking about quite a crowd. Besides The Swine and his sidekick were Maroni and his two overcoated handmaidens, my father (floating over the big TV), Josh (thankfully not closing ranks with Steven), Boyle and Hackman, the last two of whom were frozen in time on the TV. Melissa had paused the movie when she got up to leave, given that no one else in the room seemed to be paying any attention to it. Philistines. Except Josh.

Everett, Dad told me behind everyone's back but Paul's, was off looking for Maxie, who was supposed to have researched some background on Maroni that might come in useful later tonight but hadn't materialized again. He'd said he'd be "right back," but that was ten minutes earlier.

I turned the TV off altogether and looked at the assembly, which I knew was about to get considerably larger. This was a gamble, and maybe a dangerous one, but there was a lot of unraveling to do with Maurice DuBois's murder, and having everyone together seemed the fastest and simplest way to sort things out. Besides, it meant that I wouldn't have to drive anywhere far in the Volvo before Marv had performed some magic on its heater.

"Since when do you take orders from her?" The Swine asked his friend.

Bobby shrugged. "I dunno. She said if I didn't come she'd tell you I'd spilled a bunch of your secrets, so I came." The man really didn't seem to listen to anything he said.

"You told her my secrets?" Steven rose off his soft easy chair, which I knew was something of a grandstand move for him.

"She said it was important."

"You guys know I'm here in the room, right?" I asked.

True to form, they ignored my presence and continued to bicker like an old married couple about who told whom what and at what time. The idea that they were ostensibly talking about what would in their circles be classified material—and were from all appearances revealing nothing of the least bit of interest to anyone else in the room—seemed to elude them.

Finally Maroni stood up. "I'm not really seeing much point to staying," he said. In lockstep behind him the two towers rose out of their chairs and in unison shrugged in a gesture that indicated they might have to knock down a couple of buildings just to warm up tonight. "Come on, Stevie. We're leaving."

That struck The Swine by surprise; he dropped the finger he had raised in Bobby's face to make a point and seemed to sag from the hair down. He looked at Maroni. "We?"

"Yeah. You're the one who knows where the patent is. I'm the one who's going to find out. We don't have to do that here and ruin everybody's appetite. So my friends and

I will insist that you join us, and then everybody will be happy. Except you." He gestured to the two other men in his entourage and they were at either of Steven's shoulders in seconds.

"Wait. Lou." The Swine had started sweating pretty much on cue. "That's not necessary. I really don't know where that paperwork would be. No matter what you do, I'm not going to tell you, because I don't know. So why don't we forget it?"

For a man who could convince senior citizens on the very edge of poverty that giving him money would make them financially secure, that was an especially weak argument and Maroni was certainly not buying. "Forget it? Billions of dollars and we should just forget it? You are a funny man, Stevie. Let's go." Another hand gesture and there were large, somewhat hairy hands on both of my ex-husband's shoulders.

Steven and the Maroni party leaving was bad for my plan and besides, I was not going to be the one to explain to Melissa why her father had so few thumbs the next time she saw him. So I turned toward Maroni. "I don't understand something," I said.

His eyebrows rose slightly. I wasn't sure if it was what I had said or the fact that I had spoken at all that seemed to startle him. "What don't you understand?" he asked. "It's pretty simple. I want to know something he knows and he needs to tell me. How pleasant or unpleasant that experience has to be is entirely up to your hus—sorry, ex-husband. What's to understand?"

"You were pulling all your money out of the scheme and coming to collect it from Steven," I reminded him. "You didn't want to invest in this SafT thing anymore. But once this guy DuBois is shot—by someone, and we don't know whom—all of a sudden you're desperately interested in owning the patent he had. If the program doesn't work, why do you want it so badly?"

Sure, it was a stalling tactic, meant to distract Maroni from hauling Steven away, but it was an effective enough one. Everyone remained in the room.

"It's about perception," Maroni answered. He seemed to be in earnest, which was the last thing I'd expected. "If everybody on the Internet *thinks* this thing is the next Pinterest, then it doesn't matter if it works. It just matters that they'll put up the money to buy it and I'd like to own that business. That's fairly simple, isn't it?"

It was, in a sick, twisted way, but I'd been playing for time and now I was rewarded. Footsteps in the hallway led to the arrival in my movie room entrance of Constance and Harry Rendell.

The Swine's eyes opened to an uncomfortable-looking size. "Mom? Dad?" Not only was he going to be squeezed for information, but his parents were going to see him removed from a situation like the insignificant bungler they'd always suspected he was.

In some ways, this was turning into a really enjoyable evening.

Josh looked over at me and mouthed, "Mom and Dad?" I nodded. He shook his head in wonder and smiled just a little bit.

"Come in," I told the Rendells. "Have you met Mr. Maroni and company?"

Maroni, apparently now believing he was the host of the evening, reached for Harry's hand and shook it. "Nice to meet you," he said. "This your son?" He pointed at The Swine.

Harry nodded, his eyes registering sincere confusion at the whole situation. "Yeah." That was it.

"We were told we should be here tonight and so we're

here," Constance said, not looking in my direction. I hadn't even had to hint at blackmail to get her to show up and bring Harry with her.

Maxie floated down from the ceiling, saw the gathered assemblage and stopped. She's not crazy about crowds of people she doesn't know, and the group seemed to put her off her game. She lost the trench coat and if they had looked up, the civilians in the room would have seen a floating laptop computer for a moment. They didn't look up, except Josh, who was used to it and smiled. He seems to think Maxie has an impish sense of humor. I don't get that but then, Josh can't actually see or hear Maxie, which probably adds to her appeal.

"I've got something," she said to me. "I'm not sure what it means, but yeah, your DuBois guy is the one who has the patent on this SafT thing. I knew that before, but what I didn't know is that your ex's name is also on the papers."

I couldn't react, but that news came as a surprise. I looked at Dad, who was listening even as he watched Paul rise from the basement. My father was also tracing a wire from the back of the flat-screen to a small box Paul had constructed from pieces he'd dug out of my used electronics and plugged into the wall. I didn't know what it was supposed to do, but a green light was flashing on it.

I tried to say something, but Maxie was already rising back up through the ceiling. "I can't work in here," she complained. I wanted to tell her to find Everett so I could get the scoop on Josh's meeting with The Swine, but she was gone.

"Mixed success from our search," Paul said. "One of my contacts in the area of your in-laws' home managed to search the house and the garage, but could not find the paperwork Maroni is looking for."

I turned toward The Swine, but he was already looking

at me with deep suspicion in his eyes. "What's going on here tonight?" he sort of hissed.

"Dinner," I answered sweetly. "I think we're having chicken." I looked over at Maroni. "You guys aren't vegetarians, are you?"

"We'll manage," he said.

The doorbell rang, a rarity in my house, since guests are often coming and going, so I went to answer the door and found my mother already there. "Melissa doesn't need my help," she explained while we reached the front room together. "I think I'm getting in her way."

I opened the front door and there stood Susannah Nesbit looking quite annoyed. And I hadn't even said hello yet.

"Why did you call me here?" she demanded. "I have some very serious paperwork that needs to be completed tonight." She was back in businesswoman mode and her severe bun was evidence thereof. This was Executive Susannah, inconvenienced for unknown reasons.

"Well, you still have to eat, don't you?" I suggested, taking her coat. "Please, let my mom show you the movie room. We're all gathering in there until dinner is ready."

"I don't think you understand," Susannah said as Mom took her by the arm. "I don't appreciate being summoned to a place I've never been with no explanation whatsoever."

"That's nice, dear," Mom said, and made sure Susannah kept on walking.

I was hanging up her coat and hat—don't ask—when they reached the entrance to the movie room and I heard Executive Susannah's voice become that of Cheerleader Susannah, whom I believed I had met at the Harbor Haven Police Station earlier that day. "Steven!" she squealed, and Mom no longer needed to lead her by the arm, as she bounded out of my sight. Then I heard her say, "Harry!" and I remembered she knew Steven's dad. I couldn't read her inflection on that one—surprise? Confusion? Worry?

Mom gave me an eye roll and then turned back and walked into the movie room to organize the assembly.

I would have followed her, but Tony and Jeannie appeared in the doorway with both children in tow. "Couldn't get a sitter," Tony explained. "Short notice."

"I'll get Mom back into the kitchen with Liss and they can stay in there," I said. "We keep the sharp objects above toddler level."

"Alson," said Oliver. It's the best he can do with my name, and I adore it. He grabbed my calf and hugged it. "Alson."

"Hi, Ollie. Wanna see Melissa?"

"Yeah!"

"I'll take them," Jeannie told me. "But then I'm coming in to watch whatever it is you're doing. This should be fun."

Tony followed me into the movie room, where quite the crowd had gathered. He was greeted warmly by Mom and Josh, nodded at by The Swine and fairly ignored by everybody else. Of course the ghosts couldn't acknowledge him, but Maxie, back on this floor of the house, had once tried to kiss Tony and hasn't forgiven him for it, looked displeased.

Mom did indeed go to help with the kids in the kitchen, and Jeannie almost immediately took her place among us.

So there we were: The Swine and his parents, Maroni and his lifeguards, Susannah hanging off The Swine's arm while keeping an eye on Harry and being ignored for her trouble, Bobby just sitting nearby like a loyal golden retriever, Josh, Tony, Jeannie and me among the living. And the three ghosts hovering in the air over it all like a transparent Greek chorus.

I got to fulfill a lifetime ambition at that moment, and I savored it. I walked to the front of the room, stood in front of the large TV and whistled through my teeth for quiet, which surprisingly I got. All eyes were upon me. I wished Melissa could be here to witness my moment of triumph, but there were potatoes to be mashed.

Having rehearsed this repeatedly, I knew not to clear my throat ahead of time. I simply looked out over the crowd and smiled.

"So," I said. "I suppose you're wondering why I asked you all here tonight."

Twenty-two

For all my effort, I got little more than a tableau of stares.

"What is this," I asked, "an audience or an oil painting?"

Paul looked over at my father and then pointed at the wire from his homemade electrical doohickey. "Does this go straight to the power supply, or is there a breaker?" he asked.

Dad didn't blink. "Breaker. Number seven."

"What are you going on about?" Constance demanded. "Is this some kind of a joke?" Constance would have to ask because she has never been sincerely amused by anything in her life, so she wouldn't be familiar with a joke. Unless it was the reverend with the garters. He was pretty funny.

Paul stroked his goatee, but just once. Interest, not fascination. "Any way to bypass it?" he asked my father.

"Maybe," Dad said, nodding. "Want to take a look?"

He headed toward the wall, probably with the intention of entering it.

"Let me get a flashlight," Paul said. He was actually going to leave the room in the middle of an investigation to tend to this Frankenstein experiment that was likely to burn my house down. Now I was annoyed on top of feeling insulted.

"We're here to discuss the murder of Maurice DuBois," I reminded, well, everybody. I tried to regain the air of dignity and drama I mistakenly thought I'd had the minute before. "The most likely answer is that the person who shot him is in this room right now."

Josh stood up and walked to my side. That's what he does, and that's the reason I wanted to marry him. One of them, anyway. He gestured to me to lean close, so I did. "Is dinner going to be ready soon?" he asked quietly.

Saying the wedding was off would probably be an over-reaction. Instead I decided we could get married and he could keep living in his apartment. Wait. That was more convenient for him. No. He'd have to come live with me. That'd be his punishment.

"What makes you think that?" At least someone had some interest. Jeannie.

"Everyone who knew DuBois was in New Jersey is here," I explained. "He flew in from Los Angeles the same night as you, Steven, and that means he followed you. He probably wasn't planning the trip, just like you weren't."

The Swine seemed wildly interested in his shoes. He did not look up or speak. They must have been some shoes.

"I didn't know he was here," Susannah pointed out. "I never even heard about the guy until you told me his name."

"That's what you're saying," I answered. "But you couldn't possibly be stupid enough to buy that line about throwing the briefcase in the Shark River, so I'm assuming everything you say is part of an act of some kind."

"What do you mean, stupid?" she demanded.

Lou Maroni stretched as if he'd been sleeping for hours and had just awoken. "It's not that this isn't fascinating," he said, "but my original plan was to take your ex-husband here and *persuade* him to tell me about the patent documents, so if you don't have something new to tell us, why don't I just go about taking care of that?" He gestured to the statuary who had walked in with him, and they moved back over toward The Swine.

"Wait," Susannah said, voice hushed. The entire group stopped and looked at her. She pointed at me. "*You're* the ex-wife?"

I rethought my position on her not being stupid.

Harry Rendell walked to my left side, opposite Josh. "What's really going on here?" he asked me in a conspiratorial tone. "That guy wants to work Steven over?"

"It's something he's been talking about," I told him. "I've been trying to think of reasons he shouldn't."

Harry snorted just a little. "Really?"

"You're terrible." I hit him on the arm.

"You have no idea." Was he trying to tell me something? Could Harry have shot DuBois so his son would have the clear rights to SafT? I couldn't really picture that.

"I told you, Lou," The Swine chimed in. "I really and truly have no idea where those papers are. I'm not sure Maurice had them on him. Maybe the guy who shot him took them with him."

I looked up at Paul, who was deep in discussion with my father about electrical lines. I was running out of allies in this room, and pretty much everyone I'd ever met was here. "Look," I said with a new huskiness in my voice that was born of frustration. "Nobody gets any chicken until we hear some truth. So we're going to go around the room and everyone here is going to say where they were at ten o'clock on Saturday." That was roughly the time DuBois had breathed his last in an alley behind a tavern.

"I was home with the kids, and so was Tony," Jeannie volunteered. You can always count on Jeannie to get the ball rolling, something her baby daughter found seriously hilarious in other contexts.

"Thanks, Jean. Okay, Susannah. How about you?"

"I don't want to say." She was looking suddenly nervous, not making eye contact with anyone in the room, which was no small feat. "I'll pass."

"Fine, but you just became the prime suspect." I didn't think for one second that Susannah Nesbit had shot DuBois, but I'd decided I didn't like her, so I had no motivation to let her off the hook. Besides, I couldn't let the others in the room think that refusing to answer was a viable option or by my own rules, I wouldn't be eating dinner soon.

"I didn't shoot anybody," Susannah protested. "I just don't want to say where I was, okay?" Was she looking at Harry again?

"No. It's not okay. You're the only person I know for sure had the murder weapon in her possession. So you don't get to say that you don't feel like talking. That makes you sound even more guilty, and I can call Lieutenant McElone to get some more answers if you like. Her questioning carries a few more consequences."

"Okay!" She couldn't decide if she should be indignant or petulant and came down in the middle, which was essentially a sixteen-year-old being told she couldn't go to the party if her geometry grade didn't go up ten points. "The fact is I was with a guy." Her look immediately went to The Swine, who seemed not to have heard because damn, those shoes were so engrossing. "I'm so sorry, Steven."

At the sound of his name my ex-husband looked up. "Why?"

Harry, I noticed, had not reacted at all to what was being said, and seemed utterly uninterested in Susannah in any way. Which was kind of a relief.

I decided to move on. "Constance?" I asked.

She looked at me as if I'd said her name in Swahili. "Yes?" Like son, like mother. Or something.

"Where were you Friday evening around ten?" I said, voice as sweet as whatever dessert Melissa was preparing in the kitchen, which was certain to be amazing.

"Oh, don't be absurd." My ex-mother-in-law sniffed. "I don't have to justify my every movement to you."

Now, I could definitely picture Constance eliminating her son's competition without so much as a flutter, so that answer was interesting. I fixed her with a look. "Don't you?" I asked.

Constance blanched and stole a glance at her husband, who seemed just as uninterested in her questioning as he was in his son's girlfriend, who knew him first. He was strolling the perimeter of the room, stopping to glad-hand with one of Maroni's sculptures for a moment before realizing the man wasn't talking back, but was staying within grabbing distance of Harry's son in case Maroni called for that yet again.

"Fine," she said, forcing herself to look away from Harry. "I was at the movies. With *my husband*."

"What did you see?" I asked.

"What?"

You heard me. "What did you see? What movie?"

Constance looked at Harry again. "What movie did we see Saturday night?" she asked him.

He looked slightly startled, as if he'd been thinking about something else entirely, like how to find a really good sirloin in the supermarket when you couldn't see the bottom of the steak because of the packaging. "Movie?" he asked.

"Saturday night," Constance emphasized. "Remember?"

"You can't send him signals," I suggested. "He's not going to pick up on your game. Where were you really?"

She attempted to stare me down. "We were at the *movies*," she said.

I stared back. "No. You weren't. So where were you?"

"Come on." The Swine, apparently having memorized his shoes and ignored the fact that Susannah was as much a two-timer as he was, stood up. "You know for a fact that my mother didn't shoot Maurice DuBois. She didn't even know *I* was in town Saturday night. So can we get to the point, please?"

"Well, you're still the most obvious candidate, so how about telling us where you were after you left Josh's apartment Saturday night?" I said.

Steven did exactly what I wouldn't have expected. He looked over at Josh and smiled. That was creepy enough, but it got worse when he asked my fiancé, "Do you want to tell her, or should I?" There was no way anything said immediately after that could be good.

My father's head pivoted quickly to stare at Josh, but it couldn't beat mine because I had started looking at him as soon as Steven began to speak. Josh looked somewhat bemused but not seriously guilty about anything. I guessed that was a good thing, anyway.

"Well, the truth is Steven never left the apartment that night," Josh said, looking at me. "I was covering for him because he wanted people to think he was out."

"You lied to me?" The words came out of my mouth, but I hadn't planned them. It was like someone else was speaking and I was listening.

"I'm sorry, Alison. It seemed like the thing to do at the time. I didn't know someone was going to get shot."

"You lied to me," I repeated. That was a little more conscious, but not much. Then I turned toward The Swine, who I now realized was the source of all that was evil in the world and needed to be cast out before the sun rose again. Or something.

Luckily Jeannie stepped forward and took over, advancing on The Swine. "Why on earth would you make him lie to her about you being out when you were staying in?" Yeah. How did that make sense?

"There were people looking for me," Steven mumbled. "I didn't want them to find me, not then. And I knew they'd come here. So if Alison thought I was somewhere else, they wouldn't look for me where I really was." That was the purest example of Swine Logic I could recall hearing. It sounded perfectly reasonable until you thought about what the words actually meant.

But I was still stunned by Josh's part in this business. "So that's what you were talking about when he came to see you in the store today," I said.

Josh did a double take. "What?"

"When Steven drove to Madison Paints today. What was that all about?" It didn't matter who was in the room anymore; I was barely noticing there were other people despite the multitudes in front of me. All that mattered was clearing this all up with Josh, because the floorboards under my feet felt like they were shifting in an earthquake and I was finding it hard to stand straight. I had to get my balance again, and he was the source.

"Oh no, Ghost Lady." Everett had apparently shown up from . . . somewhere . . . behind me. "Mr. Kaplan wasn't at the paint store when your husband arrived today. He spent his time talking to a much older gentleman." *Josh's grandfather Sy Kaplan, the original owner of Madison Paints.*

"What?" Josh sounded puzzled.

"You went to see Sy?" I pivoted and faced The Swine before Josh could react further. He no doubt understood I'd heard that from a ghost, and was certainly putting two and two together even as I spoke. If our engagement survived this evening, the marriage would be a piece of cake.

"Joshie here had told me about him, and he sounded like quite a guy," The Swine answered. I saw Josh wince at the very idea of being called by such a juvenile nickname, one he'd hated even when I first met him at the age of twelve. "I figured I'd go and see for myself."

Well, that was certainly a crock, but I couldn't think my way around it and confronting Steven directly had led to our getting married, which was not the kind of thing I'd especially like to have happen again. So I decided to wait until the nagging feeling in the back of my mind manifested itself and then I could get him right between the eyes.

Unless Maroni and his twin giant redwoods got there first. "This isn't getting us anywhere," the (alleged) crime boss said. "I won't trouble you any further. Stevie!" He gestured toward The Swine, who could now swallow that "Joshie" and see how it tasted.

But he was stopped in his tracks and those of his minions because my thirteen-year-old daughter appeared in the entrance to the movie room. "We've got dinner for everybody in the den!" she announced, and then marched out.

It was amazing the effect that child had on this room of people discussing which one of them had shot a man in the head. There was no question or argument. The two large appendages of Maroni did not even look to their boss for acknowledgment or instruction. Everyone just immediately started filing out of the room and heading toward the den.

I held back on Josh's arm. "I'm sorry it sounded like I didn't trust you," I said.

His stare was not exactly warm and inviting. "You sent a ghost to spy on me," he said. That wasn't the case, but I couldn't argue now because Josh was following the others into the den as Melissa had commanded.

I could see it was going to be a fun dinner.

Twenty-three

The chicken, done with a mango glaze, was astonishing. The carrot-and-cauliflower soufflé, a personal favorite of mine when Melissa is feeling ambitious, was superb. There were green beans that were terrific, and I don't even like green beans.

But I could barely eat a bite of anything. My fiancé was mad at me.

Well, *mad* might be an overstatement. Josh was clearly disappointed in me, and that was as negative as he'd ever been, which was very upsetting. He wasn't looking at me with an amused twinkle in his eye, and that was unusual, especially under these bizarre circumstances.

I didn't even get to sit next to him at the enormous table Mom had set in the den. It was the largest room in the house, so we could seat the rather bloated guest list now chowing down on what was, I was sure, the dinner for four

Mom had packed for when she left the house this morning.
She and Melissa were magicians with food.

And everyone was eating. Well, besides me. You'd have
thought that Maroni or his henchmen might have opted
out just because it didn't look sinister enough to ask for
another helping of soufflé. You might assume Constance,
whom I had never actually seen taking nourishment for
fear of adding an extra pound to her petite, patrician frame,
would have eaten some green beans and declared herself
full. But no, she was packing it in (daintily, of course) with
the rest of them, something I attribute to my astonishing
daughter's culinary prowess.

Jeannie and Tony, at the other end of the huge table,
were used to dinners à la Melissa, so they were relaxed
and happy. At a separate smaller table Ollie was eating the
same food as the rest of us (Mom had not brought Cheerios,
but I had some in the cabinet; they had proven unnecessary) while Molly was in her father's lap, not so much
eating as watching the process around the table with a high
level of fascination. She wasn't ready to get there yet, but
she knew where she wanted to go.

Bobby, always at Steven's elbow, had not relinquished
that position now, but he was taking in food so quickly I
wondered if he had eaten . . . ever before. He wasn't saying
much, but was nodding enthusiastically at everything
Dr. Frankenstein (my ex) said, polishing up his hunchback
and chuckling at The Swine's lame jokes. It was sort of
disgusting.

Mom, of course, was enjoying the compliments aimed
at her granddaughter, and although she had never really
connected with Steven's parents, she was seated next to
Harry Rendell and chuckling at something he'd said. Harry
might possibly have stopped for a drink on the way to my
house this evening.

Liss, as was her habit when people—especially those

who had not done so before—were sampling her cooking, was sitting at the head of the table, the best vantage point, and taking in every reaction. She doubts her abilities the way it is said that some of the greatest actors in the world have stage fright, and so every reassurance is absolutely necessary.

The only ones besides me not eating heartily were the ghosts, including Maxie, who had dropped into the room but was staying close to the ceiling with Everett nearby. She hadn't uncovered anything else of note yet, she told me, but felt that she should watch to see if there was some question she hadn't tried to answer to this point.

Actually there was one other person not heartily digging into the meal, and that was Josh, who seemed detached and stole glances at me when he thought I was turned away.

What had I done?

To be fair, I hadn't done that much. When I sent Everett out to tail The Swine and find out what he was up to, I had not expected him to visit Madison Paints. So my intention never had been to check up on Josh at all. You had to give me points for that, didn't you?

Well?

Still, I had accepted the information I was given and jumped to an unflattering conclusion without asking for an explanation. Maybe that was the problem here. I hadn't given the man I loved the benefit of the doubt. And I knew deep down that was indeed wrong.

But hadn't Josh lied to me? Hadn't he hidden Steven's true whereabouts on the night Maurice DuBois was murdered? What about that? And besides, who would have thought The Swine was driving all the way to Asbury Park to meet Sy Kaplan?

That was the part that was weird. That didn't make sense at all. And as Paul would say, when something really stuck out as unusual or uncharacteristic, you had to take

a closer look. I knew The Swine as well as anybody, and
the idea that he would show some interest in a ninety-two-
year-old man whose grandson was about to marry me was,
at best, suspicious.

It was bothering me that I couldn't talk directly to the
ghosts in this crowd. Really, Jeannie, Tony and of course
Mom and Melissa would have been fine with it, as would
Josh when he wasn't in a grumpy mood. But with the
Rendells—all three of them—in the room just itching for
an excuse to sue for custody of my daughter, not to mention
the three representatives of at least semiorganized crime,
it seemed a bad idea to start talking to the ceiling and then
getting answers.

So when the situation isn't working for you, change the
situation. I stood up. "I need something in the kitchen," I
said. If I could get out of the room and have my spooky
friends follow me, I could start getting some answers. I
started toward the kitchen door and noted that not one
ghost was following me.

Maxie and Everett were huddled in a corner, so I tried
to catch their eyes and got nothing. My father was near my
mother, as always, so looking in his direction would have
required a full hundred-and-eighty-degree turn, and while
I adore my dad, the fact was he probably had no information that would help the investigation at all.

But Paul was the brains of the detective agency, if there
had been a detective agency. So he was my best bet and
my most reliable source of confidence. I knew he'd be able
to give me an idea of what to do next.

Except that Paul was installing another of his homemade electrical boxes into an outlet near the floor under a
window and wasn't watching me. Luckily nobody was
looking toward him or there would be questions about a
flying black box. There were none.

The only person I could count on right at this moment was Melissa. And she was engrossed in her phone, looking something more than perplexed and perhaps a hair short of frantic. I was going to ask what could possibly have been that wrong, but she got up from the table and headed toward the stairs before there was the chance. I don't usually require Liss to ask to be excused—what is my dinner table, anyway: solitary confinement?—but she pretty much always sticks around to help clean up even when she was the primary chef for the evening. Something was up.

I'd already announced my intention to go to the kitchen, so at this point not going would have sent a very strange signal. I walked to the door and pushed it open, then went inside and started to wonder what the hell I was doing here and how this whole ridiculous ball had started rolling.

I decided it was the ghosts' fault. Mostly Maxie.

There I stood in the middle of my own kitchen with absolutely nothing to do, contemplating my life. All I'd wanted was to have a nice guesthouse on the Jersey Shore where I grew up, to share the area with people for the first time and help them love it the way I always had—and maybe to make a decent living doing that.

Was that really so much to ask? Apparently so. I hadn't even gotten this very room in shape before a certain ghost had dropped a heavy bucket on my head and gotten my attention. Now I couldn't extract these dead people from my life, and every other month it seemed someone was being murdered, leading me to be called upon for some reason I couldn't fathom to investigate.

Backing out wasn't even an option. This time The Swine had entangled me, not Paul, as had become the custom. But if I stuck by my vow to vindicate Melissa's father, would I alienate the guy I really wanted to stay with for the rest of my life—and possibly beyond, for all I knew? I couldn't put my finger on it, but I had no doubt in my mind at all that Steven was responsible for the current rift between Josh and me.

Wait. I'd come in here to think about Maurice DuBois's murder. What did I know for sure?

Maurice had shown up in my house looking for Steven, who had apparently gotten into some serious debt with the guy I had thought was Maurice's employer, Lou Maroni. But as soon as the two of them were (mostly) alone, they worked out some odd détente that had them both chuckling when leaving my library and, according to Maxie, agreed on the idea that I'd sell my house and give all the proceeds to my ex-husband, which made as much sense as . . .

. . . as two dead people floating around my house. Sense didn't have much to do with anything that had happened to me in the past four years.

But then Maurice had gotten himself a little bit killed in an alley outside a local bar. According to Josh, whom I could usually trust, Steven had been with him the whole time that was happening. So DuBois must have gotten himself into trouble with someone else very quickly.

Now, though, Maroni was saying—and Maxie was confirming independently—that Maurice DuBois had actually been the mastermind who had created SafT, the program everybody (except Maroni, until recently) thought was going to be bigger than Google. So the obvious motive was that someone had wanted to claim the patent on SafT and they shot DuBois and somehow took over the rights to the software.

You have no evidence, I could hear my inner Paul saying. *You have a theory that fits the few facts we know, but you have nothing that ties anyone to the DuBois killing. Even if that was the motive, you have no way of knowing who might have been the person pulling the trigger.*

My inner Paul is really annoying.

That left me with nothing. I didn't know who killed Maurice DuBois. I doubted it was Susannah, who couldn't decide if she was a killer shark businesswoman or The Swine's bubble-headed plaything. For one thing, she didn't seem to have a motive, although her story about throwing the gun in the river was reason enough to suspect her; it was so stupid you had to figure there was no better true explanation available.

The Rendells were never really serious suspects. I had just made them show up because I wanted to see Constance squirm with the knowledge that I had some blackmail material on her and could drop it at any time, even if I wouldn't ever do it. I liked Harry too much for that.

Maroni, or by extension one of the silent twins he'd brought with him? Why would they keep looking for Steven and then the patent if they'd already killed DuBois to get the patent? That didn't seem to hold water.

I was starting to think it was possible I had killed Maurice DuBois just to give myself some aggravation, which I was now doing with a great deal of success.

Maxie floated through the wall and hovered over me. "Where did you go?" she asked.

"Portugal. This is a film of me." I wasn't in the mood for small talk. Or couldn't you tell?

"What's your problem?" she persisted. "You got up and came in here for no reason and now you're standing in the middle of the room not doing anything."

"I've decided you're responsible for everything that's gone wrong with my life," I told her. "You dropped that bucket of compound on my head and since then I've had to deal with dead people and investigate murders. It's your fault."

"It was an accident," she said, because that's what she always says when the subject is broached. "Besides, if all this hadn't happened, you wouldn't have met Josh and you wouldn't be getting married." And there were people who thought Maxie actually wasn't paying attention most of the time. Okay, not people. Me.

"Josh isn't talking to me," I said, and to my amazement there was a sob in my voice. Was I back in tenth grade? A guy didn't like me enough and so I was going to cry? This wasn't turning out to be a great day.

Maxie waved a hand. "He'll get over it. You're just difficult to deal with sometimes." What Maxie giveth, Maxie taketh away.

Maxie! "Where's Everett?" I asked suddenly, perhaps so suddenly that it startled her. "I need to know what happened exactly when Steven went to Madison Paints."

"You already know." Maxie recovers quickly and is always happy to remind me when I'm wrong. "Josh wasn't there."

"That's not the point. Get Everett."

She was so taken with my authoritative manner, it seemed, that she didn't even complain about my ordering her around like she does when I'm not actually ordering her around. Now I was and she simply obeyed, heading through the wall to go fetch her boyfriend.

This was going to be my last case, I would tell Paul. If he and Maxie wanted to quit doing the spook shows and making my guesthouse a destination for those wanting scares that didn't really exist anyway, so be it. I could run an honest inn the way I'd intended before my head started bleeding. I didn't have to put myself through this again and again.

I sort of heard a ghost coming through the wall (there wasn't really an audible "whoosh" because they were not actually displacing air at all, but there was an audible sense that something was happening in a direction so you could turn your head in time) and expected Maxie and Everett. Instead I got Paul. And I was about to launch into my speech about no more nosing around in other people's murders when he launched into one of his own.

"There's a thunderstorm on the way, Alison!" Paul was as giddy as a boy of ten when a new *Star Wars* movie is opening the next day. "It'll be here in less than an hour. I have to get my equipment ready—this is it!"

The man had gone insane. "It's February, Paul. The forecast is for maybe—*maybe*—an inch of snow tonight. Nobody said anything about you being able to electrocute yourself into the next realm. Tonight."

"You don't understand. There are lightning storms with snow. It doesn't happen often, but it does happen. Anyway, I have no time!" And down he went through the floor-boards, heading no doubt toward his pile of recycled electronics in a frantic dash to black out most of Ocean County.

There was no point in going down there to watch. I'd told Paul he could play with his toys when the time was right, and even if this was an opportunity to solve a murder and he should have been all about that, it was clear Paul's priorities were elsewhere tonight. Trying to persuade him to change his mind was like trying to convince a beagle puppy that chewing shoes didn't really make any sense when approached from a logical point of view.

That was when Maxie and Everett came phasing through, both wearing expressions of either concern or confusion. "Here's Everett," Maxie said, apparently now operating as his agent. "What did you need, exactly?"

Anne Kaminsky stuck her head through the door. "Excuse me," she said. "I don't want to interrupt the dinner party."

I gestured her in. "It's fine, Anne," I said. "This was just sort of impromptu. What can I do for you?"

"Have you seen Mel? I've been looking for him, but he's not around."

That was all I needed—a missing guest. "He's not in

his room?" Clearly he was not, so I went on. "Did he mention any plans today?"

Anne shook her head. "What do you mean, 'his room'?" she asked.

What did she mean, what did I mean? "The one downstairs. The one you were in until you asked me for a separate room."

"Oh, that's just for sleeping," she said, waving a hand. "I couldn't spend one more night in bed with that man. He snores like an outboard motor. Honestly I don't know how anybody in the house gets a wink of sleep once he gets going."

Just then the door to the basement stairs opened and Mel burst through. "Annie! You've gotta see! All the gadgets are putting themselves together in midair!" He grabbed his wife by the hand and pulled her toward the stairs. She chuckled as she went.

"Who'd want to leave that?" she said to me just before the door shut behind her.

There just wasn't time to deal with Paul's invention. I looked up at Everett. "What happened when Steven went to Madison Paints today?" I asked. "In detail."

Everett, always on task, did not hesitate. "He clearly knew your fiancé would not be present. He went directly to the older gentleman and introduced himself."

"He used his real name?" I asked. You can't assume anything with The Swine other than that he'll always be a swine.

Everett nodded. "Quite accurately. He said he wanted to meet the gentleman because his grandson would be marrying you and he was particular about that sort of thing."

Yeah, like that would be true. This was the gist. "Did he bring anything? Give Sy anything or leave anything there?"

Everett thought about that. "I don't think he gave anything to the older gentleman," he said. I loved how polite

Everett was being—there were few people older than Sy. "But it is possible that while the older gentleman was attending to a customer, your ex-husband might have looked through some papers on the desk."

"Papers on the—"

We were interrupted by a loud burst of sound from the den. Maxie, always quickest, shot through the wall as Everett turned to follow and I took the conventional route toward the kitchen door.

But once I pushed the door open and looked into the den, I stopped in my tracks.

All my "guests," except of course the ones who were paying, were at the table, each looking suitably astonished or upset. Mom's face was puckered like she wanted to explain the rudeness going on but couldn't find the words. Jeannie had pushed both of her children under the table and was looking frightened. Constance seemed appalled, but that wasn't unusual. Harry was pale and his eyes were wide, and that was unusual.

Tony looked mad, like he wanted to hit someone, which was roughly the same as the way Josh's face looked. Bobby was, of course, watching Steven, but he looked especially concerned. The Swine was once again finding astonishing nuance in his shoes, but Lou Maroni and his Band of Renown appeared extra-displeased.

Standing near the head of the table, where thankfully my daughter was no longer seated, was a rather squat-looking man in a signature overcoat, cherry red scarf wrapped around his neck and hat pulled down low on his head. A few snowflakes clung to the brim of his fedora. He was holding a very efficient-looking gun in his right hand.

It was Maurice DuBois. Because apparently in my house, everybody comes back from the dead.

Twenty-four

The only trouble this time was that the guy holding the gun on everyone I had ever met was not the least bit dead; he was not transparent or floating in the air, and it was obvious from the looks on every face that he was clearly visible to the gathered group.

I stared. Lieutenant McElone had said the identification was positive and Phyllis Coates had confirmed it—the dead man was Maurice DuBois and yet there he was, holding my entire den full of people at bay. I wondered if it was time for Maxie to get her shovel.

Actually no. I knew it was time for Maxie to get her shovel.

But I had come in after the festivities apparently got started. Maroni was looking even more discontented than usual, which was something of a scary thought. He glared at DuBois and said, "Who told you it was okay for you to be in charge?"

DuBois pointed to himself with his free thumb. "I don't need you to tell me when I can go to the men's room anymore, Lou. I get to make my own decisions. And I get to make yours, too."

"That doesn't have anything to do with us," Bobby told him. "You should let me go. And Steven." Nobody paid any attention to him, but he was probably used to that.

What I felt stirring in me was not what I would have expected. I should have been petrified. I should have stood stock-still, unable to decide on a logical course of action that would resolve the situation without putting me or my loved ones (the others were secondary concerns) in any increased danger. I should indeed have been feeling my stomach dropping into my shoes.

Instead I was getting really, really mad.

"What are you doing here?" I demanded of the man with the gun. "How dare you walk into my house and wave that thing around? I have a reputation to maintain! This is a public accommodation!" It was clear I had no idea what I was talking about.

Everyone turned and looked at me with various degrees of horror on their faces. Mom very quietly admonished, "Alison," and flashed her eyes in the direction of the intruder. Like I hadn't seen he was brandishing a deadly weapon.

"My apologies, Ms. Kerby," DuBois said. "But I'm afraid I have business here that requires I act more brazenly that I might prefer. I'm sure you understand."

I was about to tell him that I understood exactly how to call the police (and get shot) when Paul rose through the floorboards, his face literally glowing with excitement.

"It's almost time!" He floated over to the box he'd installed behind the dinner table under one of the windows, completely oblivious of the situation unfolding at the other end of the room. It was a big room, but seriously. Man with gun.

"Shovel," Everett said, and Maxie, with a "here we go again" sigh, headed out through the French doors toward the shed. Everett pushed himself down toward DuBois, presumably to hold the man back if he tried to do anything. Everett's not great with tactile manipulation of objects (that's touching stuff) but he can muster the ability when he needs it.

"I have two small children," Jeannie meekly told DuBois, who looked at her as if wondering what that had to do with anything. Then he shook his head and pursed his lips.

"I'm not going to shoot your kids, lady. Calm down."

I figured it was best to get to the point. "Well, who are you going to shoot? You brought the gun. You intend to use it. Who's getting shot? I want to know which area of the rug is going to need cleaning tomorrow." I didn't know where this stuff was coming from.

"If everybody cooperates, I'm not going to shoot anyone," DuBois said. It was exactly what I would have expected he'd say given my prompt. If there's anything more annoying than having an armed gunman interrupt your dinner party, it's having to act as his straight man.

Susannah, halfway between her two personas because she couldn't decide which one would do her more good, volunteered, "I'm cooperating." DuBois, who in all likelihood had forgotten she was there, just squinted at her and then looked back toward the Maroni party.

"What do you want?" Maroni snarled at him. "Haven't you gotten enough already?"

"Not quite. I can walk out of here and live a decent life now, but I need those papers in order to be really rich. And I want to be really rich. I think I deserve it."

There was—I'm not kidding—a flash of lightning at that very moment, and the crack of thunder that followed was only a couple of seconds later. The storm was close. Paul rose and looked back at me. "You see?"

Fighting back the urge to scream at him to pay attention, I turned away and looked for Maxie in the rafters, but she had not yet arrived. Everett was still poised over DuBois, wiggling his fingers in anticipation of grabbing the man by the arms before any damage could be done. But he was clearly unsure of his skills and I didn't want him to try anything he wasn't certain about when a stray bullet could be the result. I shook my head slightly and Everett caught the gesture. He lowered his arms but stayed close.

"I don't get this," I said to DuBois. "You apparently have everything you want. Why are you here? What did you come here to do?"

"I need some paperwork these gentlemen know about, and if they produce it for me, nobody will have to suffer at all," the guy with the gun said. "It's about as simple as you can get, really."

"The patent papers?" I said. "I never heard anything about this thing until an hour ago, and this is what it was all about?"

There was a roll of thunder. Bobby squealed a little. I didn't turn around, because the sight of Paul looking as if it were Christmas Eve would have put me through the roof, and I didn't get to phase harmlessly through the wood and plaster the way he could.

"See, now everyone knows about this," DuBois said. He walked slowly toward The Swine, whose attention had shifted from his shoes to the ceiling, and he couldn't even see Dad up there, paralyzed by the same situation as Maxie would be when she got back—any sudden movement could have unintended bad consequences. There were just too many people in the room.

"Maybe we should adjourn this meeting to the movie room and just bring the people who are involved," I suggested. "There are a lot of civilians here, and you know you don't want to hurt them." I took a step toward the door and noted Josh standing and getting between me and the gun. I guessed he wasn't that mad at me.

He leaned over and got close to my ear. "Nice plan," he said, "but I don't think he's going for it."

"We're not moving anywhere," DuBois said. Josh's insistence on always being right was getting on my last nerve. "If you think I'm letting anyone get on their cell phone and call the police while we're out of the room, you're crazy, Ms. Kerby, and I don't think you're crazy."

That made one of us.

"Okay, I get that," I said. "But I don't see how this is helping."

"It would have helped if you'd let me take this mook out of here and find out where the papers are," Maroni said, pointing to The Swine. He had a decent point, but that wasn't the issue right at the moment.

But DuBois looked positively stunned when he heard Maroni. "You mean you don't know where the papers are, either?" he asked, clearly astonished.

"No. Only Stevie here knows."

Susannah, who had stood to get closer to The Swine, stopped. You could see the wheels turning in her head: Was it better to show some loyalty to the guy she thought might become very wealthy soon, or stay back if he was going to be in the line of fire? She made her decision and took the seat Jeannie had vacated to get under the table with her children, where she was organizing a game of peekaboo for Molly and I Spy for Oliver. Say what you want about Jeannie, she was all about the children.

Alas, her purse and therefore her cell phone were still

hanging from the chair she'd left, and Susannah didn't even know enough to look for the phone, as if that would have done her any good.

Constance, apparently appalled that no one was watching her be appalled, let out a disapproving sigh. Her husband, although looking not as frightened as before—you can get used to anything—had his feet up on the vacated chair next to his, which I think had been Bobby's. His shoes were off. Harry might get shot, but he'd be comfortable until then.

The Swine, taking note of the way the tides were turning in the room, did not stand up. No sense making himself a better target. But he could still talk, and that had always been his strength.

"You can't shoot me if you want those forms," he told DuBois. "If I'm dead you'll never find them."

"So you do know where they are," Maroni said. He shook his head and clucked his tongue. "Not nice keeping that from us, Stevie." He crossed his arms. "Really. Bad form." The two woolly mammoths on either side of him crossed their arms and shook their heads in a weird mirror image of their boss. I didn't know what those guys were getting paid, but they were sure worth it in loyalty.

"Let me see if I get this right," I said as Maxie, trench coat in place large enough to hide a Sherman tank, floated in through the back wall. "Almost everybody here was involved in this whole SafT thing, on the assumption that this software was going to be the next huge thing in tech. Lou here put several hundred thousand dollars in it and then got cold feet."

Maxie swung around the back of DuBois, presumably to make it less visible when she revealed whatever lethal weapon she was carrying and minimizing the chances that he'd detect the movement and randomly shoot someone. I was hoping she'd do something before Melissa decided the phone-based crisis was over and came back to get some further accolades after serving dessert.

"So Lou decided to get his money back from Steven," I continued. "Steven found out he was a wanted man, so he flew here to Jersey, thinking that would make him safe. But apparently everyone west of the Rockies knew he was here, so that didn't help and Lou sent you out to talk some sense into him." I looked at DuBois, who appeared to be listening to the story and wondering how it would come out, which was something I didn't want to think about just yet.

Maxie was looking for the precise moment to take off the trench coat. I assumed the shovel was inside, but with Maxie it was never a good idea to anticipate. She could have had anything from a pair of tweezers to a rocket launcher in there and it wouldn't have surprised me. I didn't want to talk to her if I didn't have to, but she was filling the void with a running commentary on the situation like Bob Costas calling a Mets game.

"He's moving to the left and I'm looking right at the leggy blonde," she said. "I do something now and she's gonna see it. Is that okay?" I gave my head a small shake. If there was a way to get through this without involving ghosts, it would be preferable. Made it that much easier to explain to McElone and, you know, everyone else. Cut back on the paperwork. But if it came down to a gunshot-versus-ghost exposure, Maxie was going to open her trench coat.

"That's sort of what happened," DuBois said in answer to my speculation.

"The part I don't get is how the guy in the alley got shot, and why the police think he's Maurice DuBois," I said.

The room went suddenly silent. All the alleged con-spirators in the room (that is, Maroni's group, DuBois and, yes, The Swine) stared at me with expressions that indicated I had said something really, really stupid. It's not like I'm not used to that, but I hadn't been expecting it.

Maroni grinned and broke the moment. He looked over at the man holding the gun. "Yeah. Explain that one, Richie."

Richie?

Twenty-five

"Richie?" Maxie sounded confused.

"Richie?" Tony wasn't far behind, but he didn't know it. "Who's Richie?"

"He is," Lou Maroni said, the big satisfied grin still on his face. "Always has been." He turned in Richie's (since that was who he appeared to be) direction. "How'd you get to be Maurice DuBois, Richie? I'm guessing it happened around the time you put a couple of bullets into him?"

Well, that answered one question. So Maroni hadn't actually shot Maurice DuBois, and neither had anyone else I'd suspected. The guy I knew as Maurice DuBois had shot Maurice DuBois and I was definitely going to need an aspirin very soon.

"I don't have to answer to you anymore," Richie said.

"Richie?" I looked at The Swine. "*Cousin* Richie?"

"I had to justify it somehow," Steven said to his shoe-laces. "It was a joke."

"It doesn't make sense," Maxie was musing. "I heard them. I went into the room when your ex and this guy were talking and they had this joke about call him Maurice. He had to be Maurice."

This is what happens when you send Maxie and not Paul into a room and expect an accurate report. You get the Maxie version of things, which can be easily distracted by a shiny object. So I turned and looked for Paul, but he was no longer in the room, no doubt in the basement readying his status-elevation equipment for the coming . . .

Boom! Thunder. Not terribly far away. So there was such a thing as snow thunderstorms. You learn something new every day. Now if I could just make sure everyone lived to tell someone about it.

"What was that?" Maroni spun and looked up. Because now you can see thunder, apparently.

"Thundersnow," Susannah said. She reached over to the table and picked up a small piece of chicken, which she chewed thoughtfully. "It's a thing. Usually comes from a strong upward motion within the cold sector of an extra-tropical cyclone."

There was a long moment of staring in her direction, which she didn't notice immediately because she was eyeing a dinner roll. She looked up. "What?" Nobody answered her.

Steven looked at me sheepishly. "I had to meet with him quietly. We developed this idea that if he was Maurice DuBois, he could have the rights to SafT. So I told people I was visiting my cousin Richie. But I didn't know you were going to kill Maurice, Richie. I thought you were going to con him into letting you assume his identity. What happened?"

"It was a great plan, Steven," Bobby said. Then I was pretty sure he just faded back into transparency, which was something I'd only seen ghosts do before. Bobby could manage it just by being Bobby.

"I don't have to answer to you, either," Richie said. "I'm done being everybody's stooge." That didn't sound good. It sounded too final. "Now you're going to tell me where I can find those papers that say Maurice DuBois owns the patent to SafT, and I'm going to go on being Maurice DuBois."

"You can't do that." My mother, the voice of all that is fair and equitable in the world. "The police know Maurice DuBois is dead. You can't just assume his identity. They found him shot and killed. They're looking for you." *That's it, Mom. Get the guy with the gun even more nervous.*

"True, but this might not be the time," my father said to her gently.

"Oh," Mom said.

Richie turned toward her, which meant the gun turned toward her. "Oh, what?"

"Oh, sorry," Mom tried. "I was probably mistaken about that." *Way to cover, Mom.*

Maroni stood up. "No, she's right," he said, ambling casually toward Richie. "You're pretty cooked, Rich. Now, suppose I help you. Is that worth part of SafT?"

I don't know a lot about crime—I run a guesthouse on the Jersey Shore—but I did know that two bad guys making a deal with each other couldn't be a good thing. The tide was turning and The Swine knew it was coming straight at him.

"Hey, guys," he said. "This can be good for all of us. SafT is still a gold mine, and with Maurice out of the picture—may he rest in peace—there's a larger pie to divide up."

"Yeah?" Maroni asked. "The way *I* see it, you're not offering anything, and if the pie only has to be cut in two halves, we get more than if you make us cut it in thirds. So what reason do we have to include you? The patent papers?"

Steven started tapping his foot impatiently, as if waiting for the brilliant idea he knew was just on the edge of his brain to manifest itself. But the best he could come up with was "I had it first. I let you guys in on SafT or you wouldn't even know there was such a thing." That was not going to help anybody, and The Swine knew it. His foot tapped harder. I thought he might cry.

Josh put an arm around my waist, which was definitely a good sign. Then I realized he was angling to stand in front of me if there was trouble. Tony, too, was now standing up and leaning toward Mom's chair. The two Big Strong Men were going to protect us little ladies, and as comforting as the thought might have been, I was tired of being protected. I was tired of being threatened. And most of all, I was tired of The Swine.

"I know where the patent papers are," I said. "But if you want them, you have to agree to my terms."

Everyone turned toward me, each (including, I noted, Josh and my mother) with an expression of absolute amazement. They thought I wasn't capable of playing in this league? I'd show them.

Now all I had to do was figure out whether what I had said was true.

"What just happened?" I heard Jeannie call from under the dining table.

"Just stay down there," Tony told her.

"Your terms?" Maroni seemed more amused than surprised. "What are your terms?"

"Alison," Steven jumped in before I could answer. "I'm begging you, don't get in over your head. You don't know what you're saying."

If there was one thing I definitely didn't need, it was The Swine telling me I was just a silly girl and should sit and be quiet while the boys worked out their problem. "Shut up, Steven," I said. "I'm negotiating."

At the sound of the word *negotiating*, Constance perked up. "I think my husband and I should be allowed to leave," she said. "We were invited under false pretenses."

She tried to stand, but Richie waved her back into her seat with his gun hand.

Josh, hint of a smile on his face, leaned over and whispered in my ear, "Let's get married Saturday."

That didn't throw me off, but it did sidetrack me. "W-What?" I stammered.

"You heard me."

"What are your terms?" Maroni repeated. "The clock is ticking."

Josh stepped to the side. He knew I was fairly bullet-proof as long as Maroni and Richie thought I was valuable to them. He was confident enough not to worry if I took charge of a situation.

That was the man I was marrying. Saturday.

I looked at Maroni, whose men were now standing and flanking him, and Richie, whose right hand must have been awfully tired of holding that gun. His arm drooped a little. "Simple. You get what you want, but everybody here goes free and nobody gets shot. I'll tell you where to go, we'll even give you the key to get in, and I never see any of you guys again. How's that for easy?"

"And let you call the cops the second we're out the door?" Maroni sneered. "You hand us a key to some house or something and we leave. The next thing you're on your phone to the police and they get wherever we're going at least fifteen minutes before we do. Was that your plan?"

Actually it hadn't been—I was just going to let them get the forms they wanted and leave as long as I didn't have to put up with this anymore—but I could see Maroni's point. "Okay. Tell you what. You can take Steven with you."

All right, that was sort of a divorce thing. As long as

they got what they wanted, I expected no harm would come to The Swine that wasn't financial in nature.

"Oh, we're going to take Stevie, but that's not gonna stop you from calling the cops," Maroni answered. "We could take your daughter." He looked in the direction of the stairs.

"No, you can't." The words came simultaneously from me, Mom, Dad (whose vocal effectiveness was limited in this crowd), Josh and The Swine.

I stared into Maroni's eyes. "You make that a condition and I will definitely give you the address of the nearest police station instead of the place where the patent forms are sitting, just waiting for you to pick them up. You want to take that chance?"

Tony insinuated himself between one of Maroni's gorillas and the man himself. The bodyguard gave him a shove and it looked like it might devolve, but Maroni held up his hand to get his man to stop.

"Nobody's gonna get hurt unless it's necessary," he said. "Take it easy."

Richie, weariness and anger in his face, fixed his aim on Maroni. "I told you, Lou. You're not giving the orders. I am. The little girl is out of it. Steven's going and you're going. But I'm staying here."

Okay, that was unexpected. "Huh?" both Maroni and I asked. I thought it was a fair question.

"That's how it's gonna work. You take your men and Steven to wherever she sends you." He gestured at me, as if anyone thought he meant someone else. "But you stay in touch on your phone to mine every second of the way. The first time there's any trouble that I hear . . ." He walked over to me and stood only a few feet away, then raised the gun again. "I shoot her. We got that?"

I couldn't say that was my favorite possible plan, but it

did keep Melissa out of harm's way no matter what. Still, knowing that I wasn't exactly a hundred percent certain I was right about the location of the documents involved, I wasn't crazy about the possible consequences. "How about if something goes wrong, we just agree that was a possibility and chalk it up to experience?" I suggested.

Richie did not answer.

Maroni didn't look happy, but he nodded. He and his men started to gather their belongings, which no doubt included weapons of their own that you'd think they would have drawn by now. Never trust gangsters, I say.

The last person I expected to stand up for me—or anyone else—did exactly that, shaking his right foot as if it had fallen asleep.

"You don't need to threaten her," The Swine said. "Why not take Alison and leave me here in case there are issues?"

Yeah, see? He was trying to—wait. What? Take Alison! How did *that* get to be a good idea?

Luckily Maroni and Richie were having none of it. Apparently they had learned—hopefully under different circumstances—what I had about Steven: If he wanted you to do something, it was definitely not going to turn out well. For you.

"The plan goes as I said," Richie told him. "You go. She stays. That's it." Then, still standing only a couple of feet from me, he looked me straight in the eye with an expression that was not filled with warmth. "Now. Where are those papers?"

"They're in a store called Madison Paints in Asbury Park," I said. "Steven took them there this afternoon when he visited under a fake excuse."

Josh's head had turned at the mention of his business. "They're where?" he said in a low voice.

"You know the place?" Maroni asked him.

I was willing Josh to lie, but he'd pretty much already given away his position. "It's my store. I own it."

"Then you're coming along, too," Maroni said. "Get your coat. It's cold out."

One of the tree trunks in Maroni's entourage grabbed Josh's left arm, but he pulled it out of the larger man's grip. "Happy to go," he said, glaring at Maroni. "I want to make sure nothing gets damaged." He walked toward the door to the front room.

I moved quickly past Richie and got into Josh's path. He stopped. I grabbed for him and held him tightly to me. "I'm sorry," I said.

Josh held the clinch for a moment, then eased up and when I looked at him he was smiling. "If I get killed," he said, "will I be a ghost by Saturday? Because either way we're getting married."

"Can't be sure," I squeaked.

"You can be sure," Josh told me. "I'll be back."

Maroni and his two unspeaking accoutrements put on their signature overcoats, the same style and fabric as the one Richie wore. The Swine was persuaded to do the same, although his borrowed jacket was not as strong protection. Gloves and hats were donned. It took a long minute for everyone to be braced for the cold and wind—and lightning—outside, but eventually they were all ready and at the front door.

Bobby actually volunteered to go along, and I thought Maroni was going to say no just to be contrary, but Richie was happy to get rid of the toady, and I couldn't say I blamed him. I hoped Maroni had come in a large car.

Everett flew into the party. "I'll go along, Ghost Lady," he said. "Nothing will happen to your fiancé."

I nodded gratefully, not adding aloud that if something happened to my ex-husband I would not be nearly as upset.

That feeling was compounded when I got a look at The Swine's face. Walking out of the house, he turned for a moment to catch my gaze, smiled and winked. It was the most chilling moment of my life.

The door closed behind them, behind Josh, which was all that mattered, and I almost fell weeping into an easy chair in the den. I'd seen it in his face.

I was wrong about the patent papers. They weren't at Madison Paints. Steven had some kind of ridiculous plan and things were about to go very, very wrong.

Josh was going to be in danger and in all likelihood I was going to get shot.

That meant my ex was going to get custody of Melissa.

That couldn't happen.

Twenty-six

"What's the matter?" Mom asked. She'd just seen the look on my face and, being my mother, chose not to keep it to herself.

"Yeah," Maxie said. "You look like you just lost your best friend."

This was bad. This was really bad. In the annals of bad, there was very little bad that was as bad as this bad.

It was bad, is what I'm saying.

But I couldn't let Richie know that, so I put on my best neutral face and said, "A bunch of criminals and Steven just took my fiancé away and you're wondering what's the matter?" When you want to fool a man with a gun, berate your mother, I always say.

"Don't sass your mother," Dad said. "What are we going to do about this nut?" He pointed at Richie.

The nut, at that moment, was manipulating buttons on his cell phone, establishing the connection with the phone of either Maroni of one of the men with him, although I couldn't understand why guys who never spoke would need phones.

"This is a good time to clobber him," Maxie suggested. She opened the trench coat a bit and showed a baseball bat secreted inside. "He's not looking."

But Susannah gasped at the sight of the flying Louisville Slugger, so Maxie covered it back up. You could count on Susannah. Not to do anything useful, but she was at least always going to be an impediment.

"What was that?" she gaped.

"Lightning," I said. There had been a flash, so it was at least a plausible response. Susannah didn't react.

"I've got you," Richie said into his phone. The rest of us knew he had us; he had the gun and we didn't. And although there were in fact seven adult people in the room who were not Richie, rushing him while he was holding it didn't seem the best idea.

I wanted to use my ghosts. I really did. The three of them would have enjoyed it—except Paul wasn't paying attention—but you knew Maxie would have clobbered Richie happily and Dad would have applauded her efforts.

But now I knew that any serious disruption on this end of the conversation he was having (such as Richie suddenly losing consciousness and not answering) could have serious consequences for Josh and, I suppose, Steven. Telling Melissa about her dad would have been a problem. I guess.

There had to be something I could do. I'd played my best hunch and sent Josh—really the only one I cared about—after the Maltese Falcon of paperwork thinking I was being smart. But the smug grin on The Swine's face had convinced me beyond doubt that I'd been mistaken and worse, that he thought I had been trying to help by revealing the wrong address. Maroni and his men had given up squeezing the information out of Steven because I'd given it to them, except they were going to get to Madison Paints,

Josh was going to use his keys to let them in, and then they'd fail to find what they were looking for.

I couldn't see how Steven thought that was a good thing, but if he did, it was certain to be as awful as it could possibly get. I surveyed the room and saw people who had adjusted to a bad situation. Jeannie was still on the floor, although Molly was asleep and Oliver was bored, reaching for his father, who picked him up and sat him on his lap. Tony communicates with Ollie better than anyone else, and started improvising a story about a contractor whose client insisted on using thinner plywood than was necessary for the floor of a shower just to save money.

Harry, his feet assuaged, was pacing the room and gave me that same wink his son had shot from the front door when he was leaving. Somehow on the father it was charming and on the son it was the visual equivalent of fingernails on a blackboard.

Constance, who undoubtedly was trying to figure out how this was all my fault, did not realize that this was one of the only times since we'd met that I agreed with her. She had told Richie she needed the bathroom, and he had responded by confiscating every cell phone in the room and putting them in a small bag, then allowing her to leave and giving her exactly three minutes to return before he threatened to shoot her husband in the knee. Constance had managed not only to find another reason to be personally insulted, but also to get our only means of communication out of everyone's hands. Well done, Constance.

I walked to the farthest corner of the room from where Richie was standing, having put his phone (*he* got to have one) on the table next to him in speaker mode, although nothing of any interest was being said. I beckoned with my head to Maxie and she fluttered down.

"You want me to get him with the baseball bat?" she asked.

I shook my head. "We can't do anything until Josh is safe," I whispered. "Go upstairs and tell Liss not to come down under any circumstances."

"How about she calls the lady cop?" Maxie's eyes were fiery. She didn't care for anyone even getting near making danger for Melissa.

Again, I indicated no. "Anything happens here, Josh gets shot. Anything happens on Josh's end and *I* get shot. Probably everybody else, too. Tell Liss. Stay up there."

"Who are you talking to?" Richie yelled from across the room.

Maxie was already rising through the ceiling with a fist out like Iron Man. "Myself, and there's nothing you can do about it," I said. "I've seen therapists."

"Look," the gunman said. "I don't want to shoot you. Really. You seem like a perfectly nice person."

"She's better than that," my mother volunteered.

"But I need those papers and I need to be sure Maroni won't steal them," Richie went on, wisely choosing not to respond to Mom.

"What makes you think he'll bring them back here?" Harry asked.

Richie turned to face him. "What?"

"Why won't your friend just take these papers if they're so valuable? How come you think he'll drive all the way back here to give them to you?"

Richie raised the gun. "He knows I'll shoot you if he doesn't."

Harry shrugged. "What does he care?"

"You're not helping, Harry," I told him.

"It is what it is."

Constance came trotting into the room again. "It's three minutes! Don't shoot me!" she bleated. She sat back in the same chair she'd left, as if attendance were being taken and she didn't want to be marked absent.

I debated whether to tell him it would be okay if he did. I could tell Harry about the reverend after.

"They'll come back," Richie reassured himself.

The scene felt weird, as if it were from an old black-and-white movie showing how time had passed. There should have been a slowly turning ceiling fan and well-used ashtrays on the table. For all the tension about possibly being shot, mostly what was happening now was simply dull.

Maxie came back from Melissa's room, reporting that my daughter was worried but had been told with no wiggle room that she could not call for help or—definitely not—come downstairs to try to help. Maxie said she'd obtained this behavior by agreeing to fly up to the room periodically with updates. She had done so twice already, and I was afraid the reports were going to bore my daughter to tears. Nothing had changed.

At one point my mother drifted off to sleep and my father, despite not being capable of putting a foot on the ground, began to tiptoe exaggeratedly around her in fear of waking her up. The man was born to be a husband and a dad. Being dead didn't even slow him down a bit.

Throughout, Richie was sporadically talking to Maroni and his crew, now more pointedly because Harry had made him suspicious. When I got close enough, I could hear them discuss their distance from Josh's store, as well as, despite having the proprietor in the car, the instructions from the GPS Maroni had in what had to be a crowded vehicle.

Occasionally I'd hear Josh say something innocuous, giving me the impression he just wanted me to hear his voice and know it was still functioning. It wasn't the drive I was worried about. It was what was almost certainly going to happen when they arrived and didn't find the treasure they sought.

There was a flash of lightning and then some thunder.

Susannah had mentioned that thundersnow didn't often last very long, making me wonder why she'd strayed from her first true love, which had clearly been meteorology.

Paul rose through the floor quickly, positively aglow, which was due either to his state of excitement or too much exposure to all that electronic equipment. "Just a few minutes!" he shouted, as if anyone understood.

Maxie was upstairs, so just Mom and I could hear him. If Mom were awake. So it was just me, and I turned toward the ghost, who was holding a length of electrical cord he'd clearly cut from a longer extension, with the two ends stripped so they could be connected elsewhere. Susannah, luckily, was not facing in his direction or I'd have had to make up a nonsense excuse for the hovering object again.

"It's going to happen!" Paul went on. Obviously I was too dense to get his meaning, so he explained himself. "I anticipate the storm will be directly over this area in four minutes, and that increases the chances of lightning striking the device I installed on the roof. The current is going to flow through and I can evolve. Alison, this might be it. We might not see each other again!"

Now? Even if Josh or I didn't get shot, Paul was going to move on to the next level in his ghostly video game and I had to say my good-byes now? "Paul," I said.

"Paul?" Richie asked, turning toward me but luckily not toward Paul. "Who's Paul?"

This had gone far enough. I no longer cared if Susannah and Richie thought I was a lunatic, but the Rendells had The Swine's ear and Constance certainly had enough spite built up for me to use my supposed insanity as a wedge in custody hearings. But I had leverage with her and besides, I wasn't thinking straight anymore.

I looked right at Paul. "You can't leave now!" I insisted. "Look around! There's a man with a gun threatening my life!"

"We're going in now," Maroni reported through Richie's cell phone. "We should have the package in a minute." But I knew better.

"What are you talking about?" Constance demanded of me. "Who are you talking to?"

Paul took stock of the situation, and his eyes showed indecision. He looked up as a rumble of thunder sounded.

"Alison," he said intensely, "this is my chance."

I took a deep breath. "Then I can't hold you back. It's been a real gift to know you."

Paul hovered without so much as drifting, which meant he was concentrating very hard. "It has been my privilege," he said.

"Who the hell are you talking to?" Susannah said.

"The ghosts," Tony told her. "They're everywhere." Oliver laughed.

"Oh, cut it out," Jeannie said from under the table.

Richie, intent on his phone, was paying no attention to the hovering electrical wire, but Harry seemed mesmerized by it. "How do you do that?" he asked me.

"Do you have it yet?" Richie asked the phone.

Another rumble. "I have no time," Paul told me. "I'm sorry."

I shook my head. "Nothing you could do. But you should say good-bye to Melissa."

"What's she *talking* about?" Constance demanded of her husband, who waved a hand at her.

"I wish I could. But this is—" The thunder was indeed closer. A flash of lightning grabbed Paul's attention, and the crack was only a second later. He flew—really—to the window where he'd installed the strange box. Apparently the last step involved attaching it to the length of wire he had in his hands.

"Ghosts?" Susannah asked.

"Didn't you see the sign outside?" Tony said. "It's a haunted guesthouse."

"I thought that was her idea of a joke." Constance sniffed. "Haunted guesthouse, indeed."

"Well?" Richie shouted at his phone.

"Got it!" came the reply. I was astonished. The papers were really at Madison Paints? Maybe we'd be saved after all.

My elation was not long-lived. As soon as the words were out of Maroni's mouth, there was an unmistakable sound coming through the phone. A great commotion and then a voice I recognized.

McElone.

"Police! Stop what you're doing! Hands where I can see them!" I heard her yell, and my stomach sank. On the one hand, this probably meant Josh would be safe, and that was very good news for sure. On the other hand . . .

Richie's eyes narrowed to slits. He turned and faced me with rage on his face and the gun in his hand.

The rage I could have handled.

"Look, Richie . . ." I began.

"You did this," he said, advancing on me. I looked up into the ceiling for Maxie. She wasn't there. A glance at Paul: He was waist-deep in the floor tinkering with his contraption and looking up through the den window. No lightning at the moment. "You called the cops!"

Paul turned and looked. He wasn't *that* preoccupied. "Alison," he said softly.

I shook my head. This was his only chance and I could take care of Richie. All I had to do was stall until Maxie showed up or one of the others distracted him.

Lord knows, Tony tried. "Oliver!" he said, pushing his son back under the table. "What a thing to say!" Tony didn't leap to his feet, but he was standing very quickly. Jeannie grabbed her son under the table.

"Rub my leg," she instructed Oliver. "It fell asleep. Did you ever see a leg that was asleep?"

"Snoring?" Oliver asked, and then he laughed and so did Jeannie.

But throughout this vaudeville Richie's eyes never left my face. "You had to do it. Nobody else could have gotten in touch with the cops. I had all the phones." He stopped and considered, then looked upstairs. His voice dropped even more. "Your daughter?" he asked.

"No!" I shouted. "You were right. It was me. I texted Lieutenant McElone when you were fiddling with your phone, before you took mine away." There had been no such time, but logic wasn't exactly the priority at the moment.

Luckily Richie wasn't going back over the videotape of the evening to see if my explanation had been accurate. "I knew it," he said. The other end of the phone line still sounded like chaos, but quieter chaos. After a long moment, I heard Josh's voice come through, as he must have picked up Maroni's cell.

"I'm okay, Alison," he said, sounding worried. "Are you?"

Richie took the phone from the table, face contorted with anger. "No, she's not!" he yelled, and disconnected the call, throwing the phone on the table. "You took everything." He took two steps toward me. I saw Tony's body tense and lean forward.

Then so many things happened at once that I can't really tell you what order of events is correct. It was like that moment when you're in a car crash—it all seemed to go in slow motion, and none of it seemed real.

Tony jumped across the dining table, not realizing it had been constructed from three separate folding card tables because my actual one would not have been nearly large enough. The impact of his weight on the surface, and the fact that he hit squarely between two of the tables, was enough to make the near (to me) end of the structure collapse, and he ended up on the floor.

"Oof," he said.

Jeannie, under the far end of the table, was untouched by the avalanche of food, dishes, linen and Tony that landed on the other side. She looked over, saw her husband was not badly hurt and said, "What are you doing?" Tony was trying to scramble to his feet but seemed uninterested in telling her that.

Richie's phone, and mine, and Mom's, and probably a couple of the others, started to ring. Richie, holding the bag with the phones hostage on a seat next to him, made no effort to answer any of them.

Susannah, seeing Tony leap and flop, got up presumably to help him to his feet, but tried instead to reach for her cell phone. Richie hit her hand with the butt of the gun and she yelped.

Constance, now with chicken gravy saturating her lap, yelled something quite unladylike and then berated Richie. "You should have let us go an hour ago!"

"Oh, shut up, Connie," Harry answered. "Go tell your reverend about it."

Constance stared at him. Her mouth opened and closed and for the first time since I'd known her, no sound came out.

Mom, startled by the noise, woke up and saw Richie advancing on me with the gun. She didn't even comment on the table or the contractor on the floor. "Jack!" she shouted, and my father was launching himself across the room.

But even he couldn't get to Richie fast enough. "I said I'd shoot you," he said. "And I will." He raised the gun and aimed at my chest.

I figured my best chance was to not be there when the bullet arrived, so I turned to run toward the kitchen, my heart pounding in my chest. I knew I didn't have enough time, but I literally couldn't think of anything else to do.

And I saw Anne and Mel coming out of the kitchen, Mel saying something about how all the action seemed to be going on up here. They were holding hands. That was nice, I thought.

I heard Melissa's voice from the entrance to the den, where I knew she couldn't be because she was under orders not to leave her room. And of course teenagers never disobey their parents. "Mom!" she screamed. She sounded terrified. But I knew that couldn't be her. Maxie was upstairs making sure of that.

Except Maxie dropped through the ceiling, saw the situation and made the trench coat disappear. She grabbed the baseball bat and aimed at Richie's head as if it were a fat fastball in her happy zone just asking to be hit out of the park.

She hit him once, hard, and it had the effect she'd hoped for; he dropped. But on impact he fired the gun, maybe not even intentionally. And it was aimed in my direction.

At that moment, I heard Paul yell, "This is it!"

There was a tremendous flash of lightning and the thunder was simultaneous. The storm was right over my house. I saw some sparks and heard the crackling of electricity to my left. But my attention was on the gun. I looked to see its trajectory.

But I couldn't because as soon as that spark lit, the room went completely dark. The only thing I could see was Paul, who was indeed glowing. And almost immediately he seemed to be fading away. And I could hear something whirring by, which I believed to be Richie's bullet.

Then something hit me in the head and I didn't know what happened after that.

Twenty-seven

When you come out of anesthesia, your main desire is to go back to sleep. It doesn't matter how long you've been out, your body is telling you that it's not interested in doing anything at all and your eyes are absolutely not involved in the idea of being open. You have thoughts, but they're random and diffuse, moving from one topic to another like people at a speed-dating event. Hi, I'm Alison and I like to— Oh, sorry, who are you again? And what's that unicorn doing next to you?

I remembered that something had hit me in the head, but I didn't know what. There was something about a bucket of wall compound; maybe that was what had fallen on me. Yeah. I was working on the ceiling in the new house and this bucket just fell off the ladder onto my head. That was it.

My head definitely still hurt. But I didn't raise a hand to touch it; doing so would have required effort. Who needed that? Instead I just lay there, wherever I was, with my eyes closed, wondering why I had awakened at all.

"Mom?" Melissa's voice sounded small and younger. I thought it was Melissa, anyway. It might have been a baby giraffe or my grandmother on my father's side, whom I hadn't seen since she died in 1994. "You awake?"

Now, that was a perplexing question. *Was* I awake? Was anybody *really* awake? What did Goethe say about being awake? Did he say it in his sleep? Who was Goethe, anyway?

"I dunno." That was the closest I could get to an honest reply. "Where are you?"

"I'm right here," Liss said. Is that really a response to give someone whose eyes are closed? Where's "right here"? For that matter, where was I? Was I "right here," and if so, was I Melissa?

"Where's here?"

"You're in the hospital." Melissa's voice had suddenly deepened and sounded very tired. I forced my eyes open.

"Are you okay?" I asked.

"Of course I am," my mother said. "I'm not the one who has the concussion. How are *you*?"

It was, as advertised, a hospital room. I seemed to remember it from before, but not really. That bucket of compound must have hit me hard.

Wait. The bucket of compound! That was . . . four years ago! So why was I in the hospital now? Was I just waking up? How long had I been under sedation?

Had I just dreamed the whole thing? The ghosts, the guesthouse, the investigator's license, the murders?

Josh?

Had I dreamed Josh? Was I still a new divorcée with a nine-year-old daughter? How hard had I gotten hit?

But no. There was Liss and she was thirteen. And there was Mom and she was still Mom. But Josh. There was no Josh.

I hadn't actually raised my head, but I let it fall even farther back on the pillow. There was no Josh. There had been no Paul and no Maxie. Okay, the "no Maxie" part wasn't all that bad, except it was. I was going to miss her, too.

"How are you?" Mom asked again.

"I don't know," I said. "I honestly don't know."

"That's fair enough because it's my job to answer that question." A small woman with black hair walked in. She was wearing a white coat upon which was embroidered the name Dr. Dhenu Murthy.

"I'm glad you came back, Doctor," Melissa said. "I'm not sure she's entirely aware of what's going on." Like for example, I didn't know the doctor had been here before. That was one thing I wasn't entirely aware of.

"She's been asleep for a while," the doctor said, shining a light in my eyes, which was not appreciated. "That's better." What was better? Everything anybody said just confused me more.

My head was sort of clearing, but that "sort of" was important. "Can somebody tell me what happened?" I asked.

I knew what they were going to say: I had been hit with a bucket of compound and had a concussion. All the things I'd had in my mind—Paul, Maxie, my father again and mostly Josh—I'd have to keep to myself. It had been an interesting dream, but a dream nonetheless.

"Oh, she's awake." Suddenly Paul was floating over the bed. Now I knew it was a hallucination, because in any version of my reality, Paul was either a dream or he couldn't travel past my property line, and unless they'd built a hospital behind my house while I was unconscious, this was definitely not on my land. Besides, Paul had electrocuted himself into the next step up in Ghostdom, hadn't he?

"You were hit with a flying object in your house," Dr.

Murthy said, holding up her finger vertically. "Now follow this movement with your eyes. Don't move your head."

So I did that while Melissa explained. "That guy shot off his gun and must have knocked a piece of plaster loose from the ceiling when he . . . fell down," she said. "The plaster hit you on the head and we couldn't wake you up, so we called an ambulance and you've been here about seven hours now."

I was still groggy, so what I was seeing and hearing (despite Dr. Murthy's declaration that my "eye movement is good") was somewhat suspect. Paul couldn't be here. Suddenly Maxie was at his side and she was smiling at me unironically. That wasn't possible, either.

A shot of adrenaline suddenly hit me when I realized at least some of what I was seeing had to be real. "Where's—"

Josh walked into the room carrying two cups from the hospital coffee shop. "Hey! You're awake!" he told me.

"You sure?"

It was such a relief to see him. He'd been what I'd most worried would leave my life, and there he was, coffee in hand. He gave one cup to Melissa and the other to Mom, who now appeared to have Dad hovering over her shoulder. The room was getting crowded.

But the weird part was Paul, so I looked at him. "What are you doing here?" I asked.

The doctor's eyebrows lowered and she followed my line of sight toward what she saw as nothing in the air. "Who are you talking to?" she said.

Uh-oh. If the doctor thought I was hallucinating—and I wasn't sure if that was the case or not—she could turf me out to psychiatric or keep me here indefinitely. "I was talking to Josh," I said, covering. "Wasn't I supposed to keep staring ahead?"

Melissa mouthed, "Good one."

"Oh no," Dr. Murthy said. "You can look wherever you

want now." She read my monitor and probably made a mental note to have a psychiatrist consult with me. Or an ophthalmologist.

"That was the weird thing," Paul explained. "The energy experiment worked, but it didn't have the effect I expected. Instead of being elevated to the next level, I now have the ability to move around as I like. I can go anywhere!" He was like a nine-year-old if the nine-year-old were transparent and floated.

"Is there anything left of my house?" I asked him.

The doctor looked around. "I haven't seen the house," she said. "Someone else will have to tell her."

"There was just the one hole in the ceiling from the gunshot," Melissa said. "But Tony thinks it might have hit a beam, and that means doing some serious work in the rafters there."

"Looks like you're not done with that house yet, Baby Girl," my father said.

"Can I close my eyes?" I asked the doctor.

She immediately looked concerned. "Are you feeling light-headed or nauseated?"

"No. It's just the anesthesia hasn't worn off yet."

Dr. Murthy raised an eyebrow. "Anesthesia?"

"Yeah. Why'd I need surgery for a concussion?"

Everybody looked at me funny. Even Maxie, who you would normally expect to laugh out loud. "What?" I asked.

"You didn't have any surgery," the doctor said. "You were never under anesthesia. You were unconscious briefly, but then you were in pain and we gave you some medication. You slept. And now, unless there's something else you're not telling me, you're going home."

"Home?" Clearly my brain wasn't functioning properly. I needed medical observation.

"Where you live," Maxie tried. And I couldn't even answer her.

"Home," Josh said. "Where we're getting married on Saturday. You remember that?"

"Oh yes," I said as he leaned over and kissed me lightly. "I remember that."

"Okay," Dr. Murthy said. "You can go home."

Detective Lieutenant Anita McElone doesn't like to walk into my house. She'd made her peace with the fact that there are ghosts there, but she works on fact and evidence, and there is very little of those available when Paul and Maxie get involved. For example, she was now trying to piece together exactly how Richie—the ersatz Maurice DuBois— had gotten smacked in the head with a baseball bat.

"This Susannah Nesbit insists the bat just appeared in the air and clobbered Richard Attanasio in the back of the head, causing a slight crack in a thin part of his skull and a subdural hematoma," she said. She gave me a very stern look. "Now, since we both know that *couldn't happen*, what actually did?"

Maxie, floating at the other side of my bedroom, huffed a bit. "What does she mean, it couldn't happen?" she demanded. "Without me you would've gotten shot instead of having the roof fall down on you."

"I don't know, Lieutenant," I said. I was lying on the bed, no longer as punchy as I'd been at the hospital but still not exactly ready for the triathlon. "I was busy having a concussion. I'm not really even clear on why Richie shot Maurice DuBois. I mean, what did he expect to gain from it?"

"He's been awake enough to question and kept off the pain meds. He said he went out to Hanrahan's with DuBois that night to try to convince him to take your ex's name off the patent and put his on," McElone said. "Apparently that was part of the agreement he and your ex had reached about some four hundred thousand dollars owed to Mr.

Attanasio's employer, Lou Maroni. Things didn't go the way Attanasio wanted, angry words were said and DuBois ended up in the alley with a couple of bullets in him."

"But I don't understand how you even knew to show up at Madison Paints and arrest Maroni last night," I said. "I didn't call you. Nobody else could have. Who tipped you off?"

McElone looked directly at Maxie, but she didn't know it. "I'm not able to discuss that, because it was information obtained from a confidential informant."

A confidential . . . no. "The Swine?" I said aloud.

Maxie blew out her lips in an involuntary laugh.

"The what?" McElone said, looking at me again.

"It's a . . . nickname I have for my ex-husband," I said. "He was your CI, wasn't he?"

McElone drew a breath and let it out. "I can't say."

"Except you would tell me if I was wrong. It makes sense. You let him go almost as soon as you arrested him because you made a deal. So he probably arranged the arrest himself to gain cred with his buddies. He'd provide information to you in exchange for what, amnesty?"

McElone shook her head. "No need for immunity. He hadn't broken any laws, but he was in over his head and he knew it. And you didn't hear that from me. Now, about that baseball bat . . ."

"You don't want to hear my answer, Lieutenant," I said, closing my eyes. "You really don't."

She knew what I meant. "That's what I figured." She closed the notebook she used that I knew she didn't need. "You need rest. I'll come back and talk to you again later."

"Good. Something to look forward to."

My eyes were closed, but I heard her walk to the bedroom door and stop. "I hear you're getting married Saturday," she said.

That got my eyes open again. "That's right. Are you free?"

McElone raised an eyebrow. "Are we at that level?" she asked.

"If you want us to be."

She nodded. "I'll be there. I love weddings." She walked out.

"Check out the lady cop," Maxie said. "Never figured her to be a softy."

"Well, I never figured you were, either. You just don't know about some people."

Maxie puffed out her lips. "Oh, cut it out," she said as she rose into the ceiling and away.

"I'm your first phone call," Phyllis Coates said. "You know that. And do I get the phone call when a murderer is caught holding people hostage?"

"I was unconscious, Phyllis," I reminded her. "I don't see how you can hold that against me."

We sat in the library with the sun coming in through the skylight and reflecting off the window my father had installed over the door. Aside from the snow visible outside, you'd never know it was still ridiculously cold. Phyllis, voice recorder complementing her reporter's notebook, looked grumpy.

"You weren't unconscious the whole time," she said. "You could have called from the hospital."

"I guarantee you already knew about it by then."

Phyllis smiled. "Okay, you've got me there, but you know I need details. This ain't your first rodeo."

"No, but it's gonna be my last. I'm tired of having guns pointed at me. I'm hanging up my investigator's license and going back to running a guesthouse."

Yoko Takamine stopped at the open library door, her suitcase on wheels behind her. "The van will be here very soon," she said. "I wanted to thank you for a lovely stay here."

I stood up, which was still something of an adventure but definitely an improvement over the day before. "I feel like I didn't do enough for you," I told her. "Things have been kind of hectic around here the past few days."

Yoko waved a hand, dismissing the thought. "It was very peaceful for me. You were the one having the hectic time. Are you feeling better?"

Well . . . "Much," I said. "I'm glad you enjoyed yourself. Thanks for asking."

"Just one thing," Yoko said. "Did you know your daughter has a dog upstairs?"

She knew about Lester? "You've seen him?" I said.

"Of course. He's adorable."

He's also dead. "You know he's a ghost, right?"

"Of course," she repeated. "So are Maxie and Paul, and they're perfectly visible. And your father is a very charming man." She picked up the handle on her suitcase. "Thank you for the most wonderful stay, Alison. I hope I get to come back sometime."

She wheeled the bag away and I looked at Phyllis, who shrugged. "I can't help crazy people," she said. "I'm just a reporter."

I decided not to take that crazy-people crack personally. "I have to see my guests off," I said, heading for the coatrack. Phyllis followed.

The Swine was already at the front door, shaking hands with Mel Kaminsky when I arrived as if he were the host of the establishment, which he definitely was not and never would be. Josh was back at the store after a day of caring for me, just as Melissa was back in school even as she had argued that I needed rest. The fact that there was a test in earth science that day had no bearing on her argument.

She said. So if Steven wanted to pretend for a minute, that was his business. As long as he didn't think it would last more than ten minutes.

Mel and Anne were smiling at the door, watching for the van but making sure no freezing wind made its way inside. I'd never seen a happier couple. Anne had informed me Mel had an appointment with a sleep specialist when they got home to do something about his snoring problem. I marveled at their ability to remain calm and cope.

"Well, you do that," Anne said. "I've seen it. People coming and going and guests asking for special favors, and you just keep it all together. It's amazing." I immediately deducted the cost of the second room from their bill. I did it mentally because if I'd told Anne, The Swine would have heard and berated me for being a terrible business-woman as soon as they left.

The Senior Plus van arrived, in this case a minivan for only three guests, and Dave the driver got out to come grab everybody's luggage. This took roughly twenty seconds and then my three guests were loaded on the van and driv-ing off, waving to me as they went. Phyllis, still grumbling that she hadn't gotten special treatment on "the story," took off a moment later.

Steven closed the door and looked at me. "It actually sort of worked out, didn't it?" he said.

"You mean how you were informing to the police and almost got me killed? You might have mentioned that little detail before I sent you and the cast of *The Sopranos* to Madison Paints. Why'd you leave the patent stuff there, anyway?"

"I didn't. The papers were with Lieutenant McElone the whole time." He grinned an especially swinish grin and almost dislocated a shoulder patting himself on the back. "But I knew if I let you think they were there, you'd send us. I had a GPS device in my right shoe. Once I managed to get it activated, the cops could follow me to the store and you know the rest."

"With you, Steven, I never know the rest. I'm not even sure *you* know the rest. You were calling your 'cousin' Richie by the name Maurice when you came out of the library."

"It was supposed to work that way," The Swine protested. "He said if he could be Maurice he could get the patent and I'd be clear of the debt to Lou. I didn't know he was going to shoot Maurice; I thought the idea was to convince him to take a small cut because the thing wasn't going to work."

My head started to hurt and I didn't even think it was the concussion talking. I started for the den. Now that there were no guests in the house—and wouldn't be for a week— I could take a look at the damage to my ceiling and figure on what needed to be done next.

My father was already there, looking over the hole, much larger than you'd expect from just one bullet. "This is more than just Spackle," he said.

Mom had insisted Dad stick around full-time to see to my recovery, but since my recovery had consisted mostly of sleeping he'd had very little to do. So in the ensuing thirty-six hours, Dad had been doing triage on the gaping abyss in my den ceiling.

Steven had given up following me and might very well have been packing his bags. His flight for Los Angeles left in six hours. He'd spent much of his time the past day and a half giving the police depositions, and he seemed anxious to get back to a land where he could walk outside without an extra three layers of clothing. It was one of the few sentiments on which I could agree with him.

He would not, however, be returning with the patent for SafT in his back pocket. McElone and the county prosecutor's major crimes unit had confiscated it as evidence in the killing of Maurice DuBois. Legal issues would probably keep it in limbo for years. If the investors didn't get antsy, Steven might be a very wealthy man. Someday.

I looked up at the ceiling and my father. It was good he wasn't merely a dream I'd had after being hit on the head. "I know," I said. "Any ideas?"

Dad frowned, which meant he was thinking. He pointed at the hole. "The bullet went in and hit a beam," he said. "That's the real problem. The plaster we can get somebody to fix. I know a few people." The best plaster artists were on Dad's side of the continuum. "But the beam is old and it's broken enough to be compromised."

That got me frowning. "Is it going to collapse?"

He shook his head. "Not any time soon, and maybe not for years. But you might as well replace it with a steel beam and not have to worry. In the meantime, you don't have to steer clear of it or anything. It'll hold well enough for now."

"What about fixing it? What'll that take?"

He tilted his head from side to side. "It'll be a project. You up for a project?"

I laughed despite myself. "Not today, but maybe soon."

"Good enough, Baby Girl."

Twenty-eight

Melissa looked at me appraisingly and I could tell something was wrong. "What?" I asked.

"You don't look like a bride. You're getting married in twenty minutes and you don't look like a bride. You look like someone going to a wedding." She looked me up and down.

It was true that I didn't look like a traditional bride; there was no white gown or veil. This was my second wedding, and one that had been organized in less than a week. There had been no time and I'd had no inclination to guest-star on *Say Yes to the Dress*. "It's okay," I told her. "I look fine."

"Yeah, but not like a bride. Here." She walked to a vase I kept in the library, where we were getting ready because it was the best light in the house, and took out the flowers. "Hold these." She extended them to me.

"They're fake," I said. I don't keep fresh flowers in the house during the winter because . . . it's winter.

"You can sell it." Melissa, who looked wonderful in her maid of honor dress (which had also been her spring dance dress and I was fairly sure her grandma's birthday dress), took a step back and observed again. "Let me see."

I stood there exactly as before, only holding fabric flowers. "Much better," my daughter said.

"Thanks. Now go wrangle your grandmother and make sure all the chairs are set up."

She started toward the door, which admittedly wasn't far, but I couldn't let it go any farther than this. "Liss," I said, "I'm sorry I put you between me and your dad. I didn't mean to make you choose."

Her eyes indicated I might not be completely recovered from the concussion. "What are you talking about?" she asked.

"When Dad was here. I wasn't working too hard to clear his name and you seemed upset."

It took a moment to register with her and then she laughed. "That's what you thought was bothering me? Mom. I get the divorce thing; I have since I was ten. It had nothing to do with you and Dad, believe me."

"Then what was it?"

She looked away. "It's . . . do I have to tell you?"

"If something's wrong you do."

"Nothing's wrong." She turned, then turned back and let out a breath. "It was about Jared."

"Oh!" Jared. Jared. "The crush?"

Her face reddened. "Do we have to?" she asked.

"No. We don't. I don't want you to be embarrassed." Despite the fact that I'm your mother and it's pretty much my job to embarrass you.

The words seemed to fly out of her. "I found out he liked another girl and I got mad, okay? And then I found out that wasn't true and he really liked me and now I'm not sure if I like him or not. So I'm processing."

"Don't ever give a guy that much control over your feelings," I told her. "Trust me on this."

"Jared isn't Dad, Mom."

"He better not be. Will he be here today?" I'd given her permission to invite up to four friends. The den is large, but not that large.

Melissa shook her head. "Just Wendy," she said. "She's the only one important enough and the only one I don't have to explain to about the ghosts."

"So, what's the latest with Jared?" I asked.

She smiled. "He'll just have to wait to find out."

"That's my girl."

Liss smiled at me and stopped at the door. "I'm glad you're doing this," she said.

"You know what? So am I. Now scram."

I spent a couple of minutes doing absolutely nothing. You plan a day like this and then there's this time when everything's just done but it's not time to start yet. I was in the library and didn't even feel like reading a book.

Because of my agreement with some of the local restaurants that I'll recommend them to my guests, they give me a small percentage of the business they get when patrons mention the guesthouse. One of them, Belinda Rosenberg at Just Eat, had offered to provide food for the twenty guests on their way here today, at a discount.

Jenny Webb, proprietor of Stud Muffin, the local bakery, had sent a lovely cake that was also going to be delicious because that's what Jenny does. And she didn't even go the discount route—Jenny said she would not accept payment.

So the table was set, buffet-style. Marv Winderbrook, the mechanic at the Fuel Pit, was also a justice of the peace and was already in the house ready to go, having replaced the Volvo's heater "as a wedding present" earlier that day.

So were my soon-to-be-husband, my parents, Phyllis, McElone (with her husband, Thomas), Maxie's mother, Kitty Malone (whom the ghost insisted had to be on the guest list), Jeannie, Tony, Oliver and Molly, Josh's parents, Sy and Josh's friends A.J., Pollitzer (he didn't seem to have a first name) and Kenny (who didn't seem to have a last name).

Even Maxie was dressed for the occasion in her traditional black T-shirt, this one reading "Team Bride," and Everett had seen to it that she wore something other than her usual sprayed-on blue jeans, in this case a denim skirt, which I supposed was close enough. I had not seen Paul at all today, leading me to think his newfound ability to wander to his heart's content had led him to, you know, wander to his heart's content. I guessed we'd had our good-byes when I thought he was going to evolve and I was going to die.

Josh walked into the library, stood and observed. "You look beautiful," he said.

"You've actually seen me in this before."

"You looked beautiful then, too. Come on. We've got people expecting a show out there. If we don't hurry they might decide to go to another wedding."

I walked over and hugged him close. "You know you're not supposed to see the bride before the wedding," I said.

"That's silly. How would I have asked to marry you?" His arms tightened and held me closer. "You gave me a real scare that night, you know. I heard Richie on the phone and I thought . . . well. Actually I thought Maxie would hit him with a baseball bat."

I looked up into his face. "You really thought that?"

"Oddly yeah. I knew she'd have your back. She wasn't going to let Melissa grow up without a mom. From what you've told me, she's a really good friend."

"Maxie drives me crazy," I told him.

"Well, you drive me crazy, but in a good way. Let's go get married." He extended his arm and I took it, and then we went to the den.

Marv, who cleaned up nicely from his usual grease-covered jumpsuit, was standing at the far end. There would have been rows of chairs to create an aisle, but there weren't enough chairs for that, so we just walked in, me holding Josh's hand. Melissa walked to my side. Josh's dad walked to his.

Melissa had actually taught Lester "stay" because there was no point to a leash with him, and he was sitting patiently, wagging his tail, as we walked in and took our position right in front of Marv.

I couldn't see the guests once we turned to face Marv, but I could hear a few things. Jeannie kept telling Ollie to look forward because he was missing it. Ollie said he didn't care. My mother sniffed a little, which was something she had only done *after* my previous wedding. My father, situated above Marv's right shoulder so he could see my face better, actually pulled Mom's cell phone out of his pocket and took a picture. If the others noticed they did not react.

Josh smiled, though. But then, he was smiling all the way through.

We answered the questions Marv asked. Josh, who was asked first, answered, "I do." And strangely I heard the words echoed from just behind me.

I took a quick glance and saw Everett, in his dress uniform, standing in profile as Josh and I were doing to face each other. He was looking into Maxie's eyes and she was absolutely gazing into his.

She was wearing an elaborate white wedding dress with veil and train, and looked lovelier than I had ever seen her. I stood looking at her for so long that there was a pause after Marv finished asking me about marrying Josh, and there was a quick chuckle from the crowd.

"I do," Maxie said.

I turned my attention back to the man who was about to be my husband. He was still smiling, aware that something else was going on and secure that I would tell him later. He was exactly the man I needed.

"Yes," I said. "Definitely yes."

"Oh, go ahead and kiss," Marv said.

We did, and for a quick second I looked to see Maxie and Everett doing the same. When the four of us were finished, she looked at me, a small tear escaping from her left eye. "Tell my mom," she said. I nodded my agreement.

There was applause.

We were immediately surrounded by well-wishers, which was nice but overwhelming. I was completely free of any lingering concussion symptoms, thank goodness, but was still feeling a little light-headed just based on context.

Josh and I were separated by factions of friends and family. Melissa got the first hug from each of us, and I held her the longest I would anybody that day. Then she went off to stand to the side with her best friend, Wendy, and I moved on to the others.

I couldn't actually talk to Dad, Maxie or Everett just now, not with the in-laws in the room, but I made sure to give each a thankful smile. Mom stood next to me and said, "Best thing you've ever done. Except Melissa." And we fell into each other's arms for a while.

Phyllis had taken pictures for her social page and said she might run them with the story about the murder of Maurice DuBois, but she was kidding. I was pretty sure. Later when we were having dessert I heard her reiterate her offer to Melissa to start working at the *Chronicle* when she turned fourteen.

Sy Kaplan, Josh's grandfather, told me I was a "looker," and reminisced about Josh and me meeting at his store. It hadn't seemed like that big a deal at the time, but look what happened.

When I got to Kitty Malone, I whispered in her ear and she stopped, stiffened and looked into my eyes. I nodded. She gave me a very warm hug and told me to pass it on. I promised to try.

Jeannie danced the most at the party, largely because there was no band or DJ. I played a mix tape Melissa had made for me of my favorite oldies, including a couple of songs by the Jingles just to be nostalgic. Jeannie has danced the most at every party we have ever attended together. Jeannie is a force of nature. Her husband danced with her, then watched as she danced with Josh, A.J., Pollitzer and for a brief moment Lieutenant McElone.

The lieutenant came over during dessert and thanked me for inviting her and Thomas. It represented an emotional outburst for her, and then she said she had to go home because her children were probably taking the house apart by now. I thanked them both for coming. She kept looking around the ceiling as she left, but none of the ghosts was there.

By the time everyone but my parents had gone home, we were exhausted and drained. Melissa, fresh off her first glass of champagne, which she declared was "gross," was sprawled on one of the easy chairs, looking at Josh and me on the love seat, which seemed appropriate.

Mom and Dad were on the sofa. Well, Mom was on the sofa. Dad was pretending to sit but was above the cushions by about six inches. "This was a good day," Mom sighed. "A good day."

There was a tiny sense of regret for me, although it wasn't putting a damper on the events of the day. I didn't say anything, even when Maxie told us she and Everett were going on a honeymoon starting immediately.

She was back in the T-shirt and denim skirt, and Everett was in fatigues. "Where are you going?" Melissa asked.

"We're going to the airport," Everett told her. "We'll hitch a ride and once we're there, we'll choose a flight to get on."

"You've never been in an airplane," I reminded Maxie.

She shrugged. "I figure at this point, what can happen? Besides, you two need to have some time without all these people in your house." It was the first time since I'd met Maxie that she hadn't referred to 123 Seafront Avenue as "my house," because she was the owner when she'd died there and refused to acknowledge my stewardship until now.

"Our house," I said to her. She took my hand a moment—the feeling of a refreshing breeze was warmer than usual tonight—and then she and Everett rose into the ceiling and disappeared as Melissa waved.

"We're going, too," Mom said. "This is your wedding night." She had offered to have Melissa at her place for a few days, but Josh and I both wanted her around. And she had already spent enough time away recently.

Her father was back in L.A., texting that things were "great" there and promising to stay in touch. We wouldn't hear from him again for two years, and then it was an inquiry about the status of the SafT litigation. Steven was never going to be anything but The Swine.

When Mom and Dad had left and we had determined that cleaning up was not something one did after being married, Melissa took her dumbwaiter/elevator to her room and Josh and I were left alone. We were about to head upstairs when I heard something creak in the kitchen.

That couldn't be good.

Josh went in first and took a look around. "Nothing," he said. "No evidence of a mouse or anything, not even a bug. So maybe you'd better look."

I wasn't crazy about the idea, but Josh was already in the room and the lights were on. So I went in and looked around.

Sure enough, Paul was hovering just over his favorite spot by the stove.

Josh didn't even flinch when I spoke to him. "I thought you'd taken off," I said.

"Maxie?" Josh asked. I shook my head. He nodded. Of course.

"I wouldn't do that," Paul said. "I've been here all day, but I didn't want to be conspicuous. This was your day, not mine."

"That's crazy. Maxie and Everett were here."

"Yes. Getting married like you. I was just a spectator and I could watch without being seen. Don't worry."

"I'm glad you were here," I said. "It makes me feel better to know you were."

Paul smiled and stroked that goatee. "I am going to explore a little, though. I don't know for how long. But I imagine I'll be back one day."

"Unless you move on," I reminded him. "They have lightning everywhere."

Paul shrugged. "I'm not going to try too hard. Now that I can, I want to explore the world from this perspective. Travel is so much cheaper this way."

He turned to leave and I felt a little tug at my shoulder. "Say good-bye for me," Josh said.

"He can hear you."

Paul turned. "He's a good man, Alison. I'm happy for you. But I'm taking off now. It has been a privilege to live here. I will be back again."

"I'll leave the basement for you."

That crooked grin. "Thank you." And he was gone through the back wall, toward the ocean.

Josh, watching my head as I followed Paul's trajectory, held me close. "It's really been something," he said. "But everything has an end."

I kissed Josh and he kissed me back. "Oh no," I told him. "This is just the beginning."

ABOUT THE AUTHOR

E. J. Copperman is the Barry Award–winning, national bestselling author of the Haunted Guesthouse Mysteries, most recently *Ghost in the Wind, Inspector Specter,* and *The Thrill of the Haunt,* as well as the novellas *A Wild Ghost Chase* and *An Open Spook.*

Connect with Berkley Publishing Online!

For sneak peeks into the newest releases, news on all your favorite authors, book giveaways, and a central place to connect with fellow fans—

"Like" and follow Berkley Publishing!

facebook.com/BerkleyPub
twitter.com/BerkleyPub
instagram.com/BerkleyPub

Penguin
Random
House